SHARPSHOOTER

THE TALE OF BILLY THE KID AND THE TENNESSEE RAID

EDWARD J. KNIGHT

MYTHIC WESTERN PRESS LLC

ACKNOWLEDGMENTS

I couldn't have written this without the help of several people. First, my wife Sarah's continued support has been critical for my continued sanity and productivity. I also want to thank Griffin and Gwyneth for their patience with Daddy being off writing. I'd also like to thank Marcia Knight, Elizabeth Knight, Griffin Knight, Steve Hartmeyer, Mary Kay Dodson, and Matthew Dodson for proofreading. I'd also like to express my appreciation to Terry Mixon and Sam Sheddan for their on-going encouragement.

INTRODUCTION

Seven years after destroying the Confederacy and most of the Union, the Jotunheim giants threaten a defenseless New England. The Army of the West plans a bold attack on Louisville to divert them.

Billy McCarty's nightmares drove him to enlist as a sharpshooter. He just wants to put his heroics in Colorado behind him and kill giants.

Captain Mercer doesn't care. He'll use Billy's skills and reputation however he can to ensure victory.

Even if that means both their deaths.

In the Mythic West, where Civil War veterans battle nightmarish monsters, *Sharpshooter* continues the epic adventures of the hero, Billy the Kid.

Date	Event
April 12, 1861	United States Civil War begins.
April 9, 1865	Robert E. Lee surrenders the Army of Northern Virginia to Ulysses S. Grant.
April 14, 1865	President Lincoln is assassinated.
April 21, 1865	The Rift to Jotunheim is opened at Andersonville Prison, Georgia. Specific details are unknown as there are no human survivors.
April 27, 1865	General Wilson and his Union Army raiders become the first humans to encounter an army of Jotun giants in Georgia and have survivors. The human army is soundly defeated but is able to dispatch reports to Washington and Richmond.
August 6, 1865	A combined Union/Confederate Army under the command of Ulysses S. Grant, with Robert E. Lee as his second, fights a large Jotun army outside of Lynchburg, Virginia. The humans are defeated, but "Grant's Last Charge" kills the Jotun commander, halting the Jotun army advance.
July 13, 1866	Richmond, Virginia, falls to a Jotun army.
September 2, 1866	Washington, D.C., falls to a Jotun army.
December 25, 1866	The Christmas Miracle. General Lee defeats a Jotun army attempting to cross the Hudson River into New York City. The Jotun make no further attempts to invade New England or upstate New York.
June-July 1867	Jotun cross the Ohio River in multiple locations. Fighting rages throughout lower Illinois, Indiana, and Ohio. The area becomes known as the Contested Lands.
August 10, 1867	The First Battle of St. Louis. Believing he has superior numbers, General Custer crosses the Mississippi from St. Louis and attacks a Jotun army. General Custer and his army are annihilated.
August 31, 1867	The Second Battle of St. Louis. A Jotun army crosses the Mississippi and sacks the under-garrisoned city of St. Louis.
September 1867-May 1868	The Long Retreat. The Army of the West, under General Sanborn, makes multiple raids on St. Louis. The Jotun assemble a force to crush the Army of the West. The human army begins a long retreat along the Platte River. The Jotun pursue, as they believe that the Army of the West is the last capable human resistance.
May 24, 1868	The Battle of Golden City. The Army of the West lures the Jotun army into a trap between the Table Mesas outside of Golden City, Colorado. In a Pyrrhic victory, the Jotun army is destroyed.
1873	Plague sweeps New England and Europe.
June 1875	Giant Killer Cassidy returns to Golden City. Billy McCarty's adventures with him, described in *Sidekick*, occur.

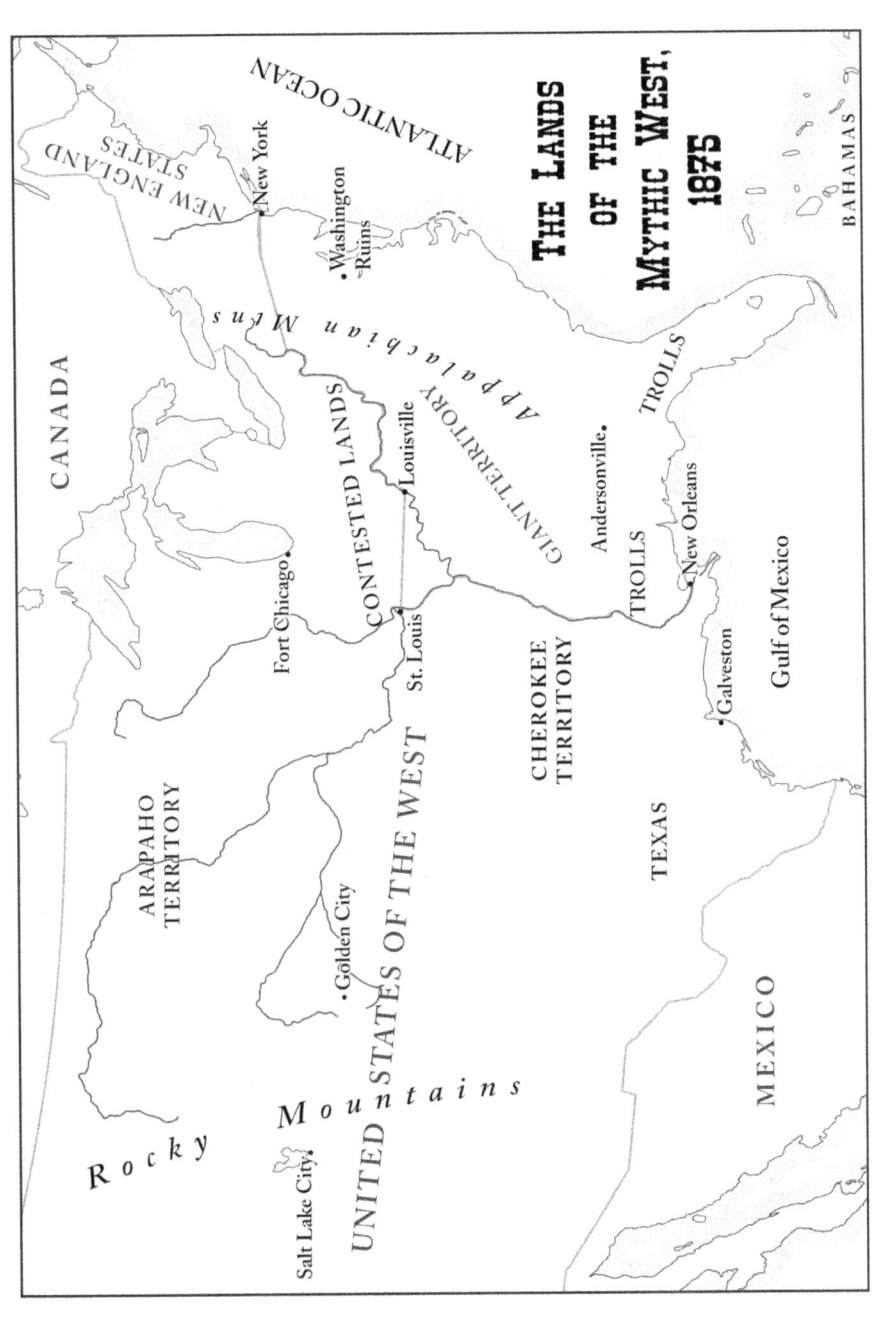

THE LANDS
OF THE
MYTHIC WEST,
1875

ATLANTIC OCEAN

BAHAMAS

NEW ENGLAND
STATES

New York

Washington
Ruins

CANADA

Appalachian Mtns

TROLLS

GIANT TERRITORY

Louisville

Andersonville.

TROLLS

TROLLS

New Orleans

Fort Chicago.

CONTESTED LANDS

St. Louis

CHEROKEE
TERRITORY

Gulf of Mexico

Galveston

ARAPAHO
TERRITORY

TEXAS

Golden City

UNITED STATES OF THE WEST

M o u n t a i n s

MEXICO

R o c k y

Salt Lake City.

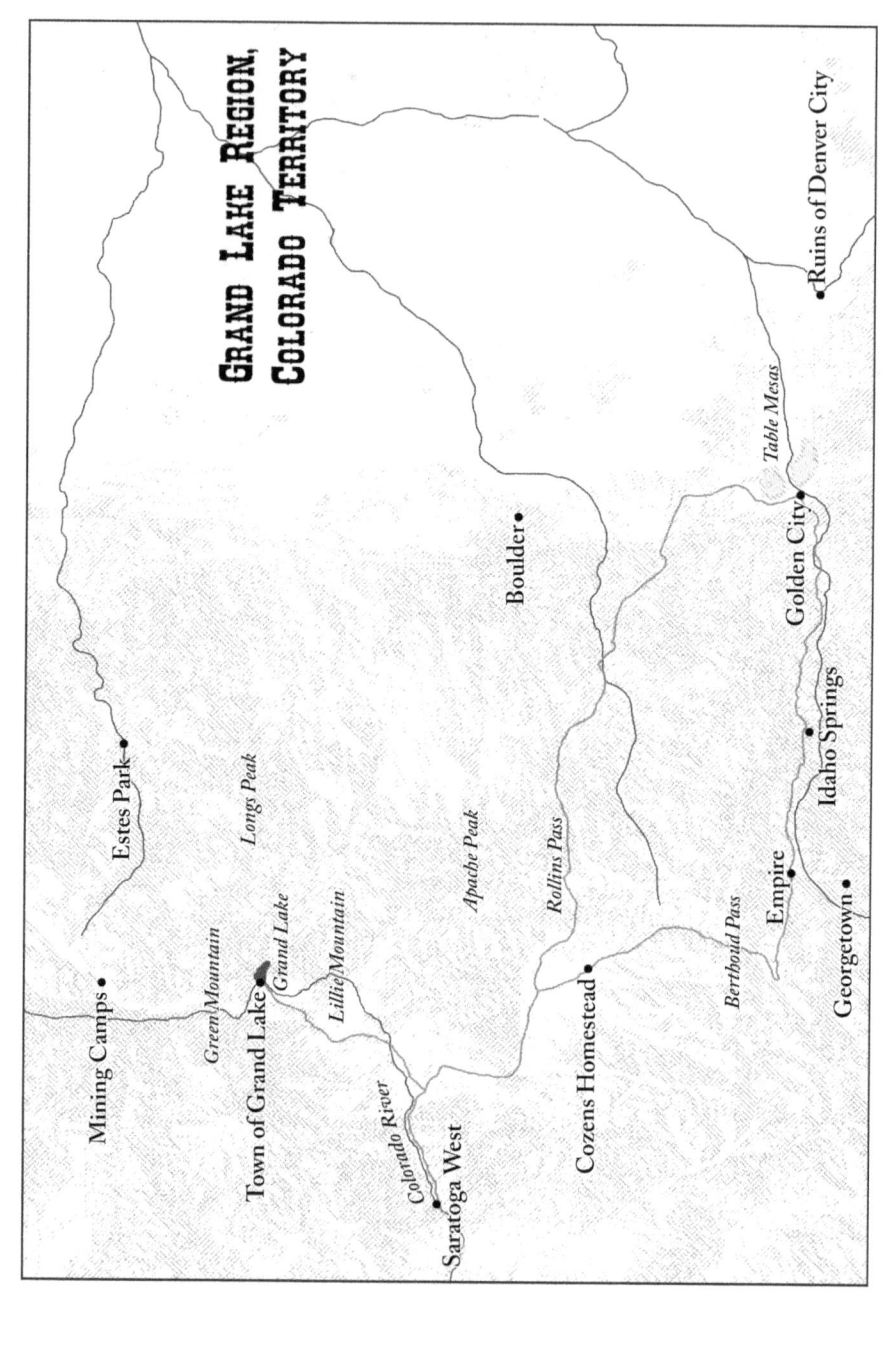

GRAND LAKE REGION, COLORADO TERRITORY

Mining Camps

Estes Park

Green Mountain

Longs Peak

Town of Grand Lake

Grand Lake

Lillie Mountain

Colorado River

Saratoga West

Apache Peak

Boulder

Rollins Pass

Cozens Homestead

Berthoud Pass

Empire

Idaho Springs

Georgetown

Table Mesas

Golden City

Ruins of Denver City

ONE

BY THE LAST day of saber training, I hated being in the army. I was sure that becoming an army sharpshooter was not the best way to kill giants. I hated army training with the same passion I'd felt when we'd confronted the witch back in Colorado. Of course, on a dusty, well-trodden field outside of Fort Chicago, there were no witches. Just a merciless sergeant, cussing us out every time we did something even the slightest bit wrong.

A sergeant I couldn't shoot.

Not like giants. Those I could shoot just fine.

It didn't help that Fort Chicago was humid and muggy in early September. My blue wool uniform clung to me from all the sweat and even that didn't stop it from scratching. The cap didn't keep the sun off my neck and left a vulnerable pink gap there when we did formation drills. At least I was comfortable during shooting practice, but that was because I was one of the best. I never missed at two hundred yards or less.

Saber practice was another thing entirely.

Besides the Winchester rifles, the army issued each of us one of the long curving swords. If we ever found ourselves in close combat with the giants, God forbid, we were to chop at their knees and ankles.

Once they were down, we could stab them wherever we could reach, but our sergeants said that keeping them from walking around was what really mattered. Upright Jotun were hard to fight. Jotun on the ground were easy pickings.

So my squad of recruits stood in a skirmish line with our sabers extended. We were far enough apart not to smell each others' stink, which was appreciated, since we'd trod through the cavalry field muck to get to this training ground. We hadn't been allowed to get out of formation, to my disgust.

My right arm ached holding my sword, but the sergeant wouldn't let us lower it until he'd individually inspected each one of us to make sure we were holding it right. The same inspection he'd done every day for the past two weeks.

But the sabers were heavier and thicker than the ones used in the War Between the States and my wrist felt like it was going to break. I grimaced and held it as best I could as the sergeant worked his way down the line. I knew he was going to yell at me because I couldn't keep the tip up. Then we'd start slashing practice, and we'd keep at it until he was either happy or convinced we weren't going to get any better that day.

That could take a long time.

For better or worse, it didn't take more than a few minutes for him to get to me. He stood a foot from my side and looked out at my blade.

"Private McCarty!" he barked. "Point higher!"

I shifted the sword as directed.

"More left! Straighter. Get that point up, McCarty!"

I ignored the string of curse words that followed. Out of the corner of my eye I'd spotted one of the HQ messengers hastening over to us. The sergeant only had time to make me do two practice slashes, both horrible according to him, before the messenger pulled up huffing in front of us.

"Sir!" he said. "Private McCarty to report to headquarters immediately, sir!"

The sergeant nodded in acknowledgement and then tilted his head while he looked at me. Out of the corner of my eye, I could see the envy in the other recruits.

"What'd you do?" the sergeant asked. "Kill someone important?"

"Yes, sir. Actually I did, but it was months ago." I saluted. "Excuse me, sir."

The sergeant stared at me in disbelief for a moment. "Fine. Dismissed."

With the glee of the paroled, I followed the messenger back to headquarters.

The sprawling Fort Chicago sat south of the actual city, with fortifications extending all the way to Lake Michigan. The army had expected the Jotun to push north once they'd crossed the Ohio, but instead the giants had targeted Saint Louis, for reasons that were still hotly debated. As a result, the original complex had grown from hastily thrown up earthworks to an immense maze of interlocking walls and buildings.

Which meant it took us over a quarter hour, even at double time, to get from the training ground to General Sanborn's headquarters. Sweat beaded on my brow and I really wished I had an opportunity to at least wash my face, but the messenger wasn't slowing or stopping. We just jogged together in silence, pounding up the dust.

But that gave me time to think.

And I couldn't come up with a single reason the general would want me. He'd been briefed on what happened in Colorado long before I'd turned up to enlist. He hadn't expressed any interest in meeting me then. There were a few stares and rumors at first, but most everybody treated me as just another soldier.

Which is how I wanted it.

I could help protect the West against the Jotun, like Cassidy had wanted. Before Cassidy had... had died. He'd said I should try to be a sharpshooter instead of a hero like him.

I'd come to believe he was right.

And so did everyone else in Fort Chicago. Heroes got people

killed. They drilled that into your head the first day. You followed orders, not your conscience. That's how you survived.

That was how we'd win the war.

Besides… after Colorado, all I wanted to do was kill giants. I wanted to aim my rifle, shoot them in the eye, and walk away knowing I'd done good.

The army thought that was just fine.

In the outer office, General Sanborn's aide sat behind a large rough-hewn oak desk. The skinny man, not much older than me, bobbled his head when he saw us enter. The rest of the room was sparse. Battalion flags covered one smooth plank wall, along with a portrait of President Stanford. The Stars and Bars stood on a pole discreetly in one corner. The room smelled of sawdust and coffee.

I pulled up in front of the desk into the stance I'd been taught and saluted.

"Private McCarty, reporting as ordered, sir."

He gave me a dour smile and a half-hearted salute in return. Clearly my fervor did not impress him.

"Go on in," he said. He gestured toward the door to his left instead of the one behind him.

I took a deep breath and marched on through.

The small conference room was nearly empty. It held a long table, and a handful of wooden chairs. Like the reception room, the walls were smooth oak planks with minimal decoration. A large map covered one side.

McNab, Cassidy's grizzled former quartermaster, stood in front of the map, casually studying it and rocking on his heels.

I took a moment to look him over. He'd trimmed the bushy salt-and-pepper hair that ringed his bald head and also shaved recently. He wore an army jacket and pants, though the high boots were decidedly his own and not government issue. Best of all, he actually looked relaxed.

He turned and gave me a broad grin.

"Billy! Good to see you!"

I snapped to position and saluted, and only then glanced at his stripes. Sergeant-Major? When did that happen?

"Sir!" I said. "Private McCarty reporting as ordered!"

"Oh, knock it off," he said with a wave. "They only gave me this," he touched his chevron, "because Mosby insisted. He said it'd make it easier for me to get him his whiskey."

I grinned. Colonel Mosby didn't drink whiskey at all, and McNab and I both knew it. But if McNab could joke about Mosby, that was a good sign.

He looked me up and down and a smirk creased his face.

"Looks like they made a regular soldier out of you," he said.

"They're trying. But I can't stand the army."

"That's too bad," he said with a grin. He nodded his head toward the table. "Your orders."

I spotted the small folded piece of paper I'd overlooked before. I picked it up and scanned it. My eyebrows went up as I did.

"Assigned to Mosby's Raiders." I set the orders down and turned to McNab. "What is this? Mosby's leaving Colorado?"

He chuckled and waved a hand dismissively. "He got his orders, too."

"And I suppose he requested me."

"You'd suppose right."

"I thought he didn't like me," I said, "after our 'talk' back at the beginning of summer."

"You weren't exactly forthcoming." McNab's grin reminded me all too well of Colonel Mosby's frown.

He was right, I hadn't been forthcoming, but not because I didn't want to tell Mosby, but because I didn't want to think about what had happened at *all*. Cassidy's face. The blood seeping from his arm. The knife.

Always the knife.

At least in my nightmares.

McNab picked up on my sudden sullen mood.

"It's okay," he said. "I don't think Colonel Mosby dislikes you for that. He wants you because he knows you're darned good in a fight."

I looked at him warily, but he just stood there, rocking a bit on his heels, clearly amused at my discomfort.

"At least according to his quartermaster." McNab couldn't hold back the teasing grin with that.

"You," I said.

He nodded.

"Fine," I said. "Who else is assigned to Mosby's Raiders?"

He held up his right hand. "Me," he said, ticking off a finger. "Jeremiah." He touched the next one. "And Luke."

I let out a deep sigh of relief. Then my mind raced.

"What about Maria?" I asked.

"Assigned to Sanborn's personal medical corps." His eyes twinkled. "But don't worry, you'll see her once we're out in the field."

I nodded. It wasn't that I was sweet on Maria, like McNab implied. I just knew how good her healing skills were and couldn't think of anyone I'd rather have around. Certainly not the sawbones I'd met here in Fort Chicago. They were way too quick to reach for the amputation saw for my comfort.

Apparently Sanborn thought so, too, if he was keeping her close. I wondered what McNab thought about that.

"Well," I said, "at least we'll be together."

"Maybe," he said. "We're all in the same regiment, but it's a big regiment. It's not gonna be like Colorado."

When it was just the six of us riding together. And Beth, the young girl we'd rescued. That I'd rescued. Of all the things that'd happened in Colorado, that was the one I was most proud of.

"Still," I said. "It'll be good to be out killing giants."

His eyes glinted knowingly, but he kept the grin off his face. I knew he felt the same.

"But first we've got a lot of work to do," he said. "Starting with recruiting."

I tilted my head and waited for him to go on.

"We got three companies at half strength," he said. "If that. We need to fill 'em with new recruits. Which is where you come in."

"Me?" I couldn't help but blink in surprise.

"Sure, kid. You've been training with 'em. Who's the best?"

"Me," I said. "Uh… at least in shooting. I'm not so good with the sword."

"You the worst?"

"Uh… no." I immediately thought of this kid from Minnesota. As skinny as he was, I was sure he'd lied about his age to join up. Not that the recruiter probably cared.

"Then you're the test. Any man who can beat you with a sword and come anywhere close to you with a rifle joins the Raiders. The rest can go to the regular infantry."

I shifted uneasily. There were easily three, maybe four, hundred new recruits in camp. And McNab wanted me to fight them all?

"C'mon." He strode toward the door. "Time's a-wasting. We've got two days to get our regiment into shape before we move out."

"Two days? That's not enough time!"

In the first two days, I'd barely learned how to march, much less how to fight. And I'd already known how to shoot.

"No, it's not," McNab said with an unsavory chuckle. "But if Sanborn doesn't attack the Jotun soon, General Lee and a bunch of his men are gonna die."

"And if he attacks with green recruits, a bunch of us are gonna die."

"You do see the problem."

He went out the door, so I hustled to catch up. As we left the building, he turned and gave me one of his most devilish smirks.

"I hope you're rested," he said. "With all the fighting you're gonna do, you're gonna need it."

I groaned. He just laughed and kept walking.

TWO

THE MAIN RIFLE range stretched out across a broad bare field west of the main fort. A large long dirt mound backed it about a thousand yards from the firing line. Wooden targets shaped like trolls could be positioned at any distance, though they generally sat about a quarter of the way back. Most were splintered and full of holes, though the carpenters did make new ones from time to time. They seemed to like two-headed troll silhouettes, but why escaped me. Everyone knew most trolls had only a single head.

The firing line itself used buffalo hides and the occasional stained sheet to provide at least a little protection from the dirt and the mud. I'd come to appreciate them a great deal on the day the sergeant had insisted we drill in a low drizzle. He'd said we should practice like we fought. I understood the idea, but we'd all complained mightily about the muck. He hadn't cared. If not for the hides, there might've been a mutiny.

As it was, the grounds were mostly dry when McNab and I arrived. Scattered clouds kept it from getting too hot, but it was still too humid for my tastes. I'd been told Chicago wasn't as bad as New Orleans, which only made me want to never visit New Orleans.

The fifteen shooting stations were filled with boys just old enough to be considered men. My age, really, though green as green could be. Their sergeant was having them practice from standing position. Their fire was ragged—ill timed and not at all on the called mark. Few of the wooden trolls seemed to be in any danger. Their sergeant walked behind them, cursing out instructions with the same words that mine had used during saber practice. I had to wonder if they traded ideas for obscenities after taps, when us privates were asleep.

The ragged roar continued as they all fired their Winchesters again.

"Awful young," McNab drawled by my side.

"So am I." I gave him a sideways glance. "A kid, remember?"

He chuckled. "Sorry about the nickname, Billy. It's too late to change it now. Jeremiah's about done writing."

"In three months?" I couldn't help my tone. It felt like just yesterday that I'd used the knife...

"Calm down, will ya?" He scowled at me. "He writes every chance he gets, but in this case he got help. He gave some of the chapters to his friend Sam Clemens in San Francisco to polish up. Jeremiah says he's a newspaperman, but he'll do right by it."

"Huh." I didn't like it, but I'd long given up on the idea that I could change Jeremiah's mind. He said the West needed tales of heroes. He didn't care that they were a pack of lies. Well, not entirely. But enough.

"C'mon," he said, "let's see how these fresh fish shoot."

McNab talked to the range sergeant and arranged for me to shoot with the next group. Then he announced to the crowd that anyone who shot as well as me would become one of Mosby's Raiders. An excited murmur went through the group—they'd heard of Mosby, even if he hadn't been at the front for a few years.

I settled into the middle of the range, where everyone could see me. I decided to shoot standing, simply because the hide was torn and I didn't feel like getting down into the dirt. The breeze was barely there, which made it easier to aim, and the sun was high enough to not give shadows or glint.

As I expected, I didn't miss with the Winchester at less than 200 yards. I switched over to a Whitworth rifle and nailed every target at 800 yards before missing one at a thousand by an inch.

I bounced the Whitworth in my hand and sighed in disappointment. The Army didn't have many of them, on account of the plague in England, and the rate of fire was far too slow compared to the Winchesters. But still, it was a delight to use. I joined McNab to watch the others.

None of the recruits in the first two groups came anywhere close to my mark. One kid in the third group managed to hit the 300 yard target twice, so McNab wrote his name down in a little notebook he'd pulled from his pocket.

The fourth group wasn't much better than the first two, with not a single soldier able to regularly crack 200 yards.

"We're supposed to win the war with this?" I asked as we watched recruits in the fifth group miss at 50 yards.

"They'll learn," McNab said. "You did."

"But we're moving out in two days," I grumbled.

"True. That's why we take the best. The rest can go in the regular infantry."

I would've grumbled more, but I realized he was right. We didn't have to take 'em all.

So we watched three more groups. They were better. McNab added ten names to his list.

We took a break for water and talked to the range sergeant a bit. Or McNab did. I just listened. Most of the conversation was about the Winchesters and ammunition supply. The army had plenty of bullets but not enough rifles. The new factory up in Milwaukee wasn't quite at full production yet. They were also having trouble getting iron from further north. The mines near Lake Superior didn't have enough men, it seemed.

There were never enough men.

The next group of trainees was late, so I decided to shoot again. Enough of a breeze had picked up to make the long distances a bit of a challenge. The bullets wouldn't blow much, but enough. To make it a bit harder, I set the Whitworth aside and picked up my trusty Winchester once again.

I settled into my stance, feet braced apart, rifle on my shoulder. I sighted at a target at 400 yards. I waited for my breathing to settle, took aim at the troll target's head, and fired.

A hit. Dead center in the target's charcoal left eye.

My second shot nailed the other eye.

For my third shot, I decided to target the crudely drawn mouth. I could barely see it at the distance, but they'd smeared the charcoal on thick enough to make the black maw stand out against the wood. Once again I let my breath settle, took careful aim, and fired.

And hit the nose of the target instead.

I lowered my rifle with a snort of disgust.

The next squadron of recruits had arrived, and with them an officer I hadn't yet met. He stood next to McNab, talking quietly and watching me. So I studied him back.

He had captain's bars, a neat black beard, long black hair to his shoulders, and a crisp brimmed cavalry hat. His uniform was pressed and fit well over his slim body. I took him to be thirty, though he stood with the confidence of an older man. He gestured with his right hand as he spoke, though his left never left the hilt of the saber at his waist.

His bushy eyebrows rose at something McNab said.

The new recruits were heading into the range, a couple of them giving me curious stares as they filed past. I gave the range sergeant a half-salute and went to join McNab and the newcomer.

"Billy," McNab said when I got close, "I'd like you to meet Captain Charles Mercer. Captain Mercer, this is Private Billy McCarty."

I gave a sloppy salute, and Captain Mercer frowned. When McNab's displeasure joined his, I came to attention and gave the Captain a proper salute.

Captain Mercer returned the salute. "A pleasure, Private McCarty."

"Captain Mercer will be with us under Colonel Mosby," McNab said.

"Commander, C Company," Captain Mercer said. "The Avenging Angels."

I raised an eyebrow at the name. Cassidy's crew had ridden with them in one of the books but they'd had a different commander then. And a longer name: "Grant's Avenging Angels."

They'd been the men who survived Grant's Last Charge.

A shiver went down my spine as I wondered if Captain Mercer had been among them.

"Sergeant-Major McNab says you're a very good shot," Captain Mercer said.

"The be— one of the best, sir," I said with a nod.

"May I have the privilege of seeing you shoot?"

"Sure—uh, yes, sir," I said. It hadn't been an order, but the sergeant had been berating us about how any officer's request should be treated as one.

"Now, uh, sir?" I asked.

He nodded and gestured toward the range. "It appears there are two openings on the end. If you do not mind, I'll shoot with you."

I nodded because, well, what could I say?

"I'll watch the rest of the recruits," McNab said. "You two go on."

Captain Mercer and I took the last two spots on the firing range. The recruits were all kneeling as they shot, but he stood. He lifted his Winchester to his shoulder and stared down the barrel at his target, which was currently set at 200 yards.

He glanced over at me. "Let's make this interesting, shall we? That target is a bit close."

"Sure, sir," I said. When the recruits had finished their round, Captain Mercer signaled the range officer.

"Move the targets to 400 yards," he said. Then he turned to me. "You first, Private."

I took a deep breath. I didn't know what his game was, but I wasn't sure I wanted to play. Did he want to show he was better than me? Was he trying to take me down a notch?

I started to seethe at the thoughts, but forced them back down. I'd faced worse, much worse than Mercer. I'd killed monsters when my life was in danger.

This was nothing.

I took a few more deep breaths to calm myself. Then I picked up my rifle. My target was now at the correct distance and was one of the two-headed troll silhouettes.

I put the first bullet into the far left eye.

Then I shifted my aim, took another deep steadying breath, and watched the rise and fall of the barrel with my breathing. My second shot hit the exact middle of the inner left eye.

With deliberate calm, I targeted the inner right eye and my bullet went true and straight. I moved over to the far right eye and waited for my breathing and arm to steady before pulling the trigger and nailing it perfectly.

Four shots. Four bullseyes.

I lowered my rifle, and looked at Captain Mercer. I dared him with my eyes, but didn't say anything.

"Quite impressive," he said. "I believe it is my turn."

The rest of the range had fallen silent. A bird called in the distance and some of the other recruits shuffled in their places, but everyone watched us.

Captain Mercer snapped his rifle to his shoulder. He squeezed off four shots in rapid succession. The first missed entirely. The second clipped the target's ear. The third hit the shoulder. The fourth smashed into its right eye.

He lowered his Winchester with a satisfied smile. Then he turned to the watching crowd.

"The target has been killed, gentlemen," he called in a loud voice. "That is the objective here. The objective of war. To kill the enemy." He pointed down the range. "It does not matter if it takes one shot or four. You will keep firing until you have killed your target. You will not stop firing until you have killed your target. Do you understand?"

A ragged call of yeses came from the watching recruits.

Captain Mercer planted his hands on his hips and glared at them. He raised his voice. "I said, do you understand?"

"Sir! Yes, sir!" they called out in unison.

Captain Mercer nodded at their response. Then he waved at the range sergeant to carry on.

My gut fell. I'd shot well—better than Captain Mercer. But his words made it clear I wasn't fast enough.

With a gesture, Captain Mercer bade me to follow him over to McNab.

"Sergeant-Major," he said. "Please have Private McCarty assigned to C Company, First Squadron. Also, this evening after dinner, please report to my quarters." He looked at me. "Both of you."

McNab raised his hand in a salute, and mine was only a second behind.

Captain Mercer turned to go, but then paused and glanced back over his shoulder at me.

"Fine shooting, Private McCarty," he said. "I look forward to having you under my command." With that, he strode off toward the main camp.

"Uh oh," McNab muttered as soon as Captain Mercer was out of earshot.

"What?" I said, not taking my eyes from the receding officer.

"I'd hoped you wouldn't be assigned to Mercer."

"Why?"

"He's good," McNab said, a note of apology in his voice. "He wins his fights…"

"Yeah, and…"

"…and a lot of his men die along the way. More than any other captain, I've heard."

I swallowed hard and took one last look at Captain Mercer. I wondered exactly why he wanted to see us that night.

THREE

I WAS WORN to the bone by the time McNab and I stood outside of Captain Mercer's office. My legs ached. The muscles in my arms were stiff and my elbow throbbed from an unlucky hit during the saber sparring, but I felt fortunate that was it. Despite his threat, McNab hadn't made me fight more than a couple of recruits. He'd only wanted to see enough to know how I stacked up, and after that he made the recruits spar with each other.

Unfortunately, dinner—some sort of stew with cabbage and beef —wasn't sitting well in my gut. I'd tried washing it down with some weak chicory coffee, but that'd only made my stomach flop worse. I wasn't sure I was in shape to be grilled by a Captain, but I didn't think I had much choice. Orders were orders, even if they weren't things I wanted to do.

I kinda hated that.

McNab seemed to handle it better. Of course, he'd just been watching instead of sparring. While I'd been dining with the recruits, he'd gone off with the other sergeants, wherever they go, and come back with an amused grin. I'd asked him what was up, but he'd shook his head and refused to say.

Captain Mercer's office was one of the tiny temporary ones on

Officer's Row. The long wooden building consisted of a series of single rooms, each with a door to the outside. Slat awnings hung over the doorways to keep the worst of the rain off, but the afternoon had been thankfully dry. We still had a bit of time 'til dusk, but the heat had broken, which helped a bit. I didn't have sweat pooling between my neck and collar.

"Do you know what he wants?" I asked McNab.

He shook his head.

"What's he like?"

"You've met him," he said. He looked at me like I'd asked something stupid.

"Yeah," I said, "but you've ridden with him."

"There were a lot of men on that mission." He frowned at the memory. "Mercer fought well, and he survived. He took down a Jotun by himself, if I remember right. Charged into it with his horse."

I choked back my surprise. Close combat with a giant was a *very* good way to get killed. Unless you were Cassidy.

And no one was Cassidy. No one was *like* Cassidy. Cassidy killed giants at close range. Until he'd... until I'd...

I choked up and fought back the salty water forming in my eyes.

McNab knocked on Captain Mercer's door.

"Enter!" we heard from within.

We walked into a bare room that held little more than the basics. Captain Mercer hadn't hung anything on the simple pine walls, unlike a lot of officers. His desk was strewn with a few papers and one large bookcase sat on the far corner. He had two rough chairs in front and another small one behind the desk which he was sitting in as we entered. A small worn leather trunk rested against the far wall behind him, but that was it.

Captain Mercer stood when we entered. McNab snapped to attention and saluted. I did too, a half second later, though not as crisp.

Captain Mercer returned the salute. "At ease. Please be seated."

I sank into the chair on the right, but my nerves overcame my weariness and so I sat on the edge.

"I do not believe in being evasive, gentlemen," Captain Mercer began as he too sat, "so I shall go straight to the point. How exactly did Captain Cassidy die?"

"Fighting the giants, sir," McNab said.

Captain Mercer waved dismissively. "That's for the books. How did he *really* die?"

"I killed him, sir," I said wearily. "I killed him. I put a knife in his heart."

Captain Mercer regarded me with a tilt of his head. Sweat started to bead on my forehead.

"And why… did you kill him, Private McCarty?"

I faltered, and nearly shed a tear. As it was, my throat caught and I had to clear it before I could speak. I lowered my head.

"Because I had to," I said flatly. I studied the grain of the wood on the floor.

"You had to," he repeated. His voice was firm, without the hint of pity I'd heard from so many.

"Yes, sir," I said. "I had to. We had to close the rift right away, sir. And Cassidy was already dying from the poison. So… I did what had to be done."

"Start at the beginning."

So I did. I looked up, met his gaze, and began.

Captain Mercer listened attentively. He didn't interrupt, and he didn't ask questions. When I choked up, he just quietly waited until I was ready to go on. His eyes never left me though, as if there was nothing more in the world that he wanted to see.

"I told all this to Colonel Mosby," I said as I wrapped up. "I'm surprised you don't already have some report or another."

"I do," he said.

"Then why'd you ask?" The bile started to rise. He'd made me relive all that when he already knew? Who in the hell was this man?

He didn't speak at first, as if he was still studying me. But he didn't flinch at the growing hate in my eyes.

"The report tells me about Captain Cassidy," he finally said, flat and firm. "It does not tell me about Private McCarty."

"And what'd this interview tell you?" I practically spat. "Sir?"

"That you are a man to be reckoned with."

He turned to McNab, whom we'd both more or less ignored the entire time I'd been telling my story.

"Sergeant-Major," he said, "have you finished identifying new recruits?"

"Not quite, sir," McNab replied. "We need about twenty more, all told."

"Arrange extra drill time on the range tomorrow for the ones we have," Captain Mercer said. "As much as possible, even at the expense of other training regimes. And requisition as many Whitworths as you can."

"Those are reserved for the sharpshooter squadrons, sir."

Mercer smiled with pursed lips—the first hint of amusement I'd seen on his face.

"We *are* the sharpshooters, Sergeant-Major, and by God we're going to be the best Mosby's Raiders have ever seen."

I blinked, but before either McNab or I could speak, Captain Mercer leaned back in his chair and waved his hand at us.

"Dismissed."

———

We walked through the new-fallen night back toward the recruits' bunks, where I was still to stay for the night. McNab would start moving us into regiment quarters the next day, if they didn't just put us in tents for the road. It was warm enough that it was probably the smart thing to do, but I'd miss my lumpy mattress. It beat the flophouse floors I'd had back in Golden City.

But I seethed as I walked. Finally, I couldn't keep it inside.

"He made us come here for *that*?" I snarled to McNab as he ambled beside me. "So he could decide I was a man to be *reckoned* with?"

"You are," McNab said affably. "Even if you're more kid than man."

"Don't start," I snapped. Then I sucked in my breath and realized who I was talking to. "Sorry, McNab. Uh, sorry, sir."

"It's fine, Billy," he said. "No one's around. Besides, at times I think the army's as silly as you do."

"You do?"

"At times," he said. "But I don't let it show. You should learn not to, either."

I frowned, but then nodded. Then my gut sank.

"He's my commanding officer now, isn't he?"

"Yes he is," McNab said. I could sense the edge of disappointment in his voice. He wasn't happy.

I wasn't either, but I didn't see anything I could do about it. I didn't like Mercer, and I suspected the feeling was mutual.

The next morning at breakfast, new orders arrived for most of the recruits in my bunkhouse. Soldiers grumbled over their coffee and johnny cakes and compared what they'd heard about their new commanders. A few kept shooting glances at me. When I caught them, they looked away.

They'd been at the range the day before, when Mercer'd shot after me, making my own careful marksmanship look wasteful.

My own commander had made me look bad.

I bristled at the thought.

I stewed all through morning drill, which, despite Captain Mercer's orders to McNab, we apparently still had to do. When we got to the range just before noon, they didn't have the Whitworths either. Neither McNab nor Captain Mercer were around, so the range sergeant put us through the usual drills.

When it was my turn, I decided to shoot lying down. I was still angry, but I'd learned long ago when hunting prairie dogs that shooting angry meant shooting wild. I had them put a single-headed wooden troll target at the Winchester's maximum range. With the wind kicking up unpredictably, it'd be a hard shot.

I took my time. Forget Mercer's lesson. I knew how to shoot.

I emptied the magazine one careful shot at a time.

All fifteen bullets smashed into the troll's head.

Pleased, I calmly climbed to my feet and moved out of the way for the next recruit. To my surprise, Captain Mercer now stood at parade rest off to the side. He appeared to notice me, but then his eyes rested on the soldier taking my place.

I shouldered my rifle and moved to the irregular gallery of men who'd already shot. I shuffled my feet and tried not to glare at Captain Mercer. I didn't want him noticing and deciding to humiliate me again. I looked for McNab, but he was nowhere to be seen.

What I did see was another squad marching toward us. They were as ragged as we'd been two weeks ago. Their blue uniforms and caps looked crisp, though, and I blinked and looked again.

They were all Negroes.

I knew there were some in the army, but I hadn't met any yet. Most Negroes lived down around New Orleans these days. Those that weren't still trapped in Jotun territory, of course. But here was a full squad, including a regal Negro sergeant.

Whom I knew, I realized.

I shaded my eyes and squinted. As they came closer, it became unmistakeable. It was my old pal Jeremiah, the man who'd written the dime store novels about Cassidy that I'd loved. The man who'd fought with Cassidy until…

I took a deep breath. Here he was, marching as a regular army sergeant and calling out orders for his troop.

I was relieved as much as I was confused. McNab was a Sergeant-Major. Why was Jeremiah just a Sergeant?

But the relief at seeing him won out. I drifted to the edge of the milling men and waved. Jeremiah didn't see me so I waved harder.

"Jeremiah!" I called. "Over here!"

He looked my way and smiled, but quickly turned back to his own men.

A few minutes later, the soldiers around me noticed the newcomers. The crowd eased its way away, giving the Negro squadron plenty of room to come onto the range. The recruits who'd been shooting finished up and scrambled to the side.

"Halt!" Jeremiah ordered. He then directed his squad to take their places on the range. Only then did he turn to me.

"Billy," he said and extended his hand.

It wasn't enough. I pulled him into a big hug. He laughed and let me before pulling back.

"It's good to see you too," he said. "But that might not be the way to show it." His eyes darted sideways.

I quickly looked over at Captain Mercer. He watched us, his face unreadable. Next, I scanned the soldiers nearby. Most weren't paying attention, but a couple were watching us. Some of them had faces filled with disgust. I glared at one, but turned back to my friend.

"I don't care," I said. "How're you doing?"

"I'm doing as well as one might expect," he said. He gestured toward his squad, now getting into their stances on the range. "I wish they learned as quickly as you."

"You should see me in saber practice," I chuckled.

"Perhaps I shouldn't." He said with a smirk.

"Well, well," A voice said behind me, "the Sergeant-Major's pet is also a Nigger lover."

I whirled. "Who said that?"

The men there looked at me, some with surprise, some with disgust, some with pity. The nearest, a big scraggly-bearded guy puffed his chest and glared at me, challenging almost. But his eyes darted past me and I could see he was biting his tongue.

My hands clenched into fists.

"Is there a problem, gentlemen?" Captain Mercer's smooth voice caused me to spin about. He slowly strolled up to us. He eyes were narrowed, steel hard.

"Uh," I said, "no, sir. No problem." I gave the big scowling man the evil eye even as the words left my mouth.

He grunted but that was it. He gave one last look at Jeremiah before looking off at the range.

"Sergeant Freeman," Captain Mercer said to Jeremiah, "please continue on. I wish to see your squadron shoot."

"Yes, sir," Jeremiah replied. He saluted, and, after Captain Mercer's returned salute, took his men over to the range.

Then Captain Mercer looked at the other men, still shuffling and watching and waiting.

"You men are dismissed to the mess hall," he said. When I started to move, he held me back with a nod.

"Private McCarty," he said once the others were all out of earshot. "It appears your… friendship with Sergeant Freeman has survived your adventures in Colorado, has it not?"

"It has," I said warily.

"Then you will have no issues in assisting in the training of his troops while we are on the road. Good. You are reassigned to Third Squadron."

I swallowed hard, wondering exactly what that meant.

FOUR

FOR THE REST of the day, I wondered what Captain Mercer had in mind. After my squad ate, we skipped saber drill and spent the afternoon moving out of the recruit barracks. We had to clean them first, which got harder as each new sergeant came to collect his men. I was sweeping around my bunk, and kicking up clouds of dust that made my nose itch, when a soldier by the door yelled out my name.

"McCarty! Your sergeant's here!"

I gave the dirt one last brush and leaned the straw broom against the barrack wall. I grabbed my haversack and my bedroll and tied them onto my backpack. As usual, the combined load was a bit heavy, but I was able to wrestle my arms through the straps and get it on without too much delay. I cinched the straps, grabbed my rifle, and headed out.

To my surprise, Jeremiah awaited me.

I blinked. "Where's McNab?"

Jeremiah raised his eyebrows and then slowly his hand moved up in a salute.

Realization hit me fast. I quickly snapped the salute I should've given him before he could finish his.

"At ease, Private," he said. Then he gestured for me to follow him.

I glanced back at the recruits still waiting. A couple gave me dark looks. I shook 'em off and quickened my pace so I could walk at Jeremiah's side.

"Where's McNab?" I asked quietly.

"He's making sure the entire regiment is organized. He reports to Colonel Mosby, remember?"

"Oh, yeah." Since Captain Mercer outranked McNab, I'd forgotten that McNab wasn't actually under Mercer. But if Jeremiah was my sergeant...

"You report to Mercer too?" I asked.

He nodded, but didn't reply.

We double-timed through the Fort to the large main gates. Those steel-bound doors had been open the entire time I'd been in Chicago, but now the flow of men and horses and wagons clogged and congested them. I was itching to ask Jeremiah more, but I needed to keep my wits about me unless I wanted to get jostled hard or ran into.

Once we were through the gates, Jeremiah led me down the main road headed out of the fort towards the southeast. We passed several squads already camped out before he turned down a small track to the left across some grassy scrub. We passed three more campsites before he indicated one on the right that nestled into some scattered oak trees.

"Our squad," he said with a gesture toward the smattering of canvas tents in front of us.

I swallowed hard. Three Negroes sat around a small cook fire where a coffee pot bubbled. One was whittling something and a second poked at the coals with a thin stick. The third looked at me with raised eyebrows. He stood and walked over.

"Private McCarty," Jeremiah said, "meet Private Washington."

Private Washington reminded me of Boggs, the merchant back in Golden City I'd traded a rifle for a horse with, except for the deep black skin. Private Washington had the same dense, muscular frame, and though he wasn't much taller than me, he probably weighed twice as much. He had piercing eyes and a shaved head and his mouth pursed into a thin smile.

He just stopped and nodded without a salute, which was good

because I didn't know if privates should salute each other. I just nodded back.

"Where's the rest of the squad?" Jeremiah asked.

"Sleeping," Private Washington said with a nod toward the tents, "or fetching water." He squinted at me. "You're the sharpshooter supposed to train us, right?"

I gave Jeremiah a questioning look and he nodded.

"Good," Private Washington said. "We saw you shoot. You're good."

I nodded. That was a fact.

"We've," he continued with a gesture toward the other men sitting by the fire, "only been on the range twice. You better teach good."

I swallowed hard. I'd only gotten good with years of practice, mostly hunting. I didn't know how to *teach*.

And we didn't have years. We were supposed to move out tomorrow.

Jeremiah introduced me to the rest of the squad—all Negroes and all with barely any training. Their names flew by me except for Private Washington, who asked that I call him Zeke, short for Ezekiel. Most of them had come up from Arkansas and Texas looking for work and found the army. Zeke himself had been born a slave outside of Little Rock, but was still a young boy when The War Between the States had been fought. His master's widow had freed him after the arrival of the Jotun, to his amusement.

"Said they was the scourge sent for our sins," he said with a chuckle as we sat around the fire eating salty fried pork and some black beans for our mid-day meal. "The South's sins, she meant. Her sister was an abolitionist, which mighta been why she came to think that."

"Do you think that?" I asked.

"Oh Lord, no," he said with a chuckle. "After what the trolls did to Memphis, I know they be from the Devil. If the Lord above sent 'em, then He's a terrible Lord. A truly terrible Lord. And He's not. Not according to my Bible. He is a God of Love. I know that."

I blinked. Ma hadn't made me go to church. Not after my brother Josie died. I knew the Bible, but I'd never thought much about it.

"We," Zeke said, with a firm pat on his thigh for emphasis, "are the agents of the Lord. We will do His work by driving the Devil's Jotun from the lands."

I blinked and my disbelief must've shown on my face. He grinned and shoveled another forkful of pork into his mouth. I glanced at the other soldiers sitting around but they just focused on their own food, as if they'd not heard a thing Zeke had said.

Or they'd heard it enough to pay it no mind.

So I shrugged and worked on finishing my own meal.

We had marching drill that afternoon, in a wide field where the wheat had been harvested a few weeks before. It made the footing tricky, with all the dirt clumps and plowed rows in places. We struggled to stay in formation, but we managed. With the cool breeze blowing the general mugginess away it actually was a pleasure to march instead of have saber training.

The entire company drilled together, with Captain Mercer in the lead, calling orders loud and crisp. Too bad our turns weren't so crisp, with so many ragged and slow. Captain Mercer called out to the sergeants to correct things, but without heat or obscenity. Apparently he didn't care to swear like so many of the others.

I lined up between Jeremiah and Zeke as the only white soldier in our squad. My shoulders twitched a bit, but I tried to shake off any feelings of discomfort. They were men, just like me, after all, and Jeremiah was a friend. Still, the stares of some of the soldiers in the other squads unsettled me.

I caught a glimpse of McNab, off to one side, talking with Colonel Mosby. They were deep in their conversation and only glanced our way once or twice. I never spotted Luke, Cassidy's old scout, though McNab had said he was part of the Regiment.

After we finished the marching drill, Captain Mercer had us form up close. He stood at parade rest in front until we were all settled and quiet.

"Men," he called out loud enough for us all to hear. "Tomorrow we march to Louisville." He paused until the murmur that rippled through the crowd died. "General Sanborn intends to take the city and destroy the Jotun garrison there. We attack in two weeks."

I tried not to let the surprise show on my face. We'd barely get there in two weeks, and that was assuming we didn't run into any Jotun in the Contested Lands along the way.

"I have requested," Captain Mercer continued, "the honor of being the first to cross the river. That has been granted. Mosby's Raiders will cross south of the city the day before the attack. Our orders are to cut off the city from reinforcements. We, the Avenging Angels, will be the vanguard."

Muted voices ran through the ranks as the implications sunk in. If the battle went badly, we'd be trapped on the wrong side of the river.

I suppressed a shudder.

"We are the Avenging Angels!" the Captain shouted. "We destroy our enemies! We bring terror to their hearts! We do not stop. We do not surrender. We do not *lose*! We win, and then we win again!"

A ragged cheer went up from some of the soldiers.

"May God have mercy on the Jotun," Captain Mercer said more evenly, "for we shall have none."

We all fell silent.

"None."

Then the Captain waved his hand. "Dismissed. We march at dawn."

All we talked about around the dinner campfire was the coming attack. We wolfed down our baked beans and bacon and hardtack and made our guesses about how we'd proceed. Jeremiah remained quiet, off to one side, but he kept a watch on the rest of us.

One of the privates in our squad, Joe Johnson, a scraggly Negro missing his left pinky finger, had lived in Louisville before the Jotun War.

"The river's wide," he said. "No place to hide. They'll see the boats for sure."

"So?" Zeke said. "Nuthin' they can do about 'em 'til they're in close. They can't throw rocks far."

"They can throw them plenty far," I said, remembering some that had nearly missed me, back in Colorado.

"Won't matter with the ironclads," Zeke said. "Heard the Army's bringin' 'em up from New Orleans."

"Where'd you hear that?" Jeremiah interjected. His brow furrowed in worry.

"Telegraph guy in my prayer group," Zeke said.

I blinked in surprise. I hadn't heard anything about a prayer group before. "Is it true?"

Jeremiah frowned, but then nodded. "It is. There's supposed to be twenty of them coming. They'll provide cover for the troop ships."

"Except we'll already be across," I said.

"We will," Jeremiah said. He glanced around at the squad, most of whom were scraping the last bit of food out of their tin plates or finishing their tack. "Which means... time for training." He raised his voice. "Third Squadron! Form up in five minutes for rifle training!"

The men grumbled, but sped up finishing their dinners.

"Where we gonna train?" I asked Jeremiah. "The range is back at the Fort and we're surrounded by other camps."

"Right here," he said. "With their rifles unloaded so they can't shoot anyone accidentally."

"How are they gonna learn anything that way?"

"Good question," he said with a devilish grin. "I look forward to seeing what you teach them."

I rolled my eyes before stuffing the last of my salty beans into my mouth.

I was pleased to discover that all of the squadron at least knew the right way to hold a rifle. They set the butt of their Winchesters into their shoulders the right way and each of them did a good job of aiming down the barrel.

At least standing. It took a long time for a couple of them to get it right while lying down. Joe Johnson looked like he was taking a nap on his stomach, his head leaning on his rifle's stock. I corrected him twice, and then he at least looked like he was awake.

Jeremiah didn't like how slowly some of them sank to their knees and spread out. He stood in front of the squadron with his hands on his hips.

"When I say 'Down!' you get down fast!" he barked. "You don't, and you may find a spear in your belly."

"Or a bullet," I added. "If you're down, other men can fire over your head."

Jeremiah shot me a pointed look, and I remembered that I wasn't supposed to interrupt someone of higher rank.

"We will now practice," he said. "On your feet." He waved me into the line with the rest.

And then for the next long bit, Jeremiah made us practice dropping into a prone firing position, then standing and doing it all over again. A couple of times, a few soldiers moved too fast and banged their rifles on the ground, causing them to drop them. One soldier, a older Negro named Adam with short thinning curly hair, banged his knee so hard he rolled to his side, clutching it in pain.

But by the end of it, we knew how to get low fast. Even Joe Johnson got to the right position almost at once.

Then we practiced the kneeling stance, with Jeremiah and me checking that everyone held the gun the right way. Zeke's barrel was waving all over the place, so I knelt by him and grabbed it. He was panting hard.

"You have to control your breathing," I said. "Regular breaths. Like this."

I demonstrated. Then I gestured for him to try.

He let out a long breath that seemed to calm him, and then did his best to mimic me.

"Good," I said after a bit. "Your rifle moves with your breathing. Get into the stance and watch the tip."

He did, and as his barrel slowly lifted and fell, a light seemed to come on in his eyes.

"That's enough," I said.

He lowered the rifle and stared into the distance.

"Oh my," he said at last. "I wish I'd known that back in Little Rock."

He seemed unfocused, like he wasn't with me. I nudged him gently on the arm. "Why?"

"'Cuz then maybe Georgie'd still be alive."

FIVE

DUSK HAD BEGUN to set in, casting shadows across Zeke's face. Wrinkled lines appeared in the dark creases around his eyes. For a moment, I thought I saw a tear.

"Georgie?" I asked.

Zeke grimaced and turned to me. "My baby brother," he said as he wiped his eye. "A troll got 'em."

"Ah," I said. My heart wrenched at memories of Josie. "The Jotun got my baby brother, too."

"Then you know what it's like," he said. "Watching someone you care about die."

"Yeah," I said. "Yeah I do." But my mind hopped from Josie to Cassidy. I hadn't seen Josie die—just his body when we went to bury him. But Cassidy...

I suppressed a shudder.

"Attention!" Jeremiah called. "Fall in!"

We scrambled to line up. When we were done, he told us we were finished for the night and to hit the sack. We'd be up before dawn to get ready to march. I lingered, so I could talk with Jeremiah while the others headed to their tents. After he'd answered a question from Joe Johnson, he made his way over to me.

Belatedly, I raised my hand to salute, but his return was crisp.

"You need to do that right," he said. "It's a sign of respect."

"Uh… well, I have a hard time thinking of you as my superior," I said. "You're my friend."

He smiled. "A friend, really?"

"After what we've been through together…" I let out a sigh. "That's what I wanted to talk about, actually."

"Let's sit by the fire," he suggested.

We took some seats on a small log not far from the dying campfire. We'd bank the coals later, but for now it gave a bit of warmth in the fading light. The smoke drifted up and away from us, dancing as if to the sounds of the crickets and the men getting settled to sleep.

Jeremiah stretched his legs out with a groan of relief. He clasped his hands and looked over at me as I sat by his side.

"So what's on your mind, Billy?"

"It's…. well.. this." I gestured wide to indicate the whole camp. "It's not at all like Cassidy's team. I don't know these men, and I gotta keep 'em alive? I mean, I trust you to have my back, but these guys? They can't shoot, they've never faced a giant, they…"

I took a deep breath as the realization set in.

"I miss Cassidy," I said, "but… I miss the team as much as I miss him, you know?"

"Yes, yes I do." He sadly smiled. "He was a good man and he knew how to surround himself with good people."

"He *cared*. Even when I was mad at him." I barked in ironic laughter. "Well, maybe *after* I was mad at him, when I calmed down. *Then* I knew he cared."

"That he did."

"But now…" I waved my hand at the nearest tent, where we could hear someone shuffling around. "I can't help get the feeling that if he was alive, you'd all be off on your own mission somewhere, scouting or raiding. You wouldn't be doing marching drills, or evaluating recruits, or even trying to teach new fish how to shoot."

He chuckled. "We did plenty of all of that, back in the day. I just never wrote about it."

"And what are you gonna write about now? McNab's running

around doing Mosby's errands. You're just a regular sergeant and I'm a private. I haven't even *seen* Luke or Maria."

"Yeah… about that." Jeremiah picked up a stick and stirred the coals, sparking a couple back into life.

"What?"

"You probably won't see Luke," he said. "Before he joined Cassidy, he'd been a lieutenant. So they offered him a captaincy in one of the other regiments and he took it. McNab couldn't persuade him to stay."

"He didn't want to be with us?" I exclaimed.

"More like he wanted the bars more. He told McNab that it was time for him to move on with his life and the regular army suited him fine."

"The army doesn't suit me," I grumbled.

"You have to make the best of it. This…" Jeremiah looked out at the camp and frowned. "…well, I'll do my best to make sure these men survive."

"You don't like this either," I guessed.

He snorted softly. "We have to do this. If we don't, the Jotun will destroy General Lee and all of New England."

"Yeah," I said. "There is that." That and killing Jotun, which would be good by itself.

"You'll be fine, Billy." He stirred the coals a bit more and started to push the ones that glowed into a small pile with his stick. "We get through this and who knows?"

I blinked. I hadn't thought that far ahead.

"Get some sleep," he said. "We've got a long day tomorrow and you'll need the rest."

I nodded, as he had a point.

The next day was not only long, but completely exhausting. We marched at dawn, as planned, and didn't stop until dusk. After dinner, we held more shooting practice in the dark, though once again we didn't use actual ammunition. I wasn't sure what good it did, but I hoped it helped. Zeke, at least, was getting better at controlling his breathing. When it was over, I collapsed into a deep sleep only punctuated by a single nightmare.

Then the next day, we did it again.

And the day after that, we did it again.

And the fourth day, and the fifth, and the sixth, until they blurred into a misery of marching, practicing, pitching tents, and trying to sleep.

It wasn't completely monotonous. Some nights we did saber practice instead of rifle practice. Jeremiah had Zeke teach those. I was impressed—the big man might not be able to aim a rifle, but he could toss that saber around like it was a pocketknife.

Captain Mercer marched with us some of the time. Other times, he was with other squadrons. He spoke to me twice, or maybe on three occasions. He wanted to know how the training of the rest of the squadron was going.

"It'd help if we could use real bullets and targets, sir," I said. "It feels pretty foolish without them."

"I understand, Private. But we do what we can."

It didn't reassure me.

Most of the days were hot, though the late August heat was beginning to break. We got caught in rainstorms twice, but there was nothing to do but march on. The rumor in the camps that night was that the ironclads were almost to the rendezvous location, and so we had to hurry. Sanborn wasn't going to let "a little weather" get in the way.

At one of the camps on day ten or eleven or maybe twelve, Zeke got himself stung bad by a bunch of bees. He'd been foraging and brought us back a bunch of honeycomb, for which the rest of the men were grateful, but his face and neck were a mess of welts.

"Take him to the medical tents," Jeremiah ordered me. "See if you can find Maria. She's got a salve that's good for these."

My heart skipped a beat, and I think Jeremiah noticed, because he couldn't stop the smile from creeping onto his face.

The medical tents clustered not far from Colonel Mosby's field head-quarters. The tents were larger than the ones us soldiers got, being tall enough to walk into even without stooping. They'd once been white, but mud and sun gave them a faded dullness, especially in the twilight. Each tent opened toward a large central fire ring where pots bubbled and smoked under the watchful eye of a skinny pale girl with a white nurse's cap and apron. When I asked about Maria, she pointed me toward one of the smaller tents with the flaps down.

"Much obliged, Ma'am," Zeke said to the girl, who couldn't be more than twelve. She beamed in reply.

We paused outside the tent, not knowing quite what to do. Finally I cleared my throat.

"Maria?" I called. "You in there? It's Billy."

The tent flap opened and she stood there, smiling. In a white and blue nurse's uniform with her hair braided and flowing down her back, the small Mexican woman looked completely different than the one I'd ridden with back in Colorado. She had the same mysterious smile and twinkle in her eyes, but she looked… older. Heavier. Not her weight, but… the way she stood.

Still, I was mighty glad to see her.

"You're a sight for sore eyes," I gushed.

She nodded, and I thought I saw a bit of a smile in the corners of her mouth.

""Um… this is Zeke," I said. "He got stung by some bees."

"Still with the 'ums', Billy?" she said with a hint of amusement. She gestured toward Zeke. "Come inside."

She turned and we followed her into the tent. There, an oil lamp hung from a nail on the far tent post. A cot sat along one side and Maria pointed Zeke at it. On the other side, a small folding table overflowed with bags and small colored bottles. I recognized some of Maria's medicines, but they made up only a small portion of the bounty.

"Wow," I said as she began rummaging through her medical stash. "How'd you manage all this?"

"Pack horse," she said.

She found a brown tin can, opened it, and gave it a sniff. She nodded and took the ointment over to Zeke.

"Hold still," she said as she began smearing it over the stings. He flinched when she first touched him, but let himself relax as she worked.

I stood there, shifting my weight from foot to foot, not knowing quite what to say.

When she finished with the ointment, she stepped back and gave Zeke the once over. Then she nodded. "Go out and ask Miss Molly for some willow bark tea," she said.

"She the girl by the fire?" Zeke asked.

"Yes."

He looked at me questioningly.

"I'll be out in a minute," I said. "Maria and I are old friends."

I could tell Zeke was ready to ask something, but he swallowed the question and nodded. Then he turned to Maria.

"I'll be right outside if you need me, Ma'am."

Then he stood and left.

I watched him go with a furrowed brow. "What a strange thing to say."

"He cares about my virtue," Maria said.

"What?" I exclaimed. "He thinks... I mean, he believes I could—"

"It's all right, Billy," she said. "I'm touched, in a way." She smiled at me. "How are you?"

I let out a heavy sigh.

"Not well," I said. "The nightmares... they haven't stopped. It's every night, still."

"Did you try the poppy syrup?"

"For a few days," I said. "I gave the rest of it to Mr. Lake for his supplies." It was the least I could do for all his generosity in the days before I'd left to join the army.

"I'm sorry to hear that."

I shrugged. It hadn't helped as much as I'd hoped, actually. I fell asleep easier, but the nightmares still came.

"What else have you tried?"

"Not much. Well, a lot of stuff, but none of it worked."

She nodded. "Perhaps—"

"Hey!" a loud voice shouted outside the tent. Both our heads swiveled.

"What're you doing with that girl, Nigger?"

My eyes went wide. I didn't know the voice, but I knew he had to be talking to Zeke.

SIX

"I *SAID*, WHAT'RE YOU DOING?"

The voice was loud and defiant. Maria paused to set her medicines down, which is why I beat her out of the tent.

Outside, in the fading light, we saw two burly soldiers standing menacingly over Zeke, who sat crosslegged on the ground near the fire. His mouth hung open and his eyes stretched wide. The girl, Molly, crouched about two feet away and looked terrified.

One of the burly men made a fist and pulled back his arm.

"Hold it!" I yelled. "Leave him alone!"

The two soldiers turned and my gut fell. One of them was the same blowhard buffoon who'd made comments at the range. My pulse raced as I felt the anger rise.

He recognized me too.

"Well," he said, "if it ain't the captain's pet." He drew himself up and planted both feet firmly in the dirt.

"The nurse told him to get medicine from the girl," I snapped as I pointed at Zeke. "He's done nothing wrong. Leave him alone."

"Niggers shouldn't be using our medicines." He sneered and balled his hands into fists.

He wanted to fight. *I* wanted to fight. I shifted onto the balls of my feet and made my own fists. I looked for where I'd have to throw the first punch. He was a lot bigger than me, so I'd have to make it count.

People spilled out of the other tents and came from other places around. We soon had an audience clustered between the tents and circling the two of us. The other soldier with the Big Buffoon had nervously slid back into the crowd.

"They're *all* our medicines," I snarled.

He took a half step forward.

"What seems to be the problem, soldiers?" Captain Mercer's voice was unmistakable and a moment later he pushed his way through the crowd around us. He gave us all an appraising look before turning to Zeke.

"Soldier," he said, "are you hurt?"

"Bee stings, sir," Zeke mumbled, his eyes averted.

"Have you received treatment?" Mercer asked.

"I was," Zeke said. He pointed at Molly who held up the willow bark tea, still clutched in her hand hard enough for her knuckles to be white.

"Carry on," Mercer said. Then he turned to me and The Big Buffoon. "And you, soldiers?"

"I'm with him," I said as I pointed at Zeke. "Sir." I belatedly added.

"Just passing through, sir," the Big Buffoon said. He dipped his head and spoke softly, as if for all his bravado, he was afraid of the Captain.

"Then continue on," Mercer said. "Dismissed." He turned to the rest of the onlookers. "You are all dismissed."

With a few murmurs, the crowd dispersed. I knelt by Zeke's side.

"You okay?" I asked.

He nodded, but looked over at Molly with a pleading look. Her eyes went wide and she stuck out the tea. Her arm shook as she held it.

"Let me," Maria said suddenly appearing beside me. She took the tea from the terrified girl and handed it to Zeke. He sipped it with a look of gratefulness on his face.

I stood. Captain Mercer gave me a stern look.

"Do not kill any of my men, Private McCarty," he said. "No matter the provocation. We cannot afford the loss."

I blinked. *Kill?* The Captain was warning *me?* The other guy was twice my size!

Captain Mercer nodded, as if he'd read my mind. "Yes, you, Private McCarty. You are the deadliest soldier in my company. I do not wish to see you executed, but if I must, I will."

He gestured toward Zeke. "Take Private Washington and return to your squadron. Please inform Sergeant Freeman that I will march with you tomorrow."

With that, he turned and strode off, leaving me with my mouth agape.

Thick clouds obscured the early morning sun. A light breeze whirled through the trees as we took down our tents and packed them up. Word came down that Sanborn wanted to move quickly, so we were to eat our biscuits as we walked. Rumors soon came that a messenger had arrived from General Lee and the situation in New England looked dire.

Hearing that, I think we all had an extra hitch in our step as we got back on the road to Louisville.

As we marched, some of the men tried to get Joe Johnson to describe Louisville.

"Don't quite know what to say," he drawled. "It's a city. Got buildings. Got streets. Got people. At least I think it's got people."

"It should," Jeremiah said. "The Jotun didn't level it, so there will be human slaves."

Several of the men shuddered, all Negroes, of course. I was sure they were remembering their own time under the lash. Even Jeremiah winced a little, and he'd only been a house slave as a boy.

There weren't any slaves in Colorado Territory, so I hadn't actually met any. Just men, like Jeremiah and Zeke, who'd used to be slaves before The War Between the States. Few of them would talk about what it was like.

"We could cross at the Falls," Joe Johnson continued. When he saw our confusion, he explained, "there's waterfalls in the river there, at Louisville. It's not too deep. Of course, there's the canal. We'd have to swim that."

"We're going to be across the river long before we come to Louisville," Jeremiah said. "Remember the Captain's speech?"

"Um… yeah," Joe said.

He fell silent, and I could tell he was embarrassed, so I gave him a friendly smile when he looked my way. The rest of the talk dropped off as well as Jeremiah had us pick up the pace.

We didn't talk much for the next hour or two. The road we followed had turned to a muddy track, though we ourselves only walked in a light rain. All of us spent more time watching our step than anything else, though it was more sucking muck than slippery.

Captain Mercer appeared after our midday meal. He marched with Jeremiah at the head of the column, though they spoke little. He spoke to me not at all. Why he had thought it important to march with us escaped me.

I thought I might address him when we made camp, but instead of stopping as dusk fell, we received the order to march on. We hiked maybe two more hours until the order came to stop and camp for the night.

"No training!" Jeremiah declared. "We leave before dawn."

Joe Johnson gave me a "you gotta be kidding" look. I returned a "what can you do?" shrug. Zeke was already setting up his tent.

The next day was equally long. Our rest breaks grew shorter, as they hustled us forward whenever they could. Men complained and groused and a few had to stop and wrap rags around their feet after getting blisters. I was glad I'd bought good boots back in Golden City before I'd enlisted. At least the rain had stopped, though patchy clouds remained.

But just before noon the pace started to slow up. The regiment ahead of us seemed to come to a standstill, and then spread out.

We'd reached the Ohio River.

My chin dropped.

I'd waded through the Grand River in Colorado up near Grand

Lake, up at its headwaters. I'd crossed the upper Mississippi on my way to Fort Chicago, but that had been by ferry at night. I'd never really seen a wide river, at least not since I was a small kid.

And this was *wide*.

The trees on the far shore looked like brush hairs, sticking up against a brightening sky. Water flowed as far left and right as I could see to the bends of the shore. Grand Lake had been big, I thought, but I could've fit the entire thing in this river with room to spare.

The water was smooth, though. None of the tumbling white water I was used to. I wasn't sure if that was reassuring or not.

Zeke came up next to me and pointed downstream. "Look."

The ironclads were here.

The steamboats were both bigger and smaller than I expected. Each had twin stacks which puffed white smoke that curled around and blew east. They sat low and squat, not much taller than the Astor Hotel back home, if even that. I could probably climb from the deck to the roof without much help. Their metallic sides shone in the sunlight.

And they were long. Maybe three hundred, four hundred feet if I could guess right.

Even more, they crowded the river. Boat after boat after boat.

And then I saw that each boat also had cannons on it. They were too far away to count, but at least four per boat. Probably more.

My pulse quickened and my hopes rose. The Jotun at Louisville didn't have a chance!

"Keep moving," Jeremiah called.

I glanced around and realized we'd all come to a stop at the sight of the ships and were milling around. We needed to get out of the way so the rest of the column could advance.

Jeremiah gestured for us to follow him off to the side, downstream. We had to wind our way through some trees before we finally reached a small clearing by the shore. A small dock extended out to the river with a single smokestack small fat tugboat tied up at it.

He told us to halt and make room. A few minutes later, Captain Mercer and the rest of the squadrons under his command arrived.

We formed up ranks and Captain Mercer strode out on the dock where we could all see him.

"Men!" he called. "In a few short minutes, we shall enter enemy territory. We are taking the fight to them. We attack! And we shall be victorious!"

He drew his saber and thrust it into the air. "For General Lee!"

"For Lee!"

The ragged cheer dismayed Captain Mercer, and he raised his saber again.

"For Grant!"

The responding cheer was louder, but Mercer didn't wait.

"For the West!"

The wordless roar echoed through the river valley, so much that the rest of the army must've thought we'd all gone mad.

Instead, First Squadron, among them The Big Buffoon that had hassled Zeke, surged forward and onto the tug.

———

We lined up to be ferried across by squadron. When it was our turn to cross the river, I stood as close to the center of the tug as I could. There was a rail near the boiler, which I clung to. My knuckles turned white as I listened to the chug of the engine.

I wasn't the only one fighting to control his nerves. About half of our squadron couldn't swim. I might've been able to manage a dog paddle in still water, but the Ohio was anything but sluggish. I couldn't even look at the water.

Instead, I stared at the far shore, willing it to come faster.

There wasn't much to see. The landing area consisted of a broad shallow muddy track, with a narrow wooden dock that extended into the water. An area about thirty feet square had been cut out of the trees at the end of the dock.

One of the two squadrons that had landed before us had already moved down the dirt road leading east through the dense tall maples. The trees shaded the other squadron, Second Squadron, from the afternoon sun as they stood in rank and listened to Captain Mercer. He had his hand crossed behind his back as he spoke and looked calm, though I could not make out his words with the distance.

A cry arose down the road.

Mercer whirled in an instant. He drew his saber and held it high. With a yell over his shoulder to the Second Squadron, he charged down the road.

The soldiers all grabbed their rifles and ran after him.

Around me, men gasped.

The boat's engineer furiously shoveled coal into the boiler.

The trees about a hundred yards upstream from the landing began to shake. Then the ones closest to the shore trembled and collapsed into the river.

Gasps and cries of fright filled our little tug as a Jotun stepped into view.

Twenty feet tall, he looked human in proportion, with a leather jerkin, thick trousers, and high leather boots. He wore an iron helmet with large holes for his eyes to glare out of. His mouth hid behind his bushy brown beard. He roared something and raised his fist.

I let go the rail and gripped my rifle.

He hefted a rock the size of a sheep.

I snapped my rifle to my shoulder but lurched as the tug swerved beneath my feet. I fought to keep my balance.

The boulder came flying toward us.

SEVEN

I FIRED.

I didn't wait to see if my bullet struck the Jotun or not. I dropped to the deck and cradled my rifle while praying that the rock would fly over our heads.

The tug jerked to the sound of shattering wood.

Men screamed as the boat rocked.

I grasped desperately for the rail, but failed to grab it. I tumbled and slid, banging into other men as we all bounced like corn kernels in a hot pan.

Then the boat stopped shaking and tilted to one side. It slowly began to spin as it floated. The engine coughed, sputtered, and died.

"It's sinking!" someone yelled, his voice piercing the chaos.

Mindlessly, some men jumped into the river. I scrambled forward until I could grab a rail post. I wrapped one arm around it, still clutching my rifle with my other hand.

I can't swim, I thought. *I can't swim!* My breathing sped up and I fought to keep the panic under control.

"Lord have mercy! Lord have mercy!"

Zeke crawled across the deck until he could reach the post. He repeated his shouts, and at first I thought he was as terrified as me, but then I realized he wasn't.

"Dear Lord!" he called out. "Have mercy on us, your children!"

We clung there, sprawled like rag dolls. We hung on as the tug continued to shudder and shake. Cries and screams surrounded us.

Despite all of that, Zeke gave me a wide-mouthed grin. "The Lord will provide," he said.

Cannons roared.

I lifted my head and twisted around enough to sorta see upstream. One of the ironclads!

It'd sailed downstream and smoke rose from its barrels as it fired on the shore again. I couldn't get a good look at where the Jotun had been, but I was sure it was on the run. Cannons were the only thing that could reliably kill the giants.

"See?" Zeke said.

We clung there for a while. The tug settled at a tilt and slowly began to sink.

My heart pounded! I tried to guess how far Zeke and I were above the water. How long did we have?

The ironclad didn't fire again. Instead, it steamed right toward us.

"The Lord is merciful," Zeke said with a huge sigh.

"Thank God," I added.

"Thank God indeed."

We clung there, waiting for the ironclad. Minutes seemed like hours, in all the ways my muscles strained and my heart hammered. Every drop of mist felt like a bucketful as I feared the tug would be under the surface all too soon.

With me under the surface and drowning. I trembled at the thought and clung to the rail even tighter.

The ironclad closed agonizingly slow.

But the tug didn't sink as fast as I'd feared. Or the ironclad was faster than I thought. It got close before the water came even close to our toes. The chug of the ironclad's engine began to suffocate the sounds of the water rushing by.

It was the most welcome sound I may have ever heard!

The ironclad crew threw ropes out and one by one we all were hauled on board. I managed to get my rifle strapped around one shoulder before they pulled me up. Zeke and a few others weren't so lucky—they lost their weapons into the river.

Me, I'd lost my haversack and pack.

I was wet, but alive. I let out a long deep breath and smiled at Zeke as he knelt in prayer on the ironclad's deck.

The ironclad took us to the landing area on the south side of the river, as it was closest. Captain Mercer stood back a ways where the mud met the trees. Off to the side, a bunch of men sat on the ground, some holding their arms or heads or their comrades.

We reached the end of the dock and Captain Mercer strode down it toward us. Once he'd boarded, he looked at the rest of us bedraggled survivors of the tugboat sinking.

"Soldiers," he said crisply. "Disembark here. Sergeant," he said to Jeremiah, "I have posted lookouts down the road. Please triage the wounded and inventory our supplies. I will confer with Colonel Mosby and General Sanborn and return."

Wearily, we nodded and filed off the boat. Wet. Mostly shaken. But alive.

I sat on a dry lump of dirt and grass under one of the maples at the edge of the muddy landing and checked my rifle over. I myself was mostly dry, except for the bottoms of my pants and my socks. I'd only sloshed enough water into my boots to make me uncomfortable. I wasn't likely to risk a chill.

Others weren't so lucky. Joe Johnson and two others of our squadron had stripped off their shirts and were wringing them out on the edge of the dock. A lot of water cascaded out of their clothes, even after all the time since they'd been fished out of the river. Joe shivered despite the warm sun beating on his dark back.

Of course, it had been even worse for some. The tug had gone completely under water, and its captain had been seriously hurt. Also, one of the men who'd leaped off the tug early had drowned. That was in addition to the casualties from the two squads already ashore.

Besides Captain Mercer, the ironclad took seven wounded men and the bodies of four more back across the river. One of them was the First Squadron's sergeant, nearly sliced in half by a Jotun axe. Second Squadron's sergeant had been wounded, but word was he'd survive.

They'd driven off a Jotun, but at a huge cost.

The survivors were a sorry lot.

Men milled around, or flopped wherever it was dry. They talked in small groups and several constantly looked around with hunted looks in their eyes.

The only one that didn't seem shaken was Jeremiah, who moved from group to group, talking quietly with them and jotting things down in his little notebook.

At last he came to me.

Jeremiah paused a few feet away, where the shade just covered his head. His notebook ready, he looked me up and down. He stood straight, and I got the impression he was more sergeant than friend at the moment. He didn't make me salute, though.

"Are you injured?" he asked.

"No," I said with a shake of my head.

"Equipment?"

"I have this," I said, lifting my rifle. "That's it."

"No gear," he said as he wrote.

"No gear," I grumbled. "No food. No blankets. No dry clothes. No extra bullets either."

"We have ammunition." He tapped the end of his pencil against the notebook. "Do you think you can go forward?"

I looked at him with amused disbelief. "Why wouldn't I? I've done with worse. This is nothing."

"Not for some of these men," he said. He glanced back over his shoulder. "Some of them look like they're going to turn rabbit."

"Huh." I tried to see what he meant, but I couldn't. All the men looked pretty much the same to me. Tired and resigned, or maybe a little bit nervous.

"Come with me," he said. He started to turn, but waited for me to stand.

"Where are we going?"

"To talk to them." He gestured toward a cluster of four soldiers from one of the other squadrons standing on the far side of the landing area.

I squinted and took a better look at them. Then my muscles tightened.

The Big Buffoon, the solider that'd picked on Zeke, was there.

He and his buddies kept looking around, too. Suspicious like. As if they were up to something.

"Yeah," I said. "I can see why you might want some back-up."

"A witness," he said. "All I need is a witness."

I nodded and followed him over.

As we trod through the squishy mud, I fell a step behind Jeremiah. *He* might think he didn't need a second, but he hadn't been on the edge of throwing punches. I didn't think the Big Buffoon would care that Jeremiah was a sergeant if he thought he could get away with something.

When they spotted us coming, all four turned to stare. The Big Buffoon scowled and one of the others slid his hand to the butt of the revolver at his waist.

Jeremiah pulled up a few feet away and I stopped slightly behind him to the side. He snapped a crisp salute, which I quickly mimicked.

The soldiers glared at him, and did not return the salute.

Jeremiah dropped his hand and spoke loudly. "Captain Mercer has ordered me to inventory our supplies and equipment." He held out his notebook. "Private Forrest, are you wounded?"

"Nah," the Big Buffoon said.

"Any missing equipment?"

He scoffed. "I don't lose things."

Jeremiah wrote some things in his notebook. Then he looked at a skinny guy with big sideburns standing next to Forrest the Buffoon.

"Private Dandridge?" Jeremiah asked.

He got similar flippant answers from Dandridge and the other two soldiers. The whole time, I gave them my best serious stare. Forrest ignored me, and Jeremiah too for that matter, as if we were gnats to him.

When Jeremiah finished, he saluted again. They ignored him again. He turned sharply and marched toward the dock, me in tow. This time, I sped up a bit so we could walk side by side.

"Looks like you didn't need me," I said.

"Your presence did exactly what it was supposed to," he said. "It kept things civil."

I raised an eyebrow. If Jeremiah considered their behavior to be civil, I wasn't sure I wanted to know what he considered rude.

Captain Mercer returned on an ironclad about three hours later. He strode down the dock with a furious glint in his eye. He ignored the few soldiers sitting on the sides of the dock, dangling their feet in the water. Once he spotted Jeremiah and me sitting back under the shady maple, he stormed over.

We scrambled to our feet while he crossed the mud. This time, I stood straight and saluted as soon as he was close. Jeremiah did too.

Captain Mercer returned the salute and turned to Jeremiah. "Sergeant Freeman, your report."

"Yes, sir," Jeremiah said. He held up his notebook and looked at it. "Twenty privates and myself remain on this side. Eight have minor injuries, the worst of which is a sprained wrist. Four have lost their rifles. Eight have lost haversacks or packs or both."

"Are any squadrons complete?"

"Third Squadron," Jeremiah pointed at himself, "is nearly so." He grimaced. "Private Hanson drowned."

Mercer lowered his head. "May the Lord have mercy and accept his soul."

"Amen," Jeremiah said.

I blinked in surprise at Jeremiah's response. He'd never expressed a hint of being religious the entire time I'd known him.

"Third Squadron is the one most short of equipment," Jeremiah continued. "Lost when the tug sank."

"Third Squadron is the one I want," Captain Mercer said sharply. "The others can turn their equipment over."

When he saw the surprised reaction from us, he continued, "Colonel Mosby and General Sanborn do not wish to put the entire regiment across the river, now that the element of surprise has been lost. They fear they would be trapped."

He grimaced in frustration.

"However," he said, "I have prevailed upon them to allow me to command a single unit for the purposes of infiltration. If God wills, perhaps we can do as Grant did."

I swallowed hard. Everyone knew the story of Grant's last, suicidal charge at Lynchburg. Jeremiah seemed equally shocked.

"You mean…," he said, "…you want to kill the Jotun commander? …Sir?"

"Yes," Captain Mercer said. "Just as Grant did. If God wills."

EIGHT

WE STARED AT CAPTAIN MERCER, our eyes wide in the bright sun. Grant's charge had stopped the Jotun advance for a time, but the cost had been huge.

"That's... bold, sir," Jeremiah said after a bit. "How do we even get into the city?"

"The Jotun allow slaves to enter Louisville," Captain Mercer said with a wolfish grin. "We," he gestured to himself and then to me, "can pass for slave traders bringing in a fresh crop."

I let my eyes wander over the men in their blue uniforms, however wet or muddy they might be. I wasn't sure I shared Captain Mercer's opinion.

Jeremiah didn't seem to either. He stood stiff, and his nostrils flared. "You would put us in *chains*?"

"Ropes," Captain Mercer said. "Looped, not knotted, so you can slip out of them easily."

Jeremiah still looked indignant, but he remained silent.

"I realize this is not conventional, Sergeant," Captain Mercer continued, his eyes now hardened, and flint filled his voice. "But we shall do it. Colonel Mosby and General Sanborn agree that having a small force inside the city is too valuable to pass up."

He shifted into a parade stance. "It would be easier if I had your enthusiasm, but all I require is your cooperation."

"Yes, sir," Jeremiah said. He snapped his hand to his brow in a salute with a fury in his eye.

"Very well," Captain Mercer said with a nod. "There is a wagon on the ironclads. Please give me your inventory and then ensure it is unloaded while I speak with the rest of the men."

Jeremiah saluted, handed Mercer his notebook, and marched toward the dock.

"Private McCarty," Captain Mercer said, "you are with me."

I saluted and fell in behind him as he marched over toward the other soldiers.

"Fall in!" he called out loudly. He strode to where the road departed into the trees and then turned to face the small crowd.

I kept up with him, despite my shorter legs. He met my eye and pointed to the side of the road, which I took to be where I should stand. I took my spot and stood at parade rest. At least I'd learned how to do that well.

The soldiers formed ragged lines, roughly grouped by squadron. Some stood at attention, some at parade rest, and some just stood all casual-like.

I was pleased that most of Third Squadron was at attention. Though as I thought about it, I wondered why. I would've slouched. The order to be at attention didn't make a lot of sense, here after a battle. At least to me.

But the Negroes, other than Joe Johnson who couldn't seem to stand straight if he'd had a rod up his back, looked crisp. Even Zeke in his wet shirt and pants looked sharp.

"Men," Captain Mercer said, firm and loud so that his voice filled the landing. "We have engaged the enemy and driven them from the field."

He paused to make sure he had everyone's full attention.

"In doing so," he continued, "the element of surprise has been lost. We therefore have new orders. Third Squadron and I shall continue to Louisville at haste. The rest of you shall return to Colonel Mosby's command where you will be attached to other units."

Zeke's face lit up at this news, though the other soldiers' expressions were more guarded. A few from First Squadron looked relieved.

"Without surprise, we must make haste," Captain Mercer said. "Therefore, First and Second Squadrons: you will turn over your equipment and supplies to Third Squadron as I direct." He held up Jeremiah's notebook. "Colonel Mosby will re-provision you as required."

Outright grumbling broke out in the ranks. Captain Mercer narrowed his eyes, but it didn't seem to stop.

"Third Squadron," Mercer said. "Proceed to the dock and assist Sergeant Freeman with the wagon. First and Second Squadrons, assemble your gear and return here."

I saw Private Forrest, the Big Buffoon, give Captain Mercer a glare of pure hate. His friends didn't seem so happy either.

Captain Mercer gestured me over. He handed me Jeremiah's notebook.

"Can you do figures?" he asked.

"Yes, sir."

"We have food, water, and ammunition in the wagon," he went on. "What we do not have is blankets, tents, or cooking gear. Please determine how much of each Third Squadron requires."

I scanned down the page. Jeremiah's handwriting was quite clear, but it would take a bit to add everything up.

"What about rifles and revolvers, sir?" I asked.

"We have some in the wagon. What do we require?"

I scanned Jeremiah's notes again. "One, two, three, four, five... five rifles," I said, "and two revolvers."

"Then we are short two rifles. Follow me."

He strode over to where the survivors of First Squadron had gathered with their haversacks and packs. Private Forrest and his three friends were at the closest edge. They were talking low, in a small circle. Each held his rifle casually and had his bags around his feet.

"Private," Captain Mercer said to Forrest, "Third Squadron requires your rifle. Tell Sergeant-Major McNab that I have requested he issue you a new one."

Forrest's eyes went wide in shock and alarm.

"My rifle?" he snarled. "You ain't takin' my rifle!"

"Excuse me?" Captain Mercer said. He held out his hand to accept the gun.

Forrest jerked his rifle back. "Hell, no! You ain't giving my gun to a Nigger!"

"It's the army's gun," Captain Mercer said coldly. He snapped his fingers and held his hand out again.

"Like hell!"

My heart raced. I wasn't sure what to do and I kept shifting my weight from foot to foot.

A silence descended on the clearing. The sounds of the wagon rolling down the dock stopped. The chatter from the men in Second Squadron stopped.

Faster than I could see, Captain Mercer's hand flashed down to his waist and then back up. He now held a Colt revolver pointed directly at Private Forrest's face.

The Big Buffoon's eyes went wide. He stared at the barrel, not more than a foot from his face.

"Hand. Over. Your. Rifle. That's an order, Private. Refuse, and die."

Sweat beaded on Forrest's brow. Shock still filled his face. Slowly, jerkily, he held his rifle out.

"Private McCarty," Captain Mercer said without moving his stare from Forrest's eyes.

My knees weaker than I expected, I stepped forward and took Private Forrest's rifle from his hands. His arm dropped limply to his side.

Captain Mercer lowered his pistol. "Get on the ironclads, Private," he said to Forrest. Then his voice changed from harsh to almost comforting. "I am sure Sergeant-Major McNab can find you a better rifle. Tell him I said to try. Dismissed."

Private Forrest blinked and quickly looked at his buddies. The three of them half ran toward the dock.

All around us, the other soldiers stared.

Captain Mercer slowly turned in place. He looked at each of the remaining men individually, for just a moment, before turning to the next. His gaze was fierce. None met his eyes for long.

Captain Mercer turned back to me. "We need one more rifle, correct?"

"Yes, sir."

"Fortunately there are still some First Squadron volunteers." He glanced around until he spotted one of the soldiers from First Squadron nearby. "Come with me."

We had no difficulty rounding up the rest of the needed supplies. The second private that Captain Mercer asked for his rifle handed it over without a word. Blankets and cookware and tents got piled into the wagon after a simple request from Captain Mercer or Jeremiah.

Captain Mercer met the ironclad's captain at the end of the dock while Jeremiah and the rest of us from Third Squadron wrestled the large wooden supply wagon through the mud to the dry beginnings of the road through the trees.

We all shoved and pushed while two bay-colored horses pulled at the front. I pushed on the back edge, with Zeke beside me and Joe Johnson on the other side. The rest of the soldiers clustered around and pushed where they could. Jeremiah led the horses up front.

Grunts filled the air while the cool breeze danced along our skin. We made slow progress, but steady. The wheels turned inch by inch. They flung mud to the sides when moved through puddles, and one clot smacked Joe Johnson in the arm.

"Better than dung," he said as he brushed it off.

"When'd you get dung on your arms?" another soldier said. He was a short, wiry Negro with big buck teeth. It took me a few seconds to remember his name. Burwell. He'd said it was because his master beat him regularly as a little boy and he "bore it well."

Given the scars on his back, he was probably right.

"I worked on a hog farm as a boy," Joe Johnson said. "I got hog dung on me all the time." He shrugged. "It comes off."

"Better hog dung than chicken dung," Burwell said. "We didn't get no shovel to clean out the chicken coop. Had to do it with our hands."

"Better dung than guts," Joe Johnson said.

"Or guts and dung," Zeke chimed in morosely. "Like after some-one's died."

That killed the chatter.

It also sent me into thinking about Cassidy. The awful smell after he'd died. The way the blood had flowed out of the wound...

My gut churned and I slipped in the mud.

Zeke, pushing the wagon alongside me, grabbed my arm and stopped my fall.

"Careful," he said with a sympathetic smile. "It's just mud, but you don't wanna be in it."

"Yeah," I said. I put my shoulder into the wagon and pushed some more. I did my best not to think about anything but the wagon and the mud and pushing. I didn't want my mind to wander into the hellish places it liked to go.

After a long bit of pushing, the mud thinned and then a bit after that, the wheels hit hard ground. The horses found their footing and pulled the massive wagon onto the packed dirt road.

"At ease!" Jeremiah ordered.

Everyone found a good place to squat and catch a rest. Jeremiah had Zeke pass some water canteens around. A few men joked among themselves, but most looked nervous.

We were certainly a green group. Jeremiah, me, and eight men who could barely shoot.

Should've been nine, I reminded myself belatedly. Guilt washed over me thinking of the man that'd drowned. I hadn't really gotten to know him, other than he had a tendency to swing his rifle to the left instead of aiming straight ahead. Now he seemed forgotten.

I hoped his soul had found Heaven.

But I wasn't the only one thinking about him. After a bit, Jeremiah gestured for us to all gather around in a circle. I stood opposite him with Zeke at his right hand.

"We lost Private Hanson on the river," Jeremiah said. "Let us take a few minutes to honor his memory and pray for his soul." He nodded at Zeke and then bowed his head.

We all did the same.

"Holy Father," Zeke prayed, loud and full of strength, "Have mercy on Private Hanson. We ask you to take his spirit into your loving arms. He was a good man. He loved his sista'. He loved his mamma. He believed in You. He believed in the cause. He died, tryin' to fulfill Your will."

I balked at that, but as it was a prayer, bit back my words.

"Private Hanson was a good man," Zeke preached. "Kind, like the Lord Jesus. Loving, like his Mother Mary. He was a friend to all. He shared his food and his drink for the good of us all."

A small murmur of "amens" came from half the circle.

"Private Hanson was a good man," Zeke said again. "He would have fought the Devil's Jotun well. He believed in ridding the land of their scourge. Please, Lord, take Private Hanson into your bosom in Heaven."

"Amen," I said quietly.

"And Lord, great Lord." Zeke's voice expanded. "Let us be Your sword of vengeance. Give us the strength to fight the Devils. To destroy them in Your name. Give us the courage! Give us the power! Let us carry out Your will."

"Amen!"

I blinked. That had been Captain Mercer's voice, coming from beside me.

"Amen," Captain Mercer said again, with a note of finality.

We all looked up. His expression was grim.

"We will avenge Private Hanson," he said. He paused until all eyes were on him.

"Change your uniforms for civilian clothes. We leave when everyone is done."

NINE

A LOT of the Negroes grumbled when they heard Captain Mercer's plan. A few shot him dark looks, but after the way he'd dealt with Private Forrest, none dared to complain.

Late afternoon clouds filled the sky and the wind picked up, as it threatened to rain. Captain Mercer urged us to hurry. The further down the road we were before the deluge, the more shelter we'd have from the trees, he said.

Which, I had to agree, made sense. Not far from the landing, the road narrowed to little more than a dirt track, with tall birches and elms growing right up to the edge. In spots, the branches hung so low that a man would've been able to grab ahold of them if he stood on the wagon.

But none did. In fact, other than me and Captain Mercer, everyone walked. He wanted to spare the horses the load until we were closer, he told Jeremiah, who had not been at all happy with it. When Mercer added that it would make it easier for the Negroes to seek cover if the Jotun did attack, Jeremiah relented.

"Let me show you the loops," Captain Mercer said patiently to Jeremiah. He gestured to the side of the wagon near the front. "Put your rifle in the wagon, where you can easily reach it."

Then Captain Mercer took a long length of thick rope. He tied one end to the wagon's seat and brought the length around to the side where Jeremiah stood. "Hold out your arms."

With a frown, Jeremiah did so.

Captain Mercer looped the rope around Jeremiah's wrists, twisting it and crossing it here and there. When he was done, he tugged on the end from the wagon.

The rope pulled Jeremiah's arms forward.

"Looks secure, doesn't it?" Captain Mercer said. "Now bring your wrists together and twist." He demonstrated what he wanted.

Jeremiah did so, and the rope slipped off his hands. He blinked in surprise.

"I will not allow my men," Captain Mercer stated loudly enough for everyone to hear, "to be helpless in the face of the enemy." He looked around at the others, who'd clustered so they could see. "When I give the order, you slip your bonds, grab your rifle, and fight."

"Yes, sir!" Zeke called, followed by a ragged chorus of repeated 'Yes, sirs' from the others.

"Where'd you learn this, sir?" Jeremiah asked. He picked up the rope and started twisting it around his own wrists as best he could.

"It's an old abolitionist trick," Captain Mercer said.

"You were an abolitionist?" I blurted out.

Captain Mercer gave me an amused smirk, but his eyes were hard.

"No, Private McCarty, I was not. I hunted them."

I fell silent. So did Jeremiah. The others had already started getting rifles and guns situated and either hadn't heard Captain Mercer or were pretending they didn't.

"Excuse me, sir?" Jeremiah said after a while. His tone was as flat and controlled as I'd ever heard.

"I hunted abolitionists," Captain Mercer repeated. "And also escaped slaves, as a boy with my father." His eyes softened and he looked to the side for a moment. "But then I met my dearest Emily."

When he'd recovered, he looked Jeremiah in the eyes. "She

persuaded me of the error of my ways. After we announced our betrothal, my father never spoke with me again."

"Emily's your wife, sir?" I asked. He had never struck me as being married.

"She is," he said. "She and our girl live in Boston. I visit when duty allows."

Which couldn't be often, I realized. Not with the Contested Lands and the Jotun between us and them.

"She must be very understanding," Jeremiah murmured sympathetically.

"Emily taught me duty," he said, the flint back in his voice. "She is the steel of my soul." He chopped the air with one hand. "Enough. We have a mission. Take your places, Privates."

I felt uncomfortable riding in the wagon with Captain Mercer while all the men walked. It didn't seem right, somehow. Yet it meant I could keep my rifle. I held the Winchester across my chest as the "guard" while Captain Mercer drove the horses.

There wasn't much grumbling once we got underway, though. Well, there was a little at first. Little wiry Burwell asked why they had to have the ropes on as they walked, since they sometimes chafed his wrists.

"In case we're surprised," Captain Mercer had answered. "If the Jotun appear without warning—*again*—we need to look the part."

Burwell had been ready to complain some more, but stopped with a stricken look and just nodded.

Our losses when we'd tried to land were too fresh in all our minds.

"We also must sound the part," Captain Mercer continued. "No saluting. No use of rank. Understand?"

Heads nodded all around.

The dirt track continued under the canopy of trees for quite a ways. Then it met a wider dirt road. We turned left and continued on. The new road jogged and twisted just enough to not allow us to see far ahead, which grew even more difficult as dusk fell.

Finally, in a small clearing between two old gnarled oaks, Captain Mercer called a halt.

"We stop for food and rest," he called. "No tents. Men who wish to sleep under the wagon may do so." He turned to me. "You have sentinel duty, McCarty. You must pretend to watch the slaves, but keep an eye on the road as much you can."

I nodded and stood on the wagon seat. As I surveyed the area, Captain Mercer went and briefly spoke to each soldier. They all nodded, and then changed from what they were doing to new tasks.

We soon had a small fire going, with kettles and a pot of beans and bacon on it. We'd staked the horses off to one side where the grazing seemed best and watered them from one of the large drums we'd brought with us.

I stayed on the wagon with my gun ready as Jeremiah brought me hardtack and chicory coffee. The former was hard and tasted like glue, and the latter weak and almost flavorless. Still, I choked them down.

Captain Mercer prowled the clearing, circling the men, always looking through the trees. The clinks of dishes, the pop and crackle of the fire, and the low conversation drowned out any sounds from the woods.

A light cool breeze caused me to tighten my coat. My muscles sagged with tiredness, but I held the rifle close. I sat down and rested as best I could while still being vigilant. I yearned for sleep, but Captain Mercer hadn't given the order to turn in, and I was sure I'd have a watch to keep.

Then I saw something, moving in the gloom of the road. After a moment, it became clear.

A man on a horse, coming towards us down the track.

I stood. "Mercer! We have company!"

He drew his Colt and rushed over to the wagon.

The man became easier to see as he trotted down the track into the firelight. He had a full cloak that flowed behind him and a black stovepipe hat. Squat, he sat heavy on the black mare, though the reins were loose in his hands. His face was wrinkled with an unkempt grey beard.

"Good evening, sir!" Captain Mercer called.

The rider pulled up on the reins and stopped his horse a half dozen yards from us. He slowly surveyed the scene—me, standing on the wagon with my rifle across my chest, Captain Mercer beside me on the ground with his Colt drawn, but pointing to the ground, and of course the Negroes sitting around the fire.

"Good evening," the man said, looking at Captain Mercer. His eyes took in Captain Mercer's crisp civilian coat and trousers. "Strange to see a party on this road tonight."

"Taking slaves to Louisville," Captain Mercer said. "They're strong and should fetch a good price."

"To Louisville from where?"

"Paducah. And before that, Memphis. Is that where you might be bound?"

"My business is none of yours." He squinted at us suspiciously. "This is not the best road from Paducah."

Captain Mercer held up his hands with a shrug. "My guard thought he knew a shorter way." He gestured toward me apologetically.

"But you, sir," Captain Mercer continued, "You ride alone in Jotun territory. Surely we have as much cause for suspicion as yourself."

"I have dispensation," he said. "I am High Thrall." He reached into a pocket in his vest and withdrew a thick bundle. "My papers. Where are yours?"

I sucked in my breath. His tone was so confident, so sure of himself…

"Ah," Captain Mercer said. "In the wagon. Would you fetch them, Billy, my boy?"

I blinked in surprise, but recovered quickly and turned to rummage in a bag right behind the seat.

I slammed myself down at the sound of the gunshot. Then I quickly whipped around and reached for my rifle.

The man slowly sagged and fell off his horse. Captain Mercer still trained his Colt on the corpse.

I stood there in shock, but only for a moment.

The man's horse snorted and shifted around. Mercer ran forward and grabbed its reins. I jumped off the wagon and followed.

"What... what'd'ya do that for?" I demanded as he handed me the reins and knelt by the body.

"The mission comes first. He was too suspicious." He grabbed the man's papers and flipped through them, peering close in the low light. Then he muttered a curse and strode over closer to the fire.

Jeremiah met him halfway. "Let me," he said as he reached his hand out. "We need to know he was alone."

"Yes," Captain Mercer said with a nod, "yes, indeed. Jeremiah, you have command. Secure the camp. McCarty—with me."

Jeremiah told Zeke to take the horse from me. Captain Mercer retrieved his own rifle from the wagon and then we started walking up the road.

We fell quiet at once. The further we got from the camp, the easier it was to hear the rustle of the wind.

We didn't hear any people. Peering into the long shadows, we didn't see anyone either.

Walking with Captain Mercer felt strange. I'd headed into danger, side by side with another man before, but it'd been Cassidy.

Cassidy the Giant Killer. Cassidy the hero.

Cassidy my friend.

Whom I'd killed.

Cassidy had trusted me. I'd known that from the way we walked side by side into danger.

Captain Mercer—not so much.

He kept looking over at me, and over at my side of the road. Once or twice he gestured with his gun towards deep shadows I'd already spotted.

He also walked nervous. Not with the confidence Cassidy had always carried.

My heart tightened at the memories.

My gut also churned at Captain Mercer's murder of the man—for there wasn't any other word for it. In the dime store novels, Cassidy had killed other humans when he had to, but it was always in self-defense or as a last resort.

Captain Mercer had just done it.

That chilled my blood.

Finally Captain Mercer slowed up and paused. We'd walked a good way from our camp, and now only the sounds of our footsteps could be heard. When we stopped, just the crickets and whirring bugs filled the night.

"I figure we've gone far enough," he said. "If he wasn't alone, we'll never catch them."

"I reckon, too," I said.

He nodded and we turned to walk back. We stayed silent until we were almost halfway to the camp. Then Captain Mercer shifted uncomfortably.

"I suppose," he drawled, "you're thinking that I shouldn't have shot that man. That killing him was unjust."

My skin prickled, but I stayed silent.

"He had Jotun papers," he continued, "which makes him a traitor. He chose to work for them, and thus condemned himself."

"Maybe he didn't have a choice."

"He could move freely. Yet he did not flee their territory."

"Maybe they were holding his family, or something."

"Unlikely." He kicked a small rock in the road. "One does not become a *High* Thrall out of fear. Only traitorous desire."

The dim flicker of the campfire appeared not far ahead of us.

"Come," he said. He gestured toward the fire. "Let us see what Jeremiah has learned."

TEN

WE FOUND the men all clustered around the fire, except for Joe Johnson, who stood next to the wagon, looking not-at-all casual with his hand resting inside the bed. His hand had to be on his gun, but the way he kept looking at everyone around the fire instead of the road made him a lousy sentry.

Jeremiah stood at the center of a group of four soldiers, Zeke among them. He turned at our approach and held up the papers we'd taken from the dead man.

I glanced around. I couldn't see the corpse anywhere, but the horse now grazed with ours off to the side.

"Here," Jeremiah said when he saw us approach. "These say he was High Thrall Jorgensen, Merchant."

"Thrall?" Zeke asked.

"A thrall's a slave," Jeremiah explained. "High Thralls are trusted ones."

"Trusted, huh," Zeke said with a grunt. "The Jotun wrote that?" He pointed at the papers.

"They keep human slaves as scribes," Jeremiah said.

"And yes, trusted," Captain Mercer said. "He was allowed to ride alone, so they trusted him. Anything on where he was headed?"

"No, sir. Though I would guess Paducah from his choice of road. However…" Jeremiah tapped the papers with one finger. "If he's a merchant, where are his goods?"

"Very good question, Sergeant," Captain Mercer said. "Does he have a ledger?"

"No."

"Strange. What merchant travels without a ledger?"

No one seemed to have a good answer for that.

"Anything else of importance?" Captain Mercer asked.

"He had a large number of Jotun coins," Jeremiah said. "I suspect whatever he was selling, he sold in Louisville."

"But still no ledger," Captain Mercer mused. "Well, there's nothing more to be done." He surveyed the men. "Time to sleep, men. We move out before first light. We must make Louisville by dusk."

"Why dusk?" I asked.

"Because General Sanborn attacks at dawn the following day."

I stood in a clearing surrounded by pine trees. Darkness swallowed the sky and the space between the trees. Torches crackled and popped around the edges. A stone altar sat in the middle, with a naked man bound to it. He silently tugged at his bonds.

I approached.

The yells and clanks of battle sounded in the distance. I could smell crap and guts. My stomach churned and I could taste blood on my cracked lips.

A long curved knife appeared in my hand. I raised it as I moved next to the altar.

The merchant stared up at me. Gagged, he made no sound, but his eyes were full of terror.

I raised the knife and held it above his heart.

My pulse pounded.

My arm shook.

His face changed—Jeremiah, Zeke, McNab, Maria, Private Forrest, Captain Mercer—

I plunged the knife down.

—Cassidy. His eyes bulged in pain as the knife entered his heart.

I bolted upright, covered in sweat, and fully awake. I shook myself to try to shed the dream. Only Zeke, on watch, noticed. He didn't say a word.

We were up and walking before the sun appeared. Or walking as best we could. Too many of us had slept poor, and I tried not to nod off myself as the wagon bumped along. But I wasn't sure I wanted to sleep. Not with the nightmare still fresh in my mind.

About an hour after dawn, our road merged with an even larger one, that was better kept. That one then left the woods and ran through large wheat farms. Being early September, the golden stalks were tall with kernels already drooping. A few fields had been harvested, mown down to nearly bare dirt, leaving the pervading smell of dry grass throughout the air.

Meanwhile the sun beat down and the humid air clung to us. Captain Mercer had the rest of the men get into the wagon, figuring we were close enough to make appearances matter more than tiring the horses.

We drove the wagon at a laggard's pace, for though we were anxious to get to the city, Captain Mercer felt that too quick would draw attention to ourselves. Since the road was broad, dry, and well worn, he felt confident that our pace would suffice.

Meanwhile, we kept watch and noted all we could. We were in Jotun land now, and unlikely to escape should they discover our disguise.

Fortunately, to my relief, we saw few others and met none, human or Jotun. No one to question us. No one to have to... deal with.

The merchant sat heavily on my soul.

But as we moved, we began to see more occupied lands. The wooden farm buildings we passed, be they barns or perhaps slave barracks, sat a bit back from the road and if there was anyone within, we could not tell. The day was too overcast to note small trails of chimney smoke from the cabins, but too bright for lamps.

Several fields were already filled with human slaves—both White and Negro—harvesting the grain. They bore scythes and walked in lines, loosely roped together. We passed two groups, both hundreds of yards away from the main road, with human overseers. Those men strutted with shotguns casually held. They watched their slaves and barely gave us a glance.

I shuddered in disgust when one looked my way, but forced myself to nod my head in greeting. What sort of men could do this to their fellow men? Especially in service of the Jotun?

Then we saw one of the giants. It stood far off in one of the fields, but at its height, was the tallest thing around. It wore a huge metal breastplate and leather jerkin, though it lacked a helmet. The huge mane of golden hair and full beard made it look a bit like a majestic lion, though one that had a bow slung over one shoulder and a quiver of arrows on his back.

That made my heart race. In one of the books Jeremiah had written about Cassidy's adventures, they'd fought a Jotun with a bow. It'd shot an arrow almost a half mile with enough accuracy to kill a horse. Though I wouldn't have been surprised if Jeremiah had exaggerated for the sake of the story.

I nudged Captain Mercer and indicated the Jotun. "He's an archer."

"Hmmm," he said, with only a quick glance from the dirt road stretching ahead of us. "I thought we'd destroyed most of those."

"The archers?"

"The bows," he said. "They're from the other side of the rift. They're very hard to make here."

I nodded. There weren't very many trees tall and straight enough for the shaft that were the right type of bendy wood. I also couldn't imagine what they'd use for a string.

I studied the Jotun archer a bit more. He seemed bored. He was watching something closer to his feet, with only an occasional glance our way. He kept moving his arms around as if he didn't know what to do with them.

"What's the range on those bows?" I asked Captain Mercer quietly.

"As good as our best cannon. Better, I suspect. We must hope there are few here, for the sake of General Sanborn and the ironclads."

I swallowed hard. If a *rock* had been able to sink our tug, what could one of those huge arrows do?

Captain Mercer snapped the reins. "We'd best get into the city soon."

The city of Louisville didn't have walls. Instead, a series of forts, built by the Union back before the Jotun arrived, surrounded the city. Our road ran close to one. It sat on a squat hill high enough to be imposing with its thick stone walls. Those walls had been extended higher with new rock, roughly mortared together. The wooden door, facing our way, could've let our whole group walk through side by side. The door looked like a mishmash of sticks glued together, and I realized it must've taken a ton of trees to build it. It was closed, though it wasn't hard to imagine a Jotun walking out of it and ducking to avoid bumping his head.

But we didn't have to imagine a Jotun. One sat at the base of the fort's hill next to the road.

This one sat cross-legged on the ground. His meaty bare thighs seemed twice the length of our wagon. He didn't look comfortable in his leather jerkin. And he seemed to be sweating. His helm sat on the ground to his right and his beard and hair were damp and matted.

Most important, he looked bored as he watched us approach.

A table stood under an awning in front of the giant, right on the edge of the road. Two men in Confederate Grey uniforms sat at the table and paid us a lot more attention, watching us like hawks. One fidgeted with his hands as we approached.

Captain Mercer stopped the wagon about twenty yards away. "If there's trouble, shoot the Jotun first," he murmured as he tied the reins.

I tightened the grip on my rifle. My knuckles didn't go white, but it was close.

He climbed down from the wagon and ambled over. Between the civilian clothes and his casual gait, he didn't look like an army officer at all. He seemed to *slouch*, which was almost unimaginable for him, except I was seeing it with my own two eyes.

My blood raced as I watched him talk to the two men in the tent. I forced myself to steady my breathing, just like when I was on the rifle range. It wouldn't do to panic now.

Captain Mercer talked for a while, and then showed them the papers we'd taken from the merchant. They talked a bit more and then he ambled back.

"How'd it go?" I asked as he climbed back into the wagon.

"Fine," he said. "They wanted to know what we were going to do with the slaves. I told them we were going to sell them as construction labor. They bought it." He snapped the reins and the wagon started moving.

"So where are we headed?"

"The waterfront," he said. He gave me a nasty grin. "They said there's a master builder there that could use some help."

I chuckled. Somehow I suspected we weren't the type of help he wanted.

We spent the next two hours slowly working our way into the city. Louisville was a mix of the old human buildings—many brick and stone but many hewn timber—and new Jotun construction. The giants' homes towered over the rest, rising up like steep stone mountains among hills. Most of them clustered along the east edge of town, but a few squatted close to our road from the west.

The broad road from the fort into town still kept us a ways from the buildings, though. I'd never walked a road wide enough for six or eight wagons to travel side by side before. In a bunch of places, the rubble of destroyed buildings still lined its sides.

It was strange enough to keep my nerves on edge. Most of the men seemed the same, except Jeremiah and Captain Mercer.

I tried to keep calm like them.

We didn't encounter many people or Jotun until we got close to the center of the city. The humans, well, those we did pass gave us only a look or ignored us entirely. They seemed sullen and hurried.

The two Jotun we passed didn't pay us any attention at all, to my relief. One walked past us on the road without a glance longer than it took to avoid us. The other lounged on a huge chair just outside his house and sharpened his war axe.

Captain Mercer drove the wagon forward as if there was nothing to see. He barely turned his head, though his eyes seemed to be everywhere.

I glanced back at our men. Almost all of them gawked and stared, especially at the Jotun with the axe. A few had one hand under the tarps and blankets we'd arranged, where I was sure they were clutching their rifles. I clutched mine tighter as well.

Jeremiah, though, just looked grim. He sat still, twisting his rope-bound wrists as the wagon rolled along. Like Captain Mercer, his eyes darted everywhere.

Then just as the road seemed ready to expand into a large open square, in what looked like the center of town, Captain Mercer stopped. He peered ahead and then muttered a curse under his breath.

"What?" I said.

"They leveled the center of town." He grimaced. "Probably all the way to the river."

"Why'd they do that?"

"I don't know. But it means there's no cover. I don't like it."

I nodded. If we drove the wagon into the middle of that and something went wrong, there'd be nowhere to run. As it was, we were a good fifty feet from the nearest building, a low wooden human-sized warehouse of some kind.

"HUMANS!"

Our heads snapped toward the sound. A burly Jotun with long black hair pulled back in a braid marched toward us.

And he was looking directly at us.

My heart skipped a beat. Beside me, Captain Mercer stiffened.

A murmur ran through the rest of the men, though the road was suddenly quiet. All the low hubbub of the city seemed to stop as the Jotun strode toward us.

"Lord have mercy," Zeke said.

"HUMANS!" The Jotun said again. It stopped about thirty yards directly in front of us. Its shadow blocked the sun and I strained to stare up at it.

I trembled at first—noting his huge muscles and the leather jerkin that was thicker than my arm. He wore a sword on his belt that was taller than me. But I took a deep breath and forced my nerves under control.

"COME WITH ME!" The Jotun boomed.

"Yes, Huskarl!" Captain Mercer called, using the Jotun term for leader. "May I ask where we are going?"

"AN ARMY OF VARGR APPROACH," he snarled. "YOU WILL SERVE IN DEFENSE." He turned and gestured for us to follow. "COME!"

"Does that mean…?," I said quietly to Captain Mercer.

"Yes. He expects us to fight our own army."

ELEVEN

I STARED at the back of the Jotun as he marched down the dusty road toward the center of town, where the buildings faded off to the side. His shadow stretched scarily long.

I thought about what he'd said, in that booming voice. Then I swallowed hard and gripped my rifle even tighter.

Why did they need humans?

I shook my head. I knew that. It'd been in one of the dime novels. *Giant Killer Cassidy and the Pennsylvania Raid.* If there weren't enough Jotun around, they used trolls or slaves to fill out their ranks.

But humans fighting humans? How could the Jotun possibly expect us to do that?

But I thought of the thralls we'd passed, and the slaves. Clearly, some humans would. Some, to impress their new masters. Some, because they'd be killed if they didn't.

I swallowed hard. It was pretty clear we were the second type.

Captain Mercer didn't hesitate. He snapped the reins and started the wagon after the Jotun.

The giant strode forward briefly and then waited impatiently for us to get close. When we were about fifty yards away, he did it again. After the third time, he gestured ahead.

"GO TO THE WATER!" he said as he pointed, "REPORT THERE!"

"Yes, Huskarl!" Captain Mercer called.

The Jotun turned and marched past us, I presumed in search of more troop fodder.

The few humans within sight seemed suddenly very busy as they ran to wherever they needed to go.

Captain Mercer snapped the reins again. The horses moved a bit faster. He glanced over his shoulder to make sure everyone had a good grip in the wagon. I didn't turn to look myself. I kept my eyes ahead.

More Jotun ran past, in what had to be toward the river. It looked like others joined them. At the distance, it was hard to tell, but their size was unmistakeable.

"We can't go to the waterfront," I hissed as quietly as I could.

"I know," Captain Mercer said, "but we can't stay here." He wiped the sweat from his brow with the back of his hand. "Watch for somewhere we can hide."

I nodded and began scanning the area.

Unfortunately, the road continued to open up into a huge area without any buildings. Stone and dirt and even a few patches of grass stretched alongside the road all the way to the river, some thousands of yards away. Somewhat near the middle stood a tall stone watch tower, easily a hundred feet tall and wider than any of the forts we'd seen.

Not a single other structure was within a several hundred yards of the Jotun tower, making it an intimidating fortress. Above it, there was only the darkening sky.

Without hesitating, Captain Mercer turned the wagon left to drive closer to the buildings there. We bounced along packed dirt once we left the main road, but my eyes remained glued to the tower.

I couldn't see the top—not well. There appeared to be three to four Jotun there behind battlements, all in gleaming helms. The tower's granite sides were bare except for long narrow windows scattered here and there.

I sucked in my breath. In one of the dime novels, Cassidy's team had encountered a Jotun fortress south of Pittsburgh.

I knew what those were.

Arrow slits.

I thought of the archer we'd seen earlier, and the size of his arrows. I thought of the ironclads, floating out in the river without any cover.

And the boats carrying the troops.

And what a rock had done to our tug.

I couldn't help but shudder.

A slight breeze picked up, and the first streaks of sunset dotted the air. We bounced and jostled as the horses trotted. My mouth was dry but I didn't dare reach for my canteen.

About a third of the way down the left-hand side of the huge square around the tower, Captain Mercer spotted a human-sized black-smith shop. It had a little yard surrounded by a split rail fence with a wide gate. The yard curled around behind the shop where I presumed the forge and stables were.

Captain Mercer pulled up in front of the gate. He handed me the reins. "Get the wagon around the corner. Get the men under cover."

Then he hopped off the wagon and practically ran into the low slat-sided building.

"I'll get the gate," Jeremiah said from behind me.

He glanced quickly around, but no one was nearby. With a flip of his wrists, he slipped his fake ropes, hopped off the wagon, and went to the gate. As soon as he'd pulled it open, I drove the wagon through.

Once I'd turned the corner out of sight, the rest of the Negroes also undid their ropes. As they grabbed their guns, Jeremiah started directing them on where to go.

As I'd expected, the little courtyard was surrounded on three sides. A large stable with a second story peaked roof sat directly opposite the opening we'd come in through. Faded red paint covered the wood. The large barn door was open and four of our men raced inside.

Opposite the shop stood two small covered wooden buildings, of much the same worn slab timber. The first was open on one side and a cold forge sat within. The other had a small window in it, with gingham curtains blocking the view within.

Jeremiah led two men to the door. Without waiting, he kicked it open and they raced inside.

We heard some muffled shouts, but then all was quiet.

"Sergeant said I go with you," Zeke said from my left.

I'd been too busy watching the men race around to move off the wagon seat. Too stunned at the speed things were happening, actually.

He gestured toward Joe Johnson, who stood in front of the horses. "He's got the wagon."

I nodded and climbed down. With Zeke at my side, we headed to the back door to the blacksmith shop.

Inside, I stopped in my tracks. Zeke bumped into me, so I stepped aside so he could see as well.

Captain Mercer was holding his Colt to the blacksmith's head.

The blacksmith, a hairy dark man with a hook nose and wearing a stained apron, stood pressed against the wall. He stared wide-eyed at Captain Mercer, and his eyes only briefly flicked our way.

So did Captain Mercer's. "Any problems, Billy?"

"None," I said. "Jeremiah is securing the area."

"Good." Captain Mercer visibly relaxed, but still kept his gun pointed at the man.

"I apologize, good sir," Captain Mercer said, "but time was of the essence. I believe we can be more civil now."

"Who are you?" the blacksmith gasped. Sweat was already forming on his brow.

"Who do you think we are?" Captain Mercer replied. He put on a friendly smile and relaxed his stance, but his gun never left the poor blacksmith.

"You're not High Thralls," he said. "You'd know better—" He froze and his eyes went wide as he finally took in Zeke, who was standing at attention.

"You're... you're..." His gaze darted between the three of us before settling on Captain Mercer. "We heard the Army of the West was coming—"

"The Army of the West is here," Captain Mercer drawled. "The question is—are you with us, or against us?"

The blacksmith opened and closed his mouth a bunch of times as he stared wide-eyed at us, but no words came out.

———

We stood there for what seemed like long enough for the shadows to grow. We could hear distant shouts of men and giants from the street. Inside, all was still enough to hear the blacksmith's frightened breathing.

Now calm myself, I studied the man a bit more. His shaggy hair didn't hide old scars and burns. Newer black stains on his once-brown apron covered older, faded ones. He kept squeezing his right hand into a fist and then opening it again, as if he wanted to be holding something.

"Well?" Captain Mercer asked.

"My brother—." The blacksmith's eyes remained fixed on Captain Mercer and his Colt. "He's High Thrall. He'll… he'll make you pay for this."

"He will, will he?" Captain Mercer drawled. "And where might he be, right now, when you need him?"

The blacksmith swallowed without speaking.

"The wrath of the Almighty Lord has come," Zeke intoned from beside me. "Will you choose the path of righteousness?"

The blacksmith tore his gaze from Captain Mercer to stare at Zeke.

With a creak, the door behind me that led to the courtyard opened. I turned as Jeremiah hustled in behind me. Zeke and I stepped out of the way.

"The area's secure," Jeremiah said. "We found two young boys in the house. Privates Johnson and Burwell are watching them."

The blacksmith's eyes widened even further. His mouth dropped as he stared at Jeremiah.

"Perhaps it is time to discuss your sons instead of your brother," Captain Mercer said.

He cocked the hammer back on the Colt. "I'd hate for them to become orphans."

The blacksmith sobbed and dropped to his knees. He bobbed his head, nodding as if to some unasked question.

"Take him to the house," Captain Mercer told Jeremiah. He gestured toward the outside of the shop, "away from the windows."

Jeremiah gestured to Zeke to join him, and the two of them lifted the crying blacksmith gently by the shoulders. They walked him back toward the door. I went to Captain Mercer's side and watched with mixed emotions as they took him from the building. I wanted to feel sorry for him, but we *needed* his cooperation, and we needed it *now*.

Captain Mercer holstered his gun. "I need to interrogate that man. But we also need to know what's happening out there." He gestured toward the window and the square and tower beyond it. "Keep watch until I return."

"Yes, sir!" I said. I would've snapped a salute but my rifle was in my hand.

After Captain Mercer left, I crouched below the window, near the front door, so that only my head stuck out. I didn't think anyone could see me there, and if someone approached, I could block the door if I needed to. But to my relief, no one came close.

The air had cooled a bit, though it was still sticky hot. Outside, the setting sun continued to wane. A long shadow fell from the tower and created a gloom across the barren ground. Torches popped up along some of the far human-sized buildings, but they were just pinpricks in the distance.

The lights were also hard to see, given the commotion in the square. Now scores of men and dozens of giants raced toward the river. Shouts of all sorts rang out, though most of the words were lost in the din. I saw two field wagons full of humans in ragged clothes gallop through. Their drivers whipped the horses and the men hung on tight to the sides.

Then I let out a hiss. Not one, not two, but four Jotun strode steadily from the road toward the river. Each one carried a huge axe at his belt and a long bow across his shoulders.

Not one archer. Four.

To my surprise, they didn't go to the tower. They marched past it, toward the river itself, off at the edge of my view.

But there *were* Jotun in the tower. Two appeared on the top battlements. One shaded his eyes and stared toward the river. The other lifted a large battle horn to his lips.

The loud notes rang out deafeningly.

I clamped my hands over my ears. In the square, men dropped to their knees and did the same.

Then the notes faded.

Men stood and ran. More Jotun poured into the square, all headed for the river. I tried counting, but lost track around thirty. There wasn't any method or order. They just ran.

Captain Mercer appeared by my side. He crouched as well, so as to stay out of sight.

"What's happening?" he asked.

"Everyone's running toward the river," I said quickly. "Our army must be here."

"Anything of note?"

"Four archers. They went that way." I pointed. "No one's gone into the tower. I haven't seen any Jotun that looked like a commander."

"The blacksmith says the commander lives in the tower. He's decided to cooperate, by the way."

I swallowed hard. I didn't want to think about how he'd come to that decision.

We heard cannons thunder from the direction of the river.

Captain Mercer cursed under his breath. "Too soon! Not at dusk!"

"Maybe they didn't have a choice," I pointed out. "They weren't expecting the archers."

"Of course," he agreed. "The ironclads were supposed to move into position tonight, before the attack in the morning. They probably were spotted."

"And the archers are shooting at them." My blood went cold.

"We can't wait," he said. "If those archers sink the ironclads, the battle will be lost." He cursed again. "We have to go after them."

My mind raced as I tried to guess where they'd gone when they'd left my sight. Then I thought of something.

"But our orders are to go after the commander," I said.

"Our *mission*," he said, "is to win the battle. By whatever means required."

"So what do we do?"

He grimaced and looked out the window once again. A squad of Jotun jogged toward the river in perfect formation. They carried war axes and swords and looked grim.

"We have to stop the archers and find the commander simultaneously. We therefore have no choice but to divide the squad," Captain Mercer said at last. "I'll lead a group to find the archers. You and Sergeant Freeman will go for the commander."

Eyes wide, I nodded.

TWELVE

THE DISTANT CANNONS THUNDERED AGAIN. Jotun yelled in the square. As we knelt there, crouched behind the window in the sticky evening air, the battle seemed distant, like some stage production down at the dance hall back in Golden City.

But it wasn't distant. It was just outside the window. I just wasn't looking at it.

Instead, I kept my eyes fixed on Captain Mercer's.

His were cold and firm. They peered at me, deep into me.

Finally, he curled his lip and said, "You're the most dangerous man in this squad, Private McCarty. Sergeant Freeman's the most experienced. You can do this."

I slowly nodded as my blood rushed with excitement.

But then a nagging thought came to my mind.

"How do we get in?" I said. "The tower's locked. There's bound to be guards."

"Ask the blacksmith. But hurry."

I nodded and stood. Captain Mercer turned back to the window.

"Tell Sergeant Freeman to select two men to accompany you. Then send the rest to me."

I nodded.

"And Private McCarty," Captain Mercer added, "your orders are to do whatever it takes to fulfill your mission. We *must* win this battle."

"Yes, sir."

I didn't salute, though I probably should've. Instead, I strode through the back door, across the courtyard, and into the little house on the far side.

It wasn't a big place, and was crowded when I walked in. I quickly glanced around and saw Jeremiah standing with his hands on his hips. He was talking to the terrified and blubbering blacksmith who huddled on a too-small oak chair next to a rough oak kitchen table. Burwell stood behind the blacksmith, his Colt drawn but by his side.

Against a far wall sat two young boys, maybe six and eight, in dungarees and with dirty faces and unkempt black hair, obviously the blacksmith's sons. They clutched each others' hands and stared at their father. Zeke stood next to them, casually holding his pistol. He kept glancing down at them, with what looked like pity in his eyes.

Jeremiah turned at my entrance.

"Mercer wants to attack," I said. I quickly told him about the rest of the captain's plan.

Jeremiah nodded when I was done. "Burwell," he said, "go tell the other men to join Mercer in the shop and then please return here."

Burwell nodded, holstered his pistol, and took off at a trot.

Jeremiah turned back to the blacksmith. "How do we get in the tower?" he demanded.

The blacksmith sucked in his breath to stop his trembling. "You can't."

"Look," Jeremiah said. "There are ten thousand soldiers about to cross that river. Do you think they're going to be happy when they learn you didn't do everything to help?"

"But my boys...!"

"Will be safe," Jeremiah said. He put his hands on his hips and scowled. "You don't understand this, do you? There's about to be a battle here. If you want your boys to be safe, you need to be well on your way somewhere else. Delaying us only delays your departure."

"You'd let us go?" the blacksmith said, wide-eyed. He looked from Jeremiah to me to Zeke and back again.

"Are you going to help us?"

He looked at his boys, and a tear formed in his eye. They sat still and silent, their faces white with fear.

"It's… it's my other boy. The oldest," the blacksmith said at last. "They have him! In the tower!"

"Ah," Jeremiah said. "Finally, the real reason. He's… a slave?"

The blacksmith nodded. "Scribe."

"Well, we will free him if we can. But…" He gestured toward the blacksmith's sons. "Maybe you should save these two while *you* can."

"Please, Pa," the elder one said. His voice broke as he spoke.

With a final sob, the blacksmith nodded. Then he looked at Jeremiah again. "But you can't get in. Only a Jotun can open the door."

"There were arrow slits," I chimed in. "I could probably squeeze through one."

"Too high," Jeremiah replied. "Even if we could climb up, you'd be spotted."

In the distance, cannons thundered, a bit louder than before.

"What about his brother?" I asked, pointing at the blacksmith. "He's High Thrall, right? Is he in the tower too? He could let us in."

The blacksmith shook his head. "My brother is in charge of farms east of town along the river."

Jeremiah's eyebrows went up, and then he grinned evilly. "I know exactly what we're going to do."

I stayed with the blacksmith for some time while Jeremiah hurriedly completed the preparations. Dusk had deepened so Zeke lit an oil lamp, but otherwise stayed quiet as he stood by the young boys.

The cannons continued to thunder in the distance. The yells of men and Jotun did too. It made an eerie quiet.

The blacksmith stopped blubbering, which soothed my nerves more than I'd expected. I hadn't liked the sight of him being all emotional. Maybe he had cause. I was just happy he was calm.

He did give me a full description of his eldest son, a swarthy dark-haired kid about my own age named Hank. The Jotun were keeping him and another handful of boys as slave clerks. He didn't know exactly where inside the tower, as he'd never been allowed in.

But otherwise he wasn't much help. He just stared at his younger sons, his eyes full of sadness and held-back tears, unless I asked him a direct question.

I didn't have the heart to truly interrogate him.

Finally, Jeremiah bustled back into the room. He gave me a nod and joined me by the blacksmith.

"What's your brother's name?" Jeremiah asked the blacksmith.

"Henry Tanner." He seemed to spit the name.

"Good," Jeremiah said. "Now you take your boys, get on a horse, and ride west out of town. Keep going for at least a full day. Then, cross the river if you can and go to Fort Chicago."

"What about Hank?" the blacksmith asked. "My other son?"

"The army will treat him well," Jeremiah assured. "You'll see when the battle's over. They'll take him to Fort Chicago if they can."

"If they can," the blacksmith grumbled.

Jeremiah pointedly looked at the two younger sons.

The blacksmith blinked and choked back a sob. "We'll go! We'll go!"

Jeremiah nodded. "Best get moving."

Jeremiah, Zeke, Burwell and I stood in the blacksmith's shop, checking our final preparations. Captain Mercer and the rest were long gone.

We wore long coats, inside-out to hide their Western Army markings, and broad-brimmed hats pulled down low. We'd ripped the insignia off, though Zeke had grumbled when we did.

Me, I would've grumbled about how hot the coats were. I couldn't stop sweating and feeling like I was rolled in honey.

Jeremiah had us slide our sabers and pistols back behind our hips so they'd be harder to see. The others also had their rifles slung over their backs under their coats. The tips of the barrels stuck out behind their necks and looked obvious to me, but Jeremiah assured me that no one would look close.

My rifle was out in the open, but Jeremiah assured me that was all right.

"They won't be surprised at a High Thrall's foreman being armed," he reassured me, "and they don't think a single armed man is a threat."

"I'm not much of a threat anyway," I grumbled. The brass buttons now inside the coat rubbed my wrists wrong. I shook my arms in irritation.

"You just have to convince them you're from High Thrall Tanner well enough to open the door."

I dourly nodded in agreement. I was "sent by High Thrall Tanner" to tell our Jotun masters about "an army crossing the river" near our farm. We, meaning the four of us, could provide more details of what we'd seen if they let us in.

I was sure it'd never work.

Still, as the near constant sound of cannons reminded us, we didn't have much time.

So we strode out into the square.

The tower and the whole side of the square near the river were lit by torches, with even a few bonfires here and there. There wasn't as much commotion as before. All of the Jotun and men seemed to be down by the river, with only a few sentries at the top of the tower staring that way.

We marched with purpose. "Look like you belong," Jeremiah told Zeke when the big man started to fall out of step.

Zeke nodded. Then he quickly bowed his head. "Dear Lord have mercy on us, as we enter the lion's den to do Your work."

No one replied. We set too fast a pace to talk.

We crossed the several hundred yards of cleared ground to the tower, then headed around to the huge door on the side that faced the river. Twenty yards away, we came to a stop.

I stared up at the door and the tower, and swallowed hard. The door was five times my height, and the tower twenty times.

The tower soared into the sky.

I hadn't truly realized how high until I stood in front of it.

The door consisted of a lot of thick timbers each as wide as a tree. Together, they looked like different colored matchsticks glued together.

I saw wood of all types just shoved together. A forest smashed into a tall, wide board.

About halfway up the door was a large wooden handle made of three tree trunks. It looked sturdy and completely out of reach. Two thirds the way up the door was a square opening—a crude window of sorts. Light leaked around the edges of some sort of curtain hanging on the inside.

"There's no bell," Jeremiah muttered. "No servant's door."

I scanned the base of the tower. He was right—there was no way to let the folks inside know that we were here.

"We could knock," Zeke said. He slid up close behind me, looking not at all like the slave he was supposed to be.

"And they'd hear us over this?" Burwell said. He waved his hand in a circle, just as another round of cannons rang out, making his point.

Jeremiah quickly glanced around. "No one's paying attention to us. Let's go closer."

We walked up to the door itself, but that didn't change anything. My heart beat a little faster, but that was it. I'd hoped that a door this large might have an equally large crack beneath it, but the door scraped the ground. I knocked just for the heck of it, but I couldn't hear it myself so I knew no one inside could.

"There's got to be a way for humans to get in," Jeremiah muttered.

"Why?" I said.

"I doubt they want to have to open that door every time a thrall appears. Maybe there's a servant's entrance around back."

He gestured for me to lead the way.

We circled the entire tower, which took quite a bit of time, and didn't find anything other than the main door. Other than it and the arrow slits higher up, there didn't seem to be any way in or out of the building.

As we completed the circuit to the front, the noise near the river grew. Cannons now thundered continuously. We could hear Jotun yelling and even a scream.

Then the long, loud note of a Jotun signal horn rang out.

One long note. Then three quick blasts. Then one long note.

It slowly faded away.

And was then answered by a roar of cannons. Deafeningly loud. Like the heavens opening up above us with a scream of unholy thunder.

Above us.

We all looked up, and after a minute, it happened again.

Huge, horrible roars.

And the whistle of cannon balls, large enough to block out the moon, flying toward the river.

Toward.

My eyes went wide and I turned to Jeremiah.

He stared back in equal shock.

The cannons were on the tower.

The Jotun had cannons.

The Jotun had cannons!

Which meant the Army of the West didn't have a prayer.

THIRTEEN

WE STOOD THERE IN SHOCK. The flickering fires from the waterfront and the sticky air and the booms of the cannons felt like Hell. My throat parched as my blood raced in fear.

"What do we do?" I asked Jeremiah.

He shook his head, equally as shocked as me. We just stared up, up, and up.

I snapped out of it first.

"The window," I said, "the window in the door. It's our only chance."

"It's twenty feet up!"

"The wagon," I said. "We park the wagon underneath, then you and Zeke boost me up."

"What about me?" Burwell asked.

"Lookout," I said. When he furrowed his brow, I shook him off. "Someone's gotta. Let's go!"

The Jotun cannon thundered again as we raced back to the black-smith's shop. Panting and gasping for breath, we fortunately found the wagon untouched. The blacksmith had taken only his own horses, so while Zeke and Burwell got ours hitched, Jeremiah and I furiously threw everything we thought we might need into the back.

Jeremiah grabbed plenty of rope. I threw in the blacksmith's hammer, some iron builder's spikes I found, and some of his tools. I thought about adding the anvil as a possible weight, but it was too heavy to move.

We threw off the coats—no need for disguises when we'd been completely ignored before. Meanwhile, I tried to not wince every time I heard the Jotun cannon.

Once we'd loaded everything, we paused long enough to spy at the tower again.

Two Jotun stormed out the door and slammed it behind them. Both wore full leather jerkins, studded with metal fittings, and complete helmets. They carried swords, and one wore a large gold chain around his neck that glinted in the low light.

My heart sank. We'd missed the Jotun Commander.

The two giants ran toward the river. I looked at Jeremiah.

"The cannons," he said. "They're more important."

My blood raced and I nodded in agreement.

Burwell drove the wagon. He said he'd be far better with horses than any of us yokels, and I wasn't inclined to argue. Instead, I tumbled into the wagon bed and hung on as we galloped back across the open square to the looming tower.

For a moment, I feared our own cannonballs smashing into us, but none came. Our army didn't return fire on the tower.

Maybe it was too far.

Burwell yanked up on the reins and then slowly coaxed the horses to bring the wagon next to the door. Zeke and Jeremiah jumped up in the wagon bed. They stood next to the wall and braced themselves. Zeke bent and cupped his hands to give me a stirrup to push up on.

It was no good. No good!

I could climb all the way onto Zeke's shoulders, but even standing there, I couldn't reach the window.

"Try something else," Jeremiah said. "Quickly."

"Throw a rope up?" Zeke suggested. "Maybe use the hammer as a weight?" He gestured to where I'd thrown the blacksmith tools in the wagon.

Jeremiah shook his head. "Nothing to anchor it. It'll come down as soon as Billy tugs on it."

That's when the idea hit me.

"The spikes," I said excitedly. "We use the spikes as footholds."

"It won't be fast," Jeremiah said.

The cannons above us roared again.

"But then…" He snatched up several. "Billy, tie the rope around your waist so you can pull us up. Zeke, you hammer."

The two of them quickly got to work. Zeke hammered in one spike while Jeremiah picked a spot for the next one and got it started. Then Zeke quickly banged on it.

Burwell held the reins tight. He talked to the horses, but what he said was lost to me in the din from above.

Meanwhile, as I tied the rope around my waist and checked that my rifle was strapped tight to my back, I glanced around. There was no one in the square. It was strangely still.

I could see more flames now, down at the riverfront. Some of them seemed further back, like in the river itself.

I choked up as I realized some of the boats must be burning.

Closer in, the shapes of Jotun occasionally blocked the fire as they dashed about. I could hear screams and shouts, and then, gratefully, the bark of our own cannon.

I wondered, how was Captain Mercer doing?

"Now, Billy!" Jeremiah gestured at the spikes they'd driven into the door, about head high.

Zeke boosted me up so I could stand on them. Then Jeremiah passed me two more spikes and the hammer. I nearly dropped it when he first handed it to me as I'd underestimated the weight.

"Careful," Jeremiah said with a grin. "I can't dance if you drop that on my foot."

"You can't dance now," I shot back.

We shared a grin of black humor.

The hammer had a leather thong at the end of the handle. I slid it around my wrist.

Zeke braced my legs while I pounded two more spikes into the door at shoulder height. I tested them by pulling on them as hard as I could, and they held. I started to pull myself up on them, but my arms trembled.

I needed footholds in between.

Jeremiah passed me several more spikes. I pocketed most of them and I banged two into the door at waist level. Then using the higher spikes as handholds, I pulled myself up until I could stand on them.

"That's it," Jeremiah said from below. "You've got it, Billy!"

"Jotun coming!" Burwell called.

I couldn't turn to look or I'd fall. Instead, I took a deep breath to calm myself and fished another spike out of my pocket. I started pounding it in to be a new handhold. Fortunately, the spikes didn't take much to get started between the trunk planks.

I leaned my body against the door. I tried not to think about how sturdy the spikes were.

They'd gone in easily. Would they come out easily too?

The cannons above me roared again.

"Billy!" Jeremiah called. "Keep going! We'll take care of the Jotun!"

I kept swinging the hammer.

I heard the horses neigh and then reins jangle.

I kept pounding. When the spike was in deep enough that I couldn't pull it out, I reached into my pocket for the next one.

And dropped it.

I cursed and fumbled in my pocket for another. I had only a few more. I carefully clutched the one I pulled out.

Horses screamed behind me. A Jotun roared.

I closed my eyes and forced myself to take several smooth breaths. I lodged the spike between two of the tree trunk planks and started hammering it in.

Cannons raged above.

Gunshots and a Jotun yell sounded behind me.

I focused on the spike.

I nearly bent it, but managed to knock it true again.

I pounded hard. Then I tested it and it held.

The Jotun behind me screamed.

I pulled myself up on the new spike, and one of my footholds gave. I slammed into the door and banged my shoulder, but managed to hold on for dear life.

I fumbled with my foot until I found the next foothold. Slowly I pushed up.

I could reach the window!

With all my strength I struggled up. I shoved off another spike, and this one also popped free.

But it was enough.

I pulled myself onto the window sill and gasped with relief.

The sill itself was maybe three feet wide—tiny for a Jotun but plenty of room for me. The 'curtain' looked like that thick leather they used for their jerkins—a few inches of the hide of god-knows-what beast.

Making sure not to fall, I carefully turned around.

A Jotun thrashed on the ground.

He lay on his stomach and he swung his arms to the side. Zeke and Jeremiah danced around his head. They held their sabers out.

The Jotun shot out a hand to grab Zeke. He skedaddled back and Jeremiah charged in and stabbed the giant in the shoulder.

The Jotun howled and swung his head around.

Zeke rewarded the giant's distraction by stabbing it in the arm several times. My eyebrows rose with respect. His sword danced in his hands as he slashed and stabbed and turned—far more skillfully than I'd even dreamed possible.

But I pulled my eyes away and looked for Burwell. I couldn't see him in the dark.

Crushed wood and dead horses surrounded the Jotun's legs and feet. Burwell could've been among them. I couldn't tell.

The Jotun howled again.

I realized his arms were moving but his legs weren't. That was good —real good.

I edged sideways until I reached the "wall" of the window. There, I drove one of my last spikes into the door and tied the rope around it. Now that I was able to lean against the "wall," I pulled my wrist from the hammer strap and set it down. Then I unshouldered my rifle.

I raised it to my shoulder and winced. I'd bruised it worse than I'd thought.

But the fight raged on below me.

And the cannons above roared once again.

I settled the rifle and took aim down the barrel. If I could hit the Jotun's eye—

My world shook.

The whole Jotun door rattled.

I had to throw myself flat to avoid falling off. With one panicked hand I clawed for the rope and with the other, I clutched my rifle. I rolled onto my stomach, pinning the rifle so it wouldn't slide away.

The curtain at the back of the window rose.

I gasped.

A Jotun head, half as big as me, appeared. Huge nose. Beard with hair like tree branches. Enormous round eyes.

Huge eyes.

I yanked my Colt out of its holster, still behind my hip.

The motion drew the Jotun's eyes toward me. They turned—

I fired. Again and again and again. Right at that glorious, *huge* eye.

The Jotun screamed.

I fired and fired until the revolver clicked empty.

The face disappeared and the curtain flapped back into place. A large crash and thump followed.

I panted hard.

It'd been too fast for me to be scared, but I still shook. I calmed myself with twenty breaths and listened for anything else. I couldn't hear anything from the inside of the door, but the cannons above fired again.

I rolled over and pulled myself up until I was sitting.

Jeremiah and Zeke still circled the downed Jotun—darting in to stab and then back before he could strike back. The giant's lunges at them were weaker, slower. They'd kill him soon. It was just a matter of time.

The cannons above roared again.

Time I didn't have.

I glanced at the window curtain. I couldn't see a thing inside.

It didn't matter. I started pulling up the end of the rope that dangled outside. I paused before throwing it down the other side.

I needed it to hold.

I took the last spike out of my pocket and hammered it into the window ledge, right next to the first. I tied the rope around them and gave it a quick tug. Then I pulled as hard as I could.

The spikes stayed put.

I took a deep breath and dropped the end of the rope through the gap between the curtain and the door. Then I double-checked that all my gear was secure. Another deep breath, and I started climbing down.

It took a bit of effort to slip between the bottom of the thick leather window shade and the wooden door without getting flattened or snagged on anything. Still, I managed to inch my way down. The shade weighed heavy on my legs and back and wanted to push me flat. Fortunately, it didn't extend much below the window and the squashing soon came to an end.

That didn't prevent the smell from overwhelming me. Tanned, soaked leather, and then…

Dung. The smell of dung wafting up from below. It grew stronger as I moved down.

Finally I worked my way far enough down for the curtain to slap the wood above me. My head free, I turned and looked below.

A Jotun sprawled on the floor.

He'd voided himself, so I knew he was dead. That, and the way he lay in a heap. His limbs flopped in awkward ways that no live person could've tolerated.

I let out a deep sigh of relief and triumph.

I'd killed a Jotun.

One down, several thousand more to go.

I continued my climb down, and to my relief, the rope held. A few feet from the bottom, I jumped. I landed off to the side of the body near his head.

He was an ugly brute. Even without the drool and the smashed eye. Scars criss-crossed his face and his nose had a huge notch taken out of it.

I kicked him in the face for good measure.

Other than the body, the small-for-a-Jotun room contained little else. Closed doors were in the middle of the left and right walls. These doors were as crude as the front door, but not as tightly fitted. I could see deeper shadows from the cracks underneath and around, but no light peeked through. A large tapestry hung on the wall near each door. They seemed to be of wool, but as thick as the leather curtain had been. One was dyed brown with crossed war axes on it. The other was blue with a stylized eagle. They looked like army symbols of some kind.

A hallway opened in the far wall and stretched what looked like the length of the building. At various intervals, dark openings stood on its left and right. Dim light flickered from one at the far end.

To the left of the hallway entrance, a Jotun-sized three-legged table sat along the wall, but I couldn't see the top. Its stone legs were thick and looked too sheer to climb. Above it, a large smoky torch hung in an iron sconce.

To the right of the hallway entrance—yes! A ladder leading up through a hole in the ceiling!

The sound of the cannons was muffled here, but I could still hear them. Nothing else, which both relieved and worried me in equal measures.

I ran to the ladder, but then paused. Designed for Jotun, each rung was four feet from the last one. I was a little over five feet tall.

How was I going to get up?

FOURTEEN

I STOOD there in the Jotun tower and stared at the ladder. I tried to ignore the stench of the nearby corpse and the boom boom boom of the cannons above.

My heart beat hard. I had to get up there!

I'd anchored the rope too well when I'd climbed down from the window—there was no way I'd be able to dislodge it and use it again. I didn't see anything around that I could stand on, unless I wanted to search the body, which I absolutely did not want to do.

I headed into the hallway.

I took two steps and then stopped and swore at myself. I'd emptied my revolver—what kind of stupid would I be to charge into the dark without reloading first?

I took the time to do so, and then to shift my saber to the front where I could draw it more easily. Then I took my Winchester rifle in hand and crept forward down the hall.

I glanced into the first opening I came to, but it was too shadowed to make out much. I couldn't hear anything either. Instead, the flickering light much further down drew me.

Like a cat, I crept on down. Or maybe a mouse given the size of the building.

I moved quick, but along one wall. At each opening, I stopped and peered around the edge. I never saw much in the gloom. So I scampered across as quick as I could and continued creeping toward the light.

Finally, I reached the opening with the dim light. I could almost make out voices in the room, though they were low.

I peered around the corner and stifled a gasp.

I'd found the human prisoners.

A torch flickered from a sconce above a large stone table along the far wall. The table itself stood ten feet high, but at the distance across the room I could easily see the large cages on top of it. Like jail cells, rows of thin iron bars formed a large box.

Within it the human men and boys stood or sat. They were all ages —some I was sure were the slave scribes, others must've been kept for other reasons.

They hadn't seen me yet.

I scanned the rest of the room and saw human-sized barrels and crates stacked on another stone table along a side wall. The floor itself seemed largely bare. The only other furniture was a Jotun-sized three-legged wooden stool.

No Jotun were in sight.

I dashed into the room. I didn't call out—I was afraid of making too much noise, but a boy slumped near the front of the cage perked up and then stood. He stared at me.

I reached the bottom of the stool and growled in frustration. Once again, the stupid *height* of everything was a problem. How the heck was I going to get up there?

I backed up to get a better look at the table and the cages. The men and boys now all clustered at the bars and stared down at me.

I decided to risk some noise.

"How do I get up?" I called. "How do I free you?"

A murmur ran through the men and finally they parted to allow an older, grizzled man with wavy grey hair to step forward.

"Where are the Jotun?" he asked.

"Fighting the Army of the West," I said.

A wave of excitement rippled through them.

"I need to get you out," I said, "and I need to get up to the roof to stop the cannons. Any idea how?"

"There's building tools—human building tools—on the other table," the man said. He pointed, in case I had any doubts.

I studied it. It didn't seem any easier to climb.

But I decided to give it a closer look. I approached the nearest table leg and walked around it. There weren't any handholds or obvious nooks or crannies where I could put my feet. I walked to the nearest back leg because it was closer. It'd been shoved up right against the stone wall, with only a small crack between the table leg and the wall itself.

I paused. "Small" for a Jotun, but not for me.

There weren't any handholds, but I could put my back against the wall and my feet against the table leg and work my way up. It'd be a long climb and if I fell...

I didn't want to think about "if I fell."

I couldn't do it with my rifle over my back, though, nor my saber at my side. Reluctantly, I took them off and tucked them by the side of the table leg.

Then I started to climb.

It wasn't that high, I realized once I started. Only about twice my height.

But it was slow, oh so slow.

Shove back up, grimace as the stone scraped me even through my shirt, then push back and move my feet up. Ignore the throbbing in my bruised shoulder.

Then do it again.

And again.

And again.

Finally, finally, I made it to the top. I reached over, grabbed the lip of the table, and hauled myself up.

A small cheer went up from the caged men when I appeared.

True to their word, all sorts of supplies were stacked behind the crates and barrels I'd originally seen. Saws, hammers, barrels of large nails—

—and rope.

Coils and coils and coils of glorious rope!

I dashed over to it and found five coils that I judged to be about fifty feet or so long. Plenty enough to climb the ladder to the cannons!

I swallowed hard at the memory of them.

I turned and stared at the caged men. They were safe.

The Army of the West wasn't.

Captain Mercer's orders came back to me.

Do whatever it takes to fulfill your mission.

We must win this battle.

Captain Mercer would abandon the prisoners, I realized. Or come back for them later.

Every minute I spent with them was another minute that soldiers *died* because of the Jotun cannons.

But they were hostages. If the Jotun returned, they'd surely kill them rather than let them go free.

"Hey!" one of the men called. "What're ya waitin' for?"

I jolted out of my rambling thoughts and looked at them again. About two dozen men and boys, scrawny and filthy in ragged clothes, clung to the bars staring at me. I was too far to see their eyes, but I knew they were filled with hope.

All I had to do was get down from this table, climb their table, and unlock their cage.

How many soldiers would die while I did that?

But surely it wouldn't take too long. All I had to do—

I caught myself. I looked more closely at the cage door and lock. It was huge—clearly a Jotun-sized key was required.

"How do I unlock the cage?" I called to the men.

"The Slave Master has the key," an older man called back.

"Is he an ugly Jotun with a notch in his nose?" I asked.

"No."

"Then we don't have the key."

"Bring us the tools!" one of the older boys yelled. "There's files and iron saws in one of the boxes. We can cut the bars with them. I know how—my dad's a blacksmith!"

I almost snorted at the coincidence. But it wasn't much, was it? The boy, with his dark black hair and complexion looked a bit like the blacksmith, but with none of the cowardice.

So with a nod, I began rummaging through the boxes.

It didn't take long to find the tools the boy had mentioned. I dumped three saws, a handful of metal files, and a big maul over the side of the table. Then I hooked one of the ropes around a bunch of really heavy crates. It didn't take long to lower myself to the ground.

The next rope was long enough to throw over the top of the stool and tie to the leg on the far side. That made it an easy climb, even with the various iron working tools strapped to me. Once I stood on the top of the stool, I was close enough to twirl and throw another rope toward the imprisoned men. On the third try, one of them caught it and they tied it to the bars. I scrambled up that rope and found myself face to face with the men.

They eagerly grabbed the tools out of my hands when I offered them. The blacksmith's son started explaining to the others how to use them, while the older man stared at me.

"Who are you?" he asked. His voice carried the tone of command.

"Private McCarty," I answered automatically. "Third Squadron, Avenging Angels Regiment, Army of the West."

He nodded, as if none of this surprised him. "Your mission, soldier?"

"Stop the cannons on the roof."

"Then get to it."

I almost saluted from habit at hearing an officer's tone, but instead I just nodded and ran for the rope.

Back in the entryway, I stared up at the ladder that had to lead to the roof. It disappeared into gloomy darkness, but the thunder of the cannons was louder.

I couldn't help a black-humored chuckle. It looked like Hell was up instead of down.

I threw one rope over the second rung and then tied it to the first. That gave me a loop of rope that was easy to climb. Once I reached the first rung, I used the second rope in the same way. I threw it over the third rung and tied it to the second. Then carefully, oh so carefully, I undid the first rope from the first rung. I coiled it over my shoulders and climbed to the second ladder rung.

Alternating ropes wasn't fast, but it was sure. It helped that I could almost scramble from one rung to the other since they were shoulder height. But the ropes made it safe.

The ladder reached a dark second floor. The landing had a single doorway off of it, and this one was covered by another thick curtain like the window. No light snuck out around the edges.

The ladder kept going, so I kept climbing.

The third floor landing was much like the second—a curtained doorway and no light.

Cannons roared above me.

I kept going.

About three rungs up, I realized that I was about to hit a ceiling. I stopped and tried to see exactly what was happening. My eyes had adjusted to the gloom, but there still wasn't much light from the sole torch so far below me.

The ladder ended at a trap door.

Which was closed.

I nearly screamed in frustration.

Still, there was nothing to do but keep climbing.

I reached the last rung below the trap door. It was cramped there, and I actually had to crouch because there wasn't enough space between the rung and the door. Just to be safe, I tied one of the ropes around my waist and the other end around the ladder and studied the trap door.

I couldn't see much, given how dark it was. There looked to be a two foot lip or frame running around the outside, with a darker middle. I couldn't see much at all there. I didn't see any hinges or lock, which meant it had to lift. I reached up with both hands and pushed.

It didn't budge.

With a grunt, I pushed harder. The wood under my hands nearly gave me splinters, and…

…it still didn't budge.

I nearly howled in frustration. All of the effort, all of the climbing —the door, the tables, the ladder—heck, even killing the Jotun!

And I was stopped by a heavy trap door.

I took a deep breath. Several deep breaths. Then I studied the door again.

Why was there a frame around the door?

I ran my hand over the frame and into the middle.

Leather. The same stuff as the window curtain had been. Thick, but with a little bit of give.

I let out a long, ragged relieved breath.

I could cut leather.

Carefully, I unsheathed my saber and stabbed the fabric. The blade went through and I started sawing.

The cannons fired again. A loud bark like the hounds of Hell.

I kept sawing until I had a slit wider than my body. The leather sagged, and I started cutting a perpendicular slit.

The cannons barked again.

Finally, finally, after an eternity of sawing and a sore arm and sweat beading on my brow and dripping down and worrying about my balance and the rope holding…

The fabric gave.

I had a hole.

I sheathed my saber, checked my guns, and reached through the hole. I could pull myself up on the frame.

With a deep breath to calm my nerves, I untied my rope and climbed onto the tower roof.

FIFTEEN

MY BRUISED SHOULDER screamed in pain as I pulled myself through the hole and up onto the trapdoor frame. Gasping, I collapsed onto my stomach and dragged myself across the scratchy wood to the smooth stone. I wiped the sweat from my brow and moistened my lips. For a moment, I wished I had a canteen, but, no.

I had a mission.

Determined, I rose onto my hands and knees. My rifle slid on my back and almost banged into the stone, but I caught it at the last moment. My saber did tick against the stone, but too quietly for anyone but me to hear.

I looked up.

Darkness filled the night sky, broken up by torches bigger than my head which ringed the roof about every thirty feet. Mounted on the ten foot high walls, they burned bright enough to make out the cannons and Jotun on the roof.

I let out a deep sigh. Only two cannon and four Jotun.

Only.

The cannons were huge—Jotun sized! I might've been able to stand inside the barrel. I could easily stand under one, and maybe not touch my head on its black iron. They pointed toward the river with enough upward tilt that I was sure they were hitting it.

A bare-chested Jotun was loading the nearest one. He wrestled with getting a huge cannonball the size of a sheep into the barrel. Dozens of other cannonballs stood in a pyramid nearby. He grunted and struggled and eventually rolled the ball down the long tube. At the back of the barrel, another Jotun with long blond braided hair stood by to light the cannon's fuse with a thin wisp of a torch.

The other two Jotun worked at the far cannon. One, in just a simple tunic, carried a large bag of what had to be gunpowder toward the barrel while the second used a brush to clear out the barrel. The one with the powder stood and waited for him to finish.

That heartened me. They weren't a well-oiled team like we'd been at the Battle of Golden City. They were undermanned and not trained right. But they had plenty of ammunition and plenty of time.

The first cannon fired, and my ears rang from the blast. The cannon kicked back two full lengths. The two Jotun started pushing it back into place and the bare-chested one grumbled something to the other.

None of them looked my way.

Once the two had the cannon in place, the bare-chested one stood at the front of the wall and stared out toward the battlefield. Then he started to push the cannon sideways a bit.

Adjusting its aim, I realized.

The other Jotun strode over to a large stone bin in the center of the roof. He pulled a large bag out of it and headed back toward the cannon.

My eyes went wide.

The bin was their limber—where they stored their gunpowder.

And as undermanned as they were, no one was watching it.

I climbed to my feet and glanced around. Other than the cannons and the powder bin, there wasn't much on the roof. A large stone structure stood against a far wall with what looked like pipes coming out of it. I guessed it was a cistern. But otherwise, there was nothing.

Which meant no cover for me.

Keeping my eyes on the giants the entire time, I crept toward the shadows of the closest wall.

They remained focused on their tasks, and both cannons roared once more.

I made it to the base of the wall where the shadows enveloped me. I crouched down to make myself more invisible as I studied the scene to make sure I hadn't overlooked anything.

I had to silence the cannons.

It'd be impossible to do anything to the cannons themselves. They were too massive and even if I could get to the firing pins, I doubted I could do much to them. Besides, there were two guns and I didn't think I could get to both, not with the Jotun around.

As for the Jotun themselves, I chuckled to myself in black humor. I'd be hard pressed to kill one Jotun by myself, much less four. I wasn't Cassidy.

A pang went through my heart. I'd seen Cassidy fight two giants at once and win. He'd danced between their legs, never giving either of them a clear shot at him. And then he'd used his saber to take them down. He'd been amazing.

But I was facing four, and I wasn't amazing. I couldn't wield a saber like Cassidy or Zeke.

It had to be the gunpowder.

I watched one of the Jotun as he went to retrieve another bag from the storage bin. He just reached over the top and grabbed a bag. They seemed to be made out of cloth of some type. He hefted it in one hand and carried it back to the cannon.

So there was no lid on the storage bin. All I had to do was get a torch into it, and it'd burn.

Or explode.

That thought made my heart seize.

I didn't want to be anywhere on the roof when it blew up. But there wouldn't be much time to get off before it blew.

I needed a fuse. For that matter, I needed a way to set the

gunpowder on fire anyway. The torches were far too big for me to carry.

The cannons fired again—ragged, and not together, but still enough to make me clamp my hands over my ears.

The bare-chested Jotun stood at the wall. He roared something to the other cannoneers and gestured toward the river. They all quickly started shifting the cannons' aim once again.

Watching him, I had an idea.

I quickly fumbled with my rifle straps and set it against the wall. Then I took off my shirt. It actually felt cooler to have it off, even without a breeze to break up the damp.

I rolled my shirt up tight. Now I had a fuse.

I just needed fire.

With all the torches, there was plenty around, just too far above my head to reach.

More climbing! I swore under my breath.

The wall beside me rose steep and sheer. I doubted I could climb up it, even if I got one of the ropes I'd use earlier.

There had to be another way. I started creeping along the outer wall, away from the Jotun, looking for a place that wasn't so sheer.

I found a way up by the cistern. A huge iron pipe ran down along the wall and into a hole in the roof. I scrambled up the pipe without much effort at all.

At the top, I paused. The heavy air still clung to me and just made it hard to breathe. Sweat soaked me, despite how parched my mouth was. A simple breeze would've helped.

The cannons still boomed, but I'd gotten used to it. They were slower, though, as if the Jotun were having more problems. For a moment, I hoped they would fail to clean a barrel well enough and get a misfire. I couldn't rely on that, though.

The cistern sat along the wall that faced the blacksmith's shop. I peered at it through the dark, but I couldn't make out a thing. I wondered where Jeremiah and Zeke were. I couldn't see the giant they'd been fighting from here, it was too far around the front. I prayed they'd survived. Feisty Burwell too.

Small pinpricks of light were scattered through the rest of the city. Larger blazes were down at the battlefield. The square around the tower was quiet. I didn't see a single Jotun. Other than the ones of the roof with me.

The nearest torch flickered and smoked. I could stand on the wall and just reach it. I flipped the end of my shirt into it, held it for a second, and pulled it back.

The tip had caught fire.

I scrambled down the pipe, holding the burning shirt at arm's length. I jumped the last few feet, and wobbled as I almost lost my balance.

A Jotun roared.

The bare-chested one ran toward me. He held a battle axe high above his head.

I'd been seen!

Only one thing to do! I sprinted as hard as I could toward the powder bin.

The Jotun raced to intercept me.

I ran hard.

With a snarl, he moved between me and the bin.

I swerved to the left, toward the trap door.

In a few swift strides, he towered in front of me again.

I turned and ran towards the bin.

I wasn't going to make it! His footsteps slammed behind me. I glanced over my shoulder. He'd raised his axe—

—I threw myself sideways and rolled. The axe slammed into the rooftop where I'd been, with the screech of metal on stone. Stabs of pain shot out from my bruised shoulder. I bounded quickly to my feet.

I'd dropped my burning shirt.

The Jotun turned and roared at me. He shifted his stance and raised his axe.

I ran, but towards him. I drew my saber as I did.

He swung the axe down, but I was between his legs before he

could strike. I slashed at his boot-covered ankle, but my blade bounced off without cutting deep.

I kept running.

The giant kicked at me, but I saw it coming. I was through his legs and beyond before he could turn. I circled around toward the powder bin

Another Jotun stood in front of me, blocking my way. He held a sword, its point low.

I skidded to a stop.

Then I raced toward my burning shirt.

It had nearly gone out, but still smoldered. I scooped it up with my left hand and cried out in pain.

The flames scorched my flesh.

I jumped to the side just as the bare-chested Jotun swung his axe at me again. He was closer, but still missed.

Once again, I ran toward him instead of away. He kicked his feet together, so I swerved around him.

I slashed my saber at his ankle.

It stuck in the leather of his boot and wrenched itself out of my hand.

He snarled and kicked at me.

This time he connected and I went sprawling. Pain shot through my side, but I was able to roll and bound to my feet again. I clutched the smoldering shirt to my chest and gasped in agony.

The cannons were in front of me.

The Jotun behind me roared.

I ran ahead, toward the cannon.

His axe smashed down behind me—where I would've been if I'd run towards his legs again.

Instead I raced forward.

The near cannon stood in front of me, unmanned.

I ran and I ran.

The Jotun pounded after me.

I zigzagged—left, right, right, left.

His axe clanged against the stone behind me.

The Jotun at the far cannon turned and shouted.

I focused on the cannon ahead. I could duck under it if I got there in time!

The Jotun behind me roared.

My eyes darted and then I saw it—a powder bag!

Sitting next to the cannon's wheel, the Jotun must've set it down when he'd seen me. I dashed for it, dropped my smoldering shirt on it, and dove under the cannon's barrel.

The Jotun pulled up just short of the cannon. He crouched down and held his axe ready to strike.

I ran out the other side, toward the second cannon.

Toward the two Jotun coming toward me. One jabbed a sword at me.

I threw myself sideways.

The powder bag exploded.

Wood and iron flew through the air. Something large passed over my head.

I slammed to the stone roof and skidded into the outer wall.

My head smashed into something and sparks of pain lanced through me.

Then everything went black.

SIXTEEN

EVERYTHING HURT.

It all hurt, and that was all I knew as the fog slowly left my brain. Then, slowly, the pain faded from some spots. It hurt to breathe, though. My hands hurt too. And my head screamed in agony. But I was alive. My eyelids fluttered and I slowly opened them.

Maria's beautiful face smiled down at me.

I couldn't help but smile back, even though it hurt.

Slowly, I became aware of more of my surroundings. I was lying on my back on something soft, in a room with wooden walls. A thin sheet covered me, and sunlight came from somewhere behind my head.

"How do you feel?" she asked.

"Like a horse kicked me." I smiled weakly. *Right in the skull,* I thought.

"Do you know who I am?"

"Maria."

"Do you know your name?"

"Billy." I frowned, but it hurt. "Why are you asking?"

"You hit your head hard. We were worried."

I nodded. My lip cracked.

Maria noticed and reached behind her. She held a cup of water out. "Can you sit up?"

I nodded again and started to, but then winced in pain and dizziness. I managed to make it far enough for Maria to put a supportive hand under my back and hold the cup to my lips. I drank greedily, enough that some slopped out onto my chin. I licked that up while Maria put the glass back.

"Where…?" I asked.

"The Louisville Hospital," she said. "We won."

I nodded and sank back onto the pillow. I closed my eyes and drifted off to sleep.

* * *

Low voices came from my bedside. My eyelids felt heavy, so I just enjoyed the softness of the bed for a bit. After all, I couldn't quite make out what they were saying.

After a bit, though, I recognized one of the voices. Zeke's. His unmistakeable deep bass was clear through the general murmurs.

I turned my head and opened my eyes. I couldn't help smiling, even though it hurt to do so. Zeke, Jeremiah, and Captain Mercer stood in a knot of animated conversation a few feet from my bed.

Zeke saw I was awake first. He broke into a broad grin. "The Lord is merciful!"

Jeremiah and Captain Mercer turned with relieved expressions on their faces. They approached the bed.

"How are you feeling, Billy?" Jeremiah asked.

"I hurt," I said, "but I'll live." The words almost caught in my throat. I hadn't thought about it on the roof, but I could've died then. Easily.

"Good, Private McCarty, very good," Captain Mercer said.

"What happened?" I asked.

"We won," Captain Mercer said, "in large part thanks to you."

"What happened?"

"The ironclads sailed into sight of the city at dusk, just as planned," Jeremiah explained. "They were supposed to draw the

Jotuns' attention and concentrate them at the river while the main army crossed further west. We hadn't counted on the archers, though. Our scouts and spies hadn't reported them."

I tried to snort. It hadn't been hard for *our* squadron to spot them, but maybe they were late arrivals.

"So," Jeremiah continued, "General Sanborn ordered the crossing at night instead of waiting until dawn. The ironclads engaged the archers which gave the transports cover."

"The archers...," I looked at Captain Mercer. "Did you get 'em?"

"All four," Captain Mercer said with a nod. "It was bloody work."

"Who'd we lose...?"

"Every man in Third Squadron but myself and Joe Johnson."

I sagged back into the bed and winced. I'd known these men. I'd helped train them... and they were all gone. Dead.

"Casualties were bad everywhere," Jeremiah said quietly. "But they could've been a lot worse."

"The Jotun cannon were outside our range," Captain Mercer said. "And they'd spotted the troop ships by then."

I swallowed, which hurt. My head hurt. My ribs hurt, but I had to ask.

"How bad?" I could barely croak the words out.

"They sank all the ironclads and three troop ships," Captain Mercer said. "And then they stopped."

"Your work," Jeremiah said. "You did it."

"I don't remember much," I said with a shake of my head. I winced as pain shot through my skull.

"When you do, you can tell me the full story," Jeremiah said. "The doctor says you'll live. The burns on your chest and hands were minor. You've got some cracked ribs and nearly broke your skull, but are fine otherwise."

"The Lord blessed us with a miracle," Zeke said. The big man had been silent, just watching until then. He smiled, his broad wide teeth shining against his dark skin. "You are the Lord's champion, and His hand protects you."

I snorted, but it turned into a cough, which hurt.

"You were lucky, if not blessed," Jeremiah said with a quick glance at Zeke. "We almost missed you when we got to the roof. But Zeke insisted we keep looking and I eventually spotted you against the wall near the broken cannon."

"Ah," I said. Zeke and Jeremiah had made it into the tower after all. Then I paused.

"Where's Burwell?" I asked.

"With Jesus," Zeke said solemnly. "He died a hero."

Captain Mercer and Jeremiah bowed their heads.

I felt my strength drain away. Images of Burwell—his smile, his spirit, his good nature—they all flashed through my mind.

"Time is up," Maria called from somewhere behind the men. "He needs rest."

Captain Mercer nodded with an amused grin. "Nurses. They outrank generals in the hospital. We'd best be on our way."

"I'll return after dinner," Jeremiah promised. He reached down and touched my arm.

I smiled back. Then I closed my eyes. I heard them shuffle off before I once again faded into sleep.

I awoke hungry. Long shadows filled the room. I felt strong enough to look around. Beside my bed sat a small table with an oil lamp, a pitcher of water, a glass, a small bottle, and a spoon. The label on the bottle read, "Poppy Syrup." The spoon was crusted with a dried liquid.

I sat up and winced. Waves of sharp pain came from my chest. But they dampened and dulled. I could breathe without it hurting and I could move a little. As long as I sat still, my chest didn't hurt.

So my ribs weren't as bad as I'd feared.

My head still throbbed. My temples and my eyes. I sat still with them closed and just breathed for a bit.

At least until my stomach rumbled.

I thought about getting up, but I didn't want to move.

But I also needed to pee.

"Maria?" I finally called. After a moment of silence, I called a bit louder, "Maria?"

I heard motion, like someone approaching. Then I heard clear footsteps and Maria's familiar "Mmmm."

I opened my eyes to see her concerned look.

"You sit," she said. "Good. How do you feel?"

"I hurt," I said. "And I'm hungry and I need a bedpan."

She nodded and reached for something under the bed.

"How bad am I hurt?" I asked.

"Not bad. They're waiting for you."

"Huh. Why?"

She passed me a tin bedpan and stood. "I will send food."

I nodded, and then she was gone.

I took care of my business and soon after I was done, Jeremiah appeared. He held a steaming bowl and a cup. He grinned when he saw me sitting.

"Maria said I had to bring you this if I wanted to talk with you," he said. He passed me the bowl and then the glass, both of which I set on the bed in front of me.

"She's not coming back?" I asked. I took a spoonful of the broth from the bowl. It tasted delicious—salty, beefy, and thick. Not too hot either.

"She has other patients." Jeremiah pulled over a stool and sat next to me.

"How many?" I asked as I sipped another spoonful of the delightful broth.

"For her, or total?"

"Total. How many did we lose?"

His smile faded into grimness. "About three thousand dead and wounded."

I gasped. "Three… three thousand? That's a third of the army!"

"Mmmm hmmm. The Jotun lost one hundred. And we took the city. Sanborn's sending all the civilians to Fort Chicago who want to go."

I wondered if the blacksmith and his sons were among them.

And only one hundred Jotun. We'd destroyed far more than that at the Battle of Golden City, but at a similar cost.

"How's your head?" Jeremiah asked.

"Hurts," I said. "More when I move it."

"Ah. Do you remember what happened?"

"Most," I said. "Not the end."

"Just a minute." He turned and pulled one of his leather-bound notebooks and a pencil off the table.

I couldn't help rolling my eyes, even though that hurt. Ah, Jeremiah, always working on his next dime novel.

"What are you going to call this one?" I asked.

"I haven't decided. So what happened after you climbed to the window?"

I told him as best I could remember—shooting the Jotun in the eye, rescuing the prisoners, climbing the ladder with the two ropes. My memories of the rooftop chase were fuzzier, and I couldn't remember a thing after the explosion.

"The prisoners used the rope in the window to get out," Jeremiah said when I was done. "That let me and Zeke get in. We found you against the wall, unconscious, near a destroyed cannon and four dead Jotun."

"All four?" I said, shocked.

"Mmmm hmmm. We'd heard a large explosion earlier. It looked like all their powder went up."

"I only set one bag on fire," I said. "I don't remember the rest."

"Well, whatever you did, it worked. You're a hero."

I snorted softly. But that made my ribs hurt. "That wasn't what I wanted."

"Doesn't much matter now. There's gonna be a medal ceremony as soon as you can stand. The Army of the West Medal of Valor itself, I hear. It doesn't get higher than that, and General Sanborn's going to give it to you."

"Great," I said sourly.

I'd wanted to kill Jotun. Not be paraded around in front of everyone. Cassidy'd been a hero. I…

I was no Cassidy.

Jeremiah seemed to know what I was thinking. He put a hand on my shoulder.

"Cassidy would've been proud," he said.

I grimaced. There wasn't much else to say.

For three days—or maybe four, it was hard to keep track, I rested and got stronger. The headaches started to come and go. They hurt most in the bright sun or around a lot of noise, but I felt fine lying in my hospital room. My ribs started to ache less too. Or maybe I just learned how to move without making them worse.

Maria made me get up and walk some during that time. A little longer, each time. First around my private room, which she said I got at General Sanborn's orders, and then into the hall. By the last afternoon, I made it to the main hospital ward.

That sobered me up.

The vast main hospital ward contained about five dozen cots, arranged in long lines. Almost every bed held a soldier who curled under his thin blanket or stretched out long, feet hanging wherever. The stench of blood hung everywhere, and soft moans and cries of pain filled the room.

There weren't as many wounded as I expected. Apparently, as soon as a soldier was safe to move, they loaded him up on a wagon and sent him back to Fort Chicago. The ones that were left...

...the ones that were left were miracles for having survived.

Men without arms. Men with legs hacked off. One with ugly bandages all over his face.

It churned my stomach, but I faced it. I'd seen some of the suffering after The Battle at Golden City, but being ten years old then, Ma had kept me from the worst. Now, I stood in the doorway and watched Maria and the other nurses tend to the men, moving among them like angels. I tried to keep my stomach under control and the porridge I'd had for breakfast down.

One of the soldiers on a cot close to where I stood rolled on his side to look at me. He was young, with a wispy brown beard and a flop of curly brown hair. Bandages covered his right shoulder and his left leg ended beneath the knee. Still his face was calm and his eyes clear. He looked at me curiously, and then those eyes widened in recognition.

"You…," he said, "you're Billy the Kid! Aren't you?"

I was shocked that a stranger knew that name, and I clenched my jaw to avoid saying anything. But his expression was so eager, that after a moment, I nodded. "I've been called that."

"I saw you shoot, back in Chicago. You're the best sharpshooter I've ever seen. And they say you took out the cannons…?"

"I got lucky."

"But still… you did it! I…" He looked down at his leg. "…they say I'm lucky to be alive. I suppose they're right."

"Jotun sword?"

He shook his head and his eyes narrowed in anger. "Human." Then he looked at me in shocked disbelief. "Who would fight for those monsters? Why would any man do so?"

I shrugged. I thought of the blacksmith and his brother, and of the slaves, and of the merchant we'd killed, but I didn't have any good answers.

Then his eyes narrowed and his jaw set. "Rumor is, you're going after the traitors that gave them gunpowder. You get 'em. You get 'em for all of us."

"Uh…" I couldn't stop blinking in surprise.

"We'll do that," came Captain Mercer's soft voice from beside me. He stepped forward and smiled at the soldier. "We'll get those bastards and make them pay. For all of this." He swept his hand to indicate the ward. "And for all our dead."

Then he turned to me. "Come, Private McCarty. Let's return to your room and discuss your new orders."

SEVENTEEN

THE SUNLIGHT STREAMED through the little window in my private hospital room when we arrived. It all felt clean and fresh. Maria or one of the other nurses had changed my sheets while I'd been up and there was a fresh pitcher of water on the small table by the head of the bed.

My gut tightened with guilt as I thought of the men suffering in the main room. They didn't have it so nice.

But I didn't have time to dwell on it. As soon as I'd sat down on the edge of the bed, Captain Mercer pulled the wooden chair over that Maria sat in most times and turned it around. He straddled it quickly and put his elbows on the back.

"I said you were the most dangerous man in the squadron," he said. "I was wrong. You're the most dangerous man in the army."

I scoffed and rolled my eyes.

"I know," he continued. "You were lucky. But dangerous men make their own luck. That is why you are coming with us."

"Where, sir?"

"We know where they are making the gunpowder," he said. "It is in Tennessee, not too far from here. The Avenging Angels will lead the raid to destroy the operation."

I shook my head. "They'll just rebuild it, sir."

"Perhaps," he said, "perhaps not. The freed clerks say it is owned and run by some High Thrall. There is the possibility that they have not shared the, ah, recipe, with the Jotun."

"The Jotun'll just take it."

He shrugged. "Even so, it is worth the attempt. We shall never be this close again."

I frowned and sagged where I sat. My head began to throb again, with sharp spikes jabbing around my eyes. I closed them and rubbed the bridge of my nose.

"So why a raid, sir?" I asked after a bit. "Sanborn's got the entire army here. Just attack."

"The army must stay here until the Jotun return."

"What?" I asked. "Why, sir?"

"Remember the mission, Private McCarty. This attack was to divert the Jotun army headed toward New England. It worked. They are returning to attack us. General Sanborn will stay until they are too close to turn back to their original objective."

"Uh, yeah. That's right. Uh, sir."

He scowled but ignored my sloppiness in saying "sir."

I worked out the timeline in my head. If General Sanborn waited until the last minute to escape across the river, there wouldn't be time for the Jotun Army to return to New England before the snows. Not that snow would necessarily stop them. They'd proven their willingness to attack in winter last year.

But that had been a raid and not an attack by their full army, I realized. They'd moved fast and hadn't needed a lot of supplies.

"Okay," I said. "A raid makes sense, sir. But you don't need me for that. Not if you're just up against Thralls."

"We don't know what all we are up against," Captain Mercer said, "and you *are* the most dangerous man in the army. You've killed more giants than most."

"Jeremiah's killed more than me, sir," I said, remembering the dime novels about Cassidy. "Sergeant-Major McNab too."

"Sergeant Freeman will be on this mission. I can request Sergeant-Major McNab as well."

"Then you don't need me. Sir."

He paused and raised an eyebrow. "You want to kill Jotun, do you not?"

I grimaced. He had me there. I opened my eyes and glared at him.

"Your enthusiasm is desired," he said. "The army's morale will improve knowing the Hero of Louisville conducts the raid."

He stood. "Your enthusiasm is desired, but not required. You are still in the army, under my command. We leave on the raid the day after tomorrow."

I didn't even pretend to salute as he left the room.

The next morning, the army held an awards ceremony in the plaza in front of the Jotun tower. They'd built a wooden platform tall enough for the ranks in back to at least glimpse the men on it. The soldiers stood at parade rest while those of us receiving medals sat on chairs on one side of the platform.

General Sanborn himself spoke. His full black beard offset his thinning hair, but he remained trim and in good fighting shape. He stood in the middle, pacing occasionally, as he talked about our sacrifices and triumphs.

But for me, the heat and sticky air and bright sun made my head pound. I missed most of what the General had to say, as well as most of the early awards to the men who'd fought by the river. I simply kept my eyes closed and pressed my temples with one hand while my head throbbed.

Jeremiah sat next to me. His chair wobbled as he shifted his weight, and occasionally his knee brushed mine. I ignored it until he stood to receive his award. Then I looked up to watch.

"To Sergeant Jeremiah Freeman, the Army of the West Distinguished Service Medal." General Sanborn's voice boomed over the assembled men. "For bravery in the face of the enemy." He handed Jeremiah a small box, shook his hand, and saluted.

Jeremiah returned the salute and then marched back toward the chairs.

An aide handed General Sanborn another small box. The General read something written on it and then called out, "Private McCarty!"

I stood and marched over. I winced as I walked. My skull still shot daggers of pain into me. I stopped in front of the General and saluted as I was supposed to. But after returning it, General Sanborn turned to face the assembled throng.

"Private McCarty," he called out, "fought and killed five Jotun by himself. He destroyed the cannons that ravaged our ships. We are all indebted to Private McCarty. We are thus awarding him the highest honor we can bestow, the Army of the West Medal of Valor."

He gestured to the crowd and a cheer went up.

"Private McCarty," he continued, "is also hereby promoted to Lieutenant. He and Captain Mercer will lead our attack on the gunpowder works. May the Lord bless them and bless their success!"

Another cheer went up.

Only then did General Sanborn turn to me. He handed me the box, and after I took it, extended his hand.

"Good work, son," he said as we shook.

Somewhere in there, I managed a salute and then found myself walking back to my chair. I sank into it with a sigh.

"Congratulations, Lieutenant," Jeremiah said as I hunched over my little box.

"That's wrong," I said. "They shouldn't have promoted me. They didn't promote you."

"I'm a Negro."

He said that with such flat finality that I had to look over at him. His face was grim, set hard.

I couldn't give him my new rank. I couldn't make him the lieutenant he deserved to be, and for that, I felt ashamed.

That evening after dinner, I sat outside the hospital on a small wooden bench against the wall. I cleaned my revolver carefully and slowly as I sat, but that was just an excuse. It wasn't particularly dirty, having been cleaned by someone else while I recovered. Still, it hadn't been me, and I wanted to do it myself.

Shortly after the awards ceremony, Captain Mercer had given me a short talk about the expectations that came with being an officer, now that I was one. It had mostly gone in one ear and out the other, as I was still too stunned at the promotion. It was clearly just for the army's morale—making the hero one of the leaders of the raid. It certainly wasn't because they thought I'd be a good officer.

Still, I tried to remember all that he'd said.

The sun was just starting to set, which gave the sky a few streaks of orange. A breeze had kicked up, which cooled things down, and the humidity wasn't so oppressive. The light smell of smoke wafted from the kitchens, along with the scent of cooking meat.

All in all, it was the most pleasant evening I'd had in some time.

My ribs still hurt, but I'd learned to move so they didn't stab me with pain at every breath. My headaches, too, were less frequent, and I'd warded off the last one by lying down and taking some medicine that Maria had given me.

I'd already cleaned the inside of the barrel and was wiping down the outside when McNab appeared. He looked a bit leaner than when I'd last seen him, but other than a bruise on his left cheek, none worse for the wear. He was in uniform, but the jacket was rumpled and open and his shirt showed sweat stains. Still he grinned, a happy wide grin that filled not only his face but his whole body. He gave me a casual salute and then hooked his hands into his belt and rocked on his heels.

"My my my," he said, "the Hero of Louisville."

"I don't remember it," I grumbled. "They say I killed five Jotun. I remember only one."

He chuckled. "Most don't even kill that many. Mind if I join you?" He gestured toward the bench at my side.

"Sure."

He sat and leaned back against the wall with a relieved sigh. He looked over at me, a sly look in his eyes.

"So," he said, "I understand you're responsible for my new orders."

"For the raid? It was just a suggestion."

"Your suggestion became my orders." He grinned good-naturedly.

"Sorry," I said with a casual shrug.

"Nah. This is better. Running around wiping the butts of captains and lieutenants like I've been doing? That's no fun."

"You're still gonna be wiping a lieutenant's butt," I said. "They shouldn't have promoted me."

He chuckled. "That may be so, Billy. That may be so."

He fell quiet, and we sat in companionable silence while I continued cleaning my gun. In the distance, a bird fluttered and hopped along the muddy ground, poking here and there.

I finished up and folded my rags and put them away. "You know," I said, "I didn't want to be a hero."

He nodded, without turning to look at me. "I know."

"I didn't do anything special. Just what any other man would do."

"Bull." He snorted with derision. "Most men would've given up. You're just too stubborn."

"Yeah, I get that. But stubborn don't make me a hero."

He looked at me then, and pursed his lips for a moment.

"Do you know what the difference between heroes and most men is, Billy?" he asked.

He wasn't looking for an answer, so I shook my head.

"Heroes win. Most men quit, or they decide something's too tough, or they do something stupid and they lose."

"I've done plenty of stupid stuff."

"And you won. It ain't stupid if it works."

I snorted and shook my head. Stupid was still stupid, even if luck had bailed it out.

"I was lucky," I said. "By all rights, I should be dead." My gut just sat leaden at the thought.

"Well, maybe," he said. "But we've all had our share of luck. By all rights, I should be dead too."

I thought of some of the stories I'd read, and some of the things I'd seen in Colorado. I didn't want to concede the point out loud, though.

"I heard all the things you did to take out those cannons," he continued without noticing my distraction, "well, except the last part. Best as Jeremiah can figure, some sparks from the bag you lit must've landed in their magazine and blown the roof near off. *That* was lucky."

I shrugged in agreement. I still couldn't remember. I didn't think anyone would know exactly what happened up there.

"Point is," he said, "you didn't quit. You didn't decide it was too tough, and you won. You're a damned hero all right."

"I did what I had to."

"That's what Cassidy used to say."

I winced at the memories, but McNab didn't notice. His face was filled with his own pain as he stared into space. Then he steeled himself and looked at me again.

"As someone on one of those boats, I'm damned glad you're a hero." He looked me straight in the eyes. "And nobody cares that you don't like it."

I swallowed hard, but didn't break his stare. Finally he did, looking down at his hands. He stood and brushed his pants off. Then he gave me a warmer smile.

"See you tomorrow, Lieutenant Billy. We're off to Tennessee."

EIGHTEEN

MORNING ARRIVED with its sticky heat all too soon. I dressed and ate some dull porridge with a few slices of apple in it while sitting on my bed. I was sure I'd miss the mattress, despite its lumps, once it came time to sleep on the hard ground again.

I sipped some bitter chicory coffee and looked over my gear. New haversack. New pack. Both bulged with supplies that McNab had brought me. My old hat sat on top of them, a bit worn, but clean. My old Colt too, thankfully.

But also a brand new Whitworth rifle.

Its range far exceeded my old Winchester, but I hadn't fired this one, and so I wasn't sure what quirks would throw off its aim. It had a few nicks in the stock, but someone had polished the barrel to a high shine before delivering it along with more bullets than I wanted to carry.

It was a sharpshooter's weapon. *The* sharpshooter's weapon.

I'd never even thought about owning one, and now it was mine.

I finished the coffee and set my mug down. Maria bustled in just then, her white nurse's uniform looking clean and crisp. She smiled at me and started taking medicines from the table and putting them into a large traveller's bag.

"You're leaving?" I asked, slightly amused at her hurriedness. Maria rarely moved with anything but calm grace.

"I am going with you," she said.

I raised my eyebrows. "Oh?"

"Colonel Mosby's orders. After Captain Mercer's request."

"Ah." I didn't have to guess why Captain Mercer wanted her along. Not as often as he'd been to the hospital to visit me. He'd have to have seen how good a healer she was.

"Here," she said as she handed me a small brown bottle with a faded paper label. A quick glance confirmed it was the poppy syrup she'd fed me from time to time. "If the headaches get too bad. But only a small amount. Half what you had before."

I nodded. It'd made me sleepy before, which was a good thing lying in a hospital bed and not so much riding a horse.

At least I presumed I'd be riding a horse. I realized I hadn't actually checked. I'd been moping around my room instead of trying to find out more about our mission.

"Would you like some help?" I asked Maria as she slowed and carefully packed her pouches and bottles into her bag.

"No." She gave me a warm smile, I suspected out of appreciation for my offer. "I have a bit more to do, but will see you in the plaza."

"Then I'll be on my way." I tipped my head, grabbed my gear and my new Whitworth, and walked out the door.

We mustered in the broad plaza, just south of the Jotun tower. Humans now manned its ramparts, with nearly a dozen standing atop the high walls. The ones on our side watched us with great interest.

We formed up in ranks, though our Third Squadron was notoriously thin. Mine, now that I was in command. Just me, Jeremiah, Zeke, and Joe Johnson. Well less than half our original strength.

The other squadrons weren't much better. Fourth Squadron didn't even exist—not a single survivor. Well, some might've survived and just be wounded, but none stood in the ranks. Second and Fifth

Squadrons had about half their men. First Squadron was nearly complete.

Including the Big Buffoon I'd had the run-in with earlier, to my chagrin. He and his buddies stood tall at the front of their ranks. I couldn't see their faces, but from their bearing, they had to be smirking.

All in all, the five squadrons that made up what was left of the Avenging Angels Company had maybe thirty men total. Enough for a good raid, I thought, but not enough for a serious fight.

Colonel Mosby and Captain Mercer stood at the front. Mosby's regimental bugler trilled his horn and we all snapped to attention. Colonel Mosby nodded to Captain Mercer, who stepped forward and clasped his arms behind his back.

"Men," he called out, loud enough for even the back ranks to hear, "we ride to Nickajack Cave, near Chattanooga, where we will destroy the Jotuns' gunpowder works, kill any Jotun we encounter, free any captured humans, and kill any thralls that do not wish to join our cause."

I stiffened at those last words. Did we really need to kill more humans?

"We must be swift in this endeavor," Captain Mercer continued. "Surprise and speed are our allies. They are the keys to our success. Any man who cannot ride, or ride well, must speak to me immediately so you may be reassigned to another unit."

He paused and slowly scanned the front ranks.

"But know this," he continued, "no others will earn the glory that we will. No others will be able to say they were there. No others will be able to say they rode with the Avenging Angels."

He put his fists on his hips.

"When this war is over, and the Jotun are driven from the land, they will talk of Grant's Charge. They will talk of The Battle of Golden City. And they will talk of The Tennessee Raid." He pumped his hand in the air. "For the West!"

"For the West!" we all roared.

"For the West!" he yelled again.

"For the West!"

"For Victory!"

The roars turned to cheers. Men all around raised their arms and yelled at the top of their voices.

I was among them.

We rode south an hour later—thirty soldiers, an army doctor and Maria, a dozen pack horses wrangled by McNab, and Captain Mercer in the lead. We followed the road and made no attempt to disguise our uniforms. When I asked Jeremiah about it, he said there was no point this close to Louisville. We would disguise ourselves when we got closer to Tennessee.

Not that I thought we could. We looked far too much like what we were—soldiers on the move. I doubted we could pass for Thrall, however we might try.

The hard-packed dirt road worked its way through the fields south of Louisville. Most stood empty now—the workers long gone. We passed one field where the wheat was half harvested, with rows of golden stalks that ended at a ragged row of dirt. Zeke pointed out discarded scythes leaning up against a split rail fence post.

After a while, the fields broke up, with patches of unplowed ground and copses of trees scattered here and there. The heat grew, though, as the air took on a muggy feel and the few scattered clouds didn't do enough to cool us down.

Meanwhile, my ribs throbbed as my horse ambled along. It took a long time to find a way to sit that didn't hurt, and as it was, I suspected I'd pick up some saddle sores along the way. I grumbled to myself, but decided not to complain out loud. It wasn't like anyone wanted to hear it anyway.

A little after noon, when the patches of woods grew more numerous and the fields smaller, we passed what looked like a family farmstead. A small log cabin sat back from the road, and a little boy and his mother stood in the doorway staring out at us as we rode by. The fields between the cabin and the road grew a mishmash of corn, wheat, and some smaller vegetables I couldn't quite make out at the distance.

As we rode by, a thin, raggedy-looking man in a broad-brimmed hat came around the corner of the cabin. He carried an axe and he too just stared at us.

I was riding near Jeremiah at the time, so I got his attention and pointed at the family.

"Why are they still here?" I asked. "Why haven't they fled to the West?"

"Might be a lot of reasons," he said with a shrug. "Some people couldn't, when the Jotun arrived."

"But that was years ago," I said. "Why haven't they fled since?"

"Well, if they don't know where to go, or how to get there, then leaving might be scarier than staying put."

"Yeah, but in *Jotun* territory?"

"Unlike trolls, the Jotun don't eat people." He grimaced and my mind flashed to some of the horrors that I'd heard about Memphis. "As long as they stay quiet and out of the way, it may not be that bad."

"I dunno," I said. I looked at the sharecropper family once again. They were mighty skinny. I wondered if they got enough food or if the Jotun took it all.

Still, there was nothing to be done. They didn't seem to want any part of us, and I knew Captain Mercer wouldn't stop for them. He rode anxious, like he had a burr in his pants. He didn't talk much, always looking ahead.

We pushed on well past dark. Then we camped and were up again the next dawn. Still, it was a pleasant ride, all told. Kentucky was lush and green despite it being the end of the summer, and the road broad and smooth.

I spent some time riding with Joe Johnson and Zeke the next day. At first we rode silent, but then Zeke pointed out a hawk and a little while later I spotted a rabbit. Joe Johnson was mostly silent, until he wasn't.

"Nickajack Cave," Joe Johnson said after we'd been riding for a while. "We're goin' to Nickajack Cave."

"You been there?" I asked in surprise.

"Yeah," he said with a drawl, "it's big."

"When were you there?"

"Before the war. Didn't go inside."

I paused. Joe Johnson didn't talk much about his life before the war. I knew he'd been a slave as a boy in this very region, but no one had been able to get him to say much about Louisville, much less anything else.

I tried anyway. "So whattya know?"

"It's big," he said. "I didn't go in. We didn't stay there."

"Ah. Just passing through."

"Yeah."

He just kept looking ahead, so I sensed he didn't want to talk more.

I still hadn't figured him out, though. He wasn't stupid. He knew the Bible almost as well as Zeke and more about food than any of us, which had earned him cooking chores. He was slow to pick things up, like with handling his rifle, but once he learned it, he never forgot.

And he insisted we call him by his full name. He just didn't talk much either. And his answers...

I shook my head. He'd survived, which had to count for something.

Unlike a lot of people. My mind started to run through memories of my dead, starting with my brother and Ma, but I shook myself before it got too far. Woolgathering never helped on the trail.

The trees parted and the road wandered through old fields, where weeds had long overtaken the scraggly volunteer crops that had once grown there. I spotted a decaying collapsed log cabin on our right, easily fifteen years old. A crow cawed from somewhere nearby. We rode all the way into the middle of the open area.

"Hold up," Captain Mercer called from the head of the column. He raised his hand and we all stopped and spread out a bit so we could see what was ahead.

Two of our men raced their horses back down the road toward us from the distant trees. They appeared small at first in the distance, but quickly closed. Scouts, I realized. Their expressions were grim. One man's hat flew off and he didn't even pause.

"Jotun!" they called when they were within shouting distance.

I glanced around. We were a long ways from any woods or potential cover.

NINETEEN

CAPTAIN MERCER CURSED and glanced around. The nearest trees were far to our left, a dense scrub well across a field. On the right, there was another weed-grown field behind the decayed cabin.

"Lieutenant McCarty, Fifth Squadron, with me!" he barked. He pointed toward the cabin. "Sergeant-Major, to the cabin. Look for a hunting trail into the woods!"

McNab spurred his horse forward. As he passed by, he yelled, "regroup at Munfordville!"

Captain Mercer nudged and then spurred his own horse forward. He raised one arm high.

"For the West!" he yelled.

We split into two groups, both riding forward pell-mell. The front half of the column tore off across the field and I rode fast to catch up to Captain Mercer. He slowed when he saw it was me.

"You're the sharphooter," he said breathlessly. "Find a spot and shoot for their eyes."

I nodded. The only sniper's blind around was the old cabin, so I rode hard for it, well behind the fleeing troops. They'd found a trail and disappeared into the trees.

I yanked up on the reins right behind the ramshackle ruin. The walls still standing were tall enough to hide my horse from the road. I herded it toward the middle, where it would be more out of sight, and then moved to the edge. I peered through gaps that had opened up between the logs.

I put my hand on one and yanked it back after getting a splinter. Fortunately, I was able to pick at it and pull it out. My palm still stung, though.

Captain Mercer and the six men of Fifth Squadron had come to a halt about four hundred yards from where the road emerged from the woods. They'd dismounted and stood in a firing line, with Captain Mercer at one end still on his horse, saber raised.

I looked toward the end of the road where the scouts had appeared. It was hard to see, despite the lack of trees in front of the cabin. A curve in the road and the distance made it hard to know exactly where to look. The woods down the road had several breaks that the Jotun could emerge from.

And then they appeared.

Two Jotun strode through a gap in the trees side by side. They marched fast with long strides. Each wore a full leather jerkin and the metal fittings sparkled in the sun. They also had leather caps and battle axes. Their expressions were grim.

Fifth Squadron's rifles fired as one, a thunderous roar. The lead Jotun staggered as the volley of bullets smashed into his face.

I had no time to waste. I aimed my Whitworth at the second Jotun's eye, a burly blond giant with a scraggly beard. I was at the edge of my range, and he was running, so it was a difficult shot. I fired.

And hit his cheek.

He howled but didn't slow. I concentrated on him and fired again. My shot was lost in the roar of the squadron's second volley, but the Jotun howled and fell to his knees.

My third shot was true—straight into his right eye. He dropped flat on his face.

But then two more Jotun appeared from the trees.

And then two more behind them.

And then two more. And two after that.

I sucked in my breath as my pulse raced. Eight humans against ten Jotun wasn't a fight.

It was a slaughter.

Captain Mercer and Fifth Squadron knew it too. Our men were remounting as the other lead Jotun bore down on them.

One of the Jotun at the rear threw an axe. It whirled end over end until it sliced sickeningly into one of the men trying to mount his horse.

I whipped my rifle around and fired at the axe thrower.

And missed.

He threw another axe. Another of our men died.

Captain Mercer raced his horse toward me, the surviving men who'd been able to mount hot on his heels.

They weren't fast enough. To my horror, I watched a Jotun smash his axe down on the last man in the race.

I dashed to my own horse and scrambled onto it. I rode around the edge of the cabin. I hesitated about going down the hunting trail the others had taken. I didn't want to lead the Jotun to them.

Captain Mercer must've had the same idea. As he rode closer, he pointed toward a gap in the trees closer to the road the Jotun had come from. He turned and galloped off.

I was only a few lengths behind.

A sickening human scream came from behind me. I didn't turn, but raced on.

The wind tugged at my hat, but I grabbed it with one hand and held it tight. Not too far from where the road plunged into the trees, we spotted a small gap. Captain Mercer charged for it. I was close on his heels.

The gap really wasn't more than an inlet where the sea of grass met the forest. We plunged into the dense undergrowth itself. Bushes and branches swiped at us, and we had to slow as the horses struggled to push ahead.

Loud yells and shouts came from behind us. I took a quick look back.

With horror, I realized that none of our men followed.

Only Jotun, and they were chasing fast.

We shoved through the underbrush as best we could. My horse reared up in front of two oaks where the branches were too intertwined to pass. I held tight to the reins.

Captain Mercer slipped around them to the left. I followed. We shoved through a few more dense thickets and then stumbled out onto the road, further down from where we'd been.

I glanced down it. A sharp curve through the trees hid us. The Jotun weren't in sight.

But we heard roars and the crashing of trees they way we'd just come. We didn't have much time.

"This way!" Captain Mercer cried. He raced south down the road.

I spurred my horse and followed.

I kept gasping for breath as we rode hard. I'd had to shift my balance as the horse galloped, and my ribs ached and stabbed me with pain. Water gathered in my eyes, but I still snapped the reins, urging my horse on.

Captain Mercer slowed and looked back. I caught up to him just in time to see his eyes widen.

A loud shout behind us confirmed it—the Jotun had seen us!

"Go!" Captain Mercer called.

We rode. We rode hard.

I desperately hoped it was fast enough. Jotun at a full run were about as fast as horses.

Worse, they could throw things.

But no axes or rocks came whistling by our heads. The road took a gentle turn and then opened up for a straight stretch. We galloped hard as the trees began to thin.

After more distance than I thought my ribs could handle, the road curved again, more sharply this time. I glanced back. The Jotun chasing us were a ways back. They disappeared as we took the sharp curve, blocked by the trees.

Captain Mercer slowed just a tad and turned his horse toward a gap in the trees.

Another road!

We galloped onto it.

This one was narrower, with trees closer to the edges and deep wagon ruts marring the dirt. We slowed a bit, and then after about a hundred yards, Captain Mercer yanked his horse to the left where the trees were a bit thinner. We left the road and galloped through the underbrush.

Then he slowed his horse and held up his hand.

"Quiet now," he said when I was close enough to hear.

Our horses were huffing hard after the run, as was I. I shifted my seat so as to ease up on my ribs, which helped some, but now my head was starting to pound. I still gasped and wheezed and tried to wet my cottony lips. I needed both hands on the reins, which stopped me from reaching for my canteen.

We walked the horses quietly as best we could. We went due south for a bit, away from the narrow rut-filled road, and then turned east, back toward the main road. We could hear the Jotun yelling, but they no longer sounded like war cries. More like men calling to each other, except in the Jotun tongue.

We'd lost them, I realized.

I let out a sigh of relief, and then grimaced at the pain in my ribs and head.

Captain Mercer looked over, concern in his eyes.

"Can you make it?" he asked.

I nodded. "Where are we going?"

"Munfordville, on the Green River. That's where we'll meet Sergeant-Major McNab and the others."

I nodded, having no idea where Munfordville or the Green River were.

We rode south until we found another small stream running alongside the road. We hadn't seen any giants in a while, so we stopped to let the horses drink and graze. A large oak about ten feet off the road offered a fair amount of shade, and the ground under it was clear of all but grass and a few scattered yellow flowers.

I took my canteen, some hardtack, and the poppy syrup with me and sagged to a spot on the grass. I swallowed the poppy syrup first.

All the hard riding had given me a pounding headache. It felt like my skull was about to split in pieces and my forehead fall off.

Captain Mercer lowered himself to the ground nearby. His hair was matted with sweat and he looked only a little less tired than I felt. His eyes were haunted.

Like mine, I suspected.

"Should we go back?" I asked.

He shook his head. "Not if we want to live."

"Do you think any of them made it?"

"I hope some of them survived," he said dourly, "but I doubt it." He swore. "All my fault."

I blinked, but he didn't say more. Instead, he stared off in the distance, thinking.

I thought of the lives lost too. I hadn't known the men of Fifth Squadron, but I could call up their faces.

So much death, since the Jotun came.

So much death.

I had to put it behind me.

My sense of dread grew the longer we sat there. In Louisville, we'd traded three thousand men for one hundred Jotun. Thirty humans lost for each giant. We'd done a little better on the road. Only six lost for one giant, or maybe two.

There were about twenty-five of us left. What chance did we have?

There had to be more Jotun ahead of us.

I didn't like the odds. Not at all.

The thing was, I didn't know what else we could do. If the Jotun had gunpowder, that changed *everything*. We couldn't beat their cannons. Not without doing something foolhardy or stupid.

Like I'd done.

I shouldn't have survived.

And instead of dying, they'd given me a medal and made me a lieutenant.

And not Jeremiah, like they should've.

I swallowed some water. Nearby, a bug whirred up from the grass and a few feet before setting down. Captain Mercer's horse finished greedily lapping at the stream and moved to some grass.

It was peaceful enough that I wanted to lie down until my head stopped hurting and my heart no longer felt so heavy. Yeah, the Jotun might come down the road at any minute, but I couldn't help but want to believe we'd lost them.

"We have to go on," Captain Mercer said. "We have to accomplish this mission. We *have* to."

"Yes, sir," I said slowly. "We do."

"We should've been disguised," he said. He grimaced at me. "At least civilian clothes."

"Yeah."

"I think if we go further south," Captain Mercer said after a bit, "we'll find the old railroad tracks and we can follow those to Elizabethtown, and then to Munfordville. If memory serves."

"You don't have a map?" I said with surprise.

"The Sergeant-Major has it. Besides, I came through this area once, a long time ago." He rubbed his chin as he continued to stare out ahead, instead of looking at me.

"A very long time ago," he added.

"Do you know what we're gonna find at Nickajack?" I asked.

He shook his head. "The clerks in Louisville said the Jotun brought the cannons and gunpowder themselves, about six weeks ago." He grimaced. "We still don't know where they forged the cannons. But they didn't bring enough gunpowder. One of the clerks wrote out the request for more. It was addressed to Joshua Turner, Nickajack Cave."

"Huh," I said. "Joshua. A human name."

"High Thrall. He has to be."

I shrugged in acknowledgement. "But why?"

"It does not matter. What matters is that he does not continue."

His tone was so forceful, I didn't know what to say.

He must've sensed my discomfort.

"This is not a simple war," he said. "We are not fighting for land, or independence, or even to end the scourge of slavery."

He met my eyes. His were hard.

"This war is for the very survival of humanity," he practically spat. "These Jotun will not stop with the Confederacy lands. They will not stop if they take New England or the West. Their goal is our utter destruction or slavery. And they do not care which."

He pounded a fist into the ground and turned away.

"You know this," he said more softly. "You believe in killing Jotun as much as I."

Except I didn't, I realized. Yeah, I wanted to kill them. But not with *that* much passion. They were… well… monsters to me. They'd killed a lot of people I knew, including my brother. But that had been a long time ago, and I'd largely moved on.

But Captain Mercer?

I wondered who'd died that had made him so full of cold rage. Not his wife, I knew. Or his daughter. Was there someone else who'd been close to him?

Or was it something else entirely?

I drank some more from my canteen and ate some of the tack. I tried to study him without staring. He didn't seem to notice, too lost in his own thoughts.

After a bit, though, he stirred. He gave me an amused smile. I didn't know what he'd seen in my face. But then he nodded in the direction of the horses.

"Eat up," he said. "We ride as soon as they're done."

TWENTY

WE WERE BACK on the horses within an hour. We rode them at a walk. Captain Mercer said he wanted to make progress but didn't want to overwork the animals. My beast shuffled along at a pace I quickly adapted to. My ribs were still sore, but the ride didn't make them worse. My head had gotten better.

Clouds also blew in, cutting off the bright sun. The air got sticky, even more sticky than I thought possible, but a light breeze made it bearable.

Even better, we'd seen no sign of the Jotun.

We found the railroad tracks about mid-afternoon and left the road to follow them. They'd clearly not been used in many years. While the railway was mostly clear, bushes and small seedlings grew right up to the rails in a number of spots and often between the rails themselves. Still, the way was clear enough that it might as well have been a forest path. It ran straight and true.

More than once, I looked back, but nothing followed us.

After a bit, the woods around the track opened up into a deserted, ramshackle town. Captain Mercer said it had been Elizabethtown, before the Jotun arrived, but it clearly wasn't anything now. We didn't stop for any longer than it took to water the horses again.

Late in the afternoon, the skies clouded up. I welcomed the cool and the breeze but was less happy when it started to rain. It wasn't a hard rain, but enough to create rivulets that fell off my hat onto my shoulder.

The rain also brought the darkness of night quicker than I'd expected. It soon got hard to make out whether anything was lurking in the woods on either side of the track ahead or not. When we passed a cluster of oaks without many low branches, Captain Mercer motioned for us to seek shelter under them.

"I'll take the first watch," he said. "I saw how much your head was hurting. Get some rest."

The rain had tapered off and I found a relatively dry spot. Captain Mercer went to take care of the horses while I made myself comfortable and shut my eyes.

The sun barely peeked through gloomy clouds as I rode down the road. Firs and pines crowded the edges of the path, almost suffocating me as I went. My horse trod slowly and when I pulled up on the reins, it didn't stop.

After a bit, the trees parted and the road entered a clearing. On the right lay a dead Jotun with bullet wounds and saber slashes all over his exposed flesh. A dark cloud of flies buzzed around it and the scent of spoiled blood made my stomach churn. I turned my head to look away.

And gasped.

To the left, Cassidy and Burwell sat on a large stone table, swinging their feet. The side of Burwell's head had been smashed in, but he still gave me a toothy smile. Cassidy's chest was awash in blood. The hilt of the knife still protruded from the middle.

Where I'd stabbed him.

Cassidy smiled. "Good job, Billy." He pointed at the Jotun. "Too bad you'll have to do it all again."

The Jotun stirred. It slowly pulled itself to its hands and knees and turned its head. Through bloody flesh, it grinned at me.

I screamed.

And woke up.

I snapped upright, my heart pounding. I glanced around wildly. At first I couldn't see anything in the darkness and gloom. But I heard footsteps and I turned to see Captain Mercer running down the tracks toward me. My eyes adjusted just as he arrived.

"What happened?" His head turned every direction, looking into the woods.

"Nightmare," I mumbled.

"Ah." His shoulders visibly relaxed.

"I hope no one but you heard, sir."

"No 'sir.' Not this deep in Jotun territory." He held out a hand to help me to my feet. "The rain's stopped and it looks like there's another stream up ahead."

I nodded and got up. It didn't take long to pack my stuff. Captain Mercer had us walk on foot and lead the horses. They needed their rest as much as us.

We walked quietly, using the dim light from above as a guide. We couldn't hear anything in the woods, other than the night bugs and the occasional scurry of a small animal. Nothing big enough to be a Jotun or a human. After a while, we spotted the stream Captain Mercer had mentioned earlier. It wasn't too wide—something I could've easily jumped across. But it'd do just fine for the horses.

We led them to the edge and let them drink. I scanned the trees around us—none seemed to be good candidates for shelter for the rest of the night.

"So," Captain Mercer said, "do you have nightmares often?"

"All the time," I answered. "Ever since… well, ever since Cassidy died. They're horrible."

"I know," he said. "All too well."

I was so startled, I stopped in my tracks. A small animal scurried somewhere off to the side as I turned, open-mouthed, to face Captain Mercer.

He stopped and looked at me.

"What do you mean?" I asked.

"I had nightmares after Lynchburg. Almost every night for a year."

"Did you kill someone?"

He shook his head. "No... not in that battle, at least. Unless you count Jotun. It was... honestly, there is no other way to describe it... it was Hell. Death does not scare me because I have already been to the Devil's nether regions. I have endured the Inferno."

His eyes narrowed.

"It was Hell, Billy. Hell."

"It wasn't that bad for me," I blurted, but then caught myself and clamped my mouth shut.

He chuckled at my expression. "It's not something you can compare. Does the fire burn you less from a small forge than a roaring inferno? You were burned, Billy. You were burned. As was I."

"I... I don't know what to say."

"There is nothing *to* say," he said with a soft snort. "We have been through the fire. Burned, but forged anew, like steel."

He took on a grim smile.

"It's what's made us the most dangerous men in the army," he said. When he saw my blink of surprise, he chuckled low and throaty.

"Yes," he said, "both of us, and Colonel Mosby agrees. He said I was the most dangerous man he's commanded... save one."

"But... why?"

"Because we will do what must be done. Even at the cost of our souls."

He gestured toward the horses. "When they finish, let's ride. I suspect we don't have much further to go."

As we road through the night, I thought a lot about what Captain Mercer had said. I understood "doing what must be done." Cassidy had believed the same. That's why... that's why... I didn't want to think about it, but it didn't change things. He'd told me to kill him because it had to be done.

But at "the cost of our souls?"

I shuddered. I thought I was beginning to understand what that meant. Maybe if my soul was safe, I wouldn't have nightmares.

But if they stopped, would it be because I was saved? Or damned?

I didn't have too much chance to stew on it, though, before dawn broke and we reached a spot where the tracks emerged from the woods into deserted and unworked fields. In the distance we could see dilapidated farm buildings, but no people and no giants.

We paused and let the light breeze brush our cheeks. The sky still held plenty of clouds, which now carried the orange and purple of the sunrise.

"So where are we meeting the others?" I asked.

"Where the tracks cross the river," he said. "There's a long bridge there."

"Won't the Jotun be guarding it?" I asked.

"Perhaps," he said, "but it was the only landmark the Sergeant-Major and I both knew. We will approach as best we can." He gestured toward the treeline to our left. "Perhaps we should be circumspect until we reach the river."

So we kept close to the trees as we worked our way around the fields. Not that we needed to at first. We didn't see a soul.

Tall, gangly weeds choked the fields this far from town. Any buildings we saw in the distance were as equally ramshackle as the first one we'd passed. After a bit, we stopped riding in the trees and just rode in front of them. It was easier.

It helped that the clouds stuck around. It was cool for September in the South, but still stickier than anything I'd known back in Colorado Territory. The light breeze continued, though, so at least the sweat didn't bead on my skin.

After an hour or two, we spotted a tall stone tower down where the tracks seemed to run and stopped to study it. It looked skinnier than the one in Louisville, and not quite as tall. We couldn't see any Jotun on the ramparts, either.

"They built it by the bridge instead of in town," Captain Mercer mused as he studied it.

"Why?" I asked.

"The bridge is one of the few sturdy enough for them to use. The tower defends it."

"Oh," I said, feeling a little stupid. I should've figured that out myself.

"We won't find our men close to the tower," he continued. "Nor in town. I wonder…"

"Where's the road they were following?"

"Mmmm. Good idea. They would have stopped as soon as they saw the tower. Now where would that be?" He swept his gaze across the fields.

"It should be to our right," I said.

He nodded in agreement and we began retracing our steps.

We found the rest of our company around noon. They'd camped in the woods quite a ways back from both the road and the field, but had sentries posted where they could watch both the road and the town. When one of them spotted us, he quickly escorted us into the main camp.

The camp was spread out through scattered birches and heavy underbrush alongside a small stream. The tents had been struck and most of the men sat around the low cooking fires, eating beans. One man had bacon sizzling in an iron pan as his squadron mates watched on with hungry interest. The smell made my stomach grumble, but the Captain and I pushed on until we found McNab.

"Sergeant-Major, report," Captain Mercer said.

McNab snapped to attention and saluted. "No incidents to report, sir. We arrived without encountering locals or Jotun. Sergeant Freeman has gone into the town to scout. We expect him back soon."

I breathed a sigh of relief. If anyone could glean good information, it was Jeremiah.

"Anyone scout the bridge?" Captain Mercer asked.

"Yes, sir," McNab replied. "The bridge is intact and clear of barriers. Other than the tower, it's unguarded. There may be places we could ford the river if we wished to avoid the bridge, but none close."

"We may do so," Captain Mercer acknowledged with a nod. "We will await Sergeant Freeman." He turned to me. "Go find the nurse, Private McCarty. See if she has anything that might help you sleep."

I nodded, and then remembered to salute. Captain Mercer blinked and then turned to the others. "Ah, yes. Have the men change into civilian clothes. This deep inside Jotun territory, we would be better to not be recognized."

I smiled and went in search of Maria.

I found her kneeling next to a small cook fire in a small clearing surrounded by thick leafy bushes. With an old tin spoon, she stirred a thick syrup that smelled of sour berries in a small pan. She smiled when she saw me.

"Billy," she said. "How are you?"

"I still hurt." I told her about our ride and my ribs and head, and about all the poppy syrup I'd drunk.

"Mmmm," she said. "Not good. Too much poppies will be bad for you." She handed me a small flask. "Drink this."

I took a swig. The chalky taste reminded me of aspen bark.

Then she gestured at my shirt. "Let me check your ribs."

With gritted teeth, I pulled my shirt up. It twisted, and tightened across my chest, which hurt even worse.

"All the way off," Maria said.

I frowned, but took my shirt completely off. I did it slowly, which hurt a lot less, but I felt embarrassed to be sitting there naked from the waist up.

She gently touched and pressed my chest. Her fingers worked their way down each rib, and she noted where I gasped or flinched.

"Better," she said. "More rest, when you can."

"When I can," I said with a snort. "Maybe if I'd stayed in Louisville. Maybe I should go back."

She shook her head. "You do not belong in Louisville. You are not one to quit."

"Yeah, right," I said.

She raised her eyebrows and stared at me. "You did not quit when you wanted to join Cassidy. Even after he kept sending you away. That's why he grew to admire you."

"Admire me?"

She nodded. "You did not quit then, so why do you talk of quitting now?"

I started to say something snippy, but stopped. Her eyes were so earnest, I realized it was a serious question.

I thought about it a bit.

"I... I knew what I wanted then," I said. "I wanted to ride with Cassidy. But now..."

I looked at her and saw her face still full of sympathy.

"I'm not sure I belong in the army," I said. "Actually, I know I don't. The orders. The marching. The having to do what I'm told... it's... it's hard."

I started to choke up.

"This isn't what I wanted," I finally said.

"What did you want?" she asked.

"To kill monsters," I said. "To *stop* horrible things from happening to innocent people, like the townsfolk of Grand Lake. To make... things better, I guess."

"Not to be a hero?"

"I *am* a hero," I scoffed. "At least according to the army. Got the medal and everything. It hasn't stopped the nightmares."

She nodded knowingly.

"So what do I do?" I asked.

My voice cracked and my head started to throb, just a low ache that hinted at worse to come.

"What do I do?" I repeated.

"Only you can decide that."

I knew that, but it didn't help.

"So what do you suggest?" I asked.

She shook her head. "Cassidy found his own way to get rid of his nightmares. You must find yours."

She pulled her stirring spoon up and let some of the syrup slide off it back into the pan. She nodded, pleased.

"Pass me that bottle, please." She pointed at a small glass one, much like the poppy syrup one I carried.

I did so and stood. I still didn't know what to do, but I knew the next step.

I needed to talk to Jeremiah.

TWENTY-ONE

BY THE TIME JEREMIAH RETURNED, I'd eaten my share of beans, drunk enough water to keep my lips wet for a week, and stretched out for a short nap in a shady spot on some soft grass. I didn't dream, or if I did, I didn't remember it.

Instead, I awoke to Zeke gently shaking me. His big grin was unmistakably friendly.

"Captain wants you," he said. He gestured toward the front edge of camp, toward town.

I extended a hand and as he helped me up, I asked, "Any other news?"

"'Sergeant's back," he said. "That's why they want you."

"Thanks," I said. "Where are you and Joe Johnson camped?"

"Thataway," he pointed. "Joe Johnson found us an apple tree. We're camped under it."

"Good ol' Joe Johnson," I said with a grin. "I'll find you after we're done."

"You do that," he said. "We'll have some fresh applesauce ready."

I chuckled. Trust Joe Johnson to have packed some sugar along for the raid.

Clouds still filled the sky, giving everything a shady, moody feel. I walked quick, and I found that my ribs didn't hurt near as bad as they had just that morning. I almost felt human.

I found Captain Mercer, McNab, Jeremiah, and First Squadron's sergeant, Sergeant McIlroy, standing in a small circle just outside the trees. All the remaining officers, I realized. They didn't look grim, which I took as a good sign. More determined.

"Billy," Captain Mercer said when he saw me. "I hope you are feeling better."

"Yeah," I said as I joined the circle, with Jeremiah and McNab parting to make room for me.

"Jeremiah," Captain Mercer said, pointing at Jeremiah, "says that the town is largely deserted. Only a few humans remain and most cannot leave for one reason or another."

"Many are too old or feeble to travel," Jeremiah explained.

"Those people report," Captain Mercer continued, "that there are also only a few Jotun in the tower. They believe only two, though Sergeant Freeman was unable to confirm that number. The others left a few days ago, headed north in a large group."

"The one we encountered," I said.

"Exactly," Captain Mercer said. "We seem to have done some good there." He smiled sourly and scanned the group.

"Which brings me to our plan. I want to be across the river and well away from here before dusk, in case the others return. We cannot do that if we have to find a suitable point to ford. So, given that there are but two or three Jotun left as guards, I consider using the bridge to be worth the risk."

"What if they see us?" McNab asked. "We can get close to the bridge without being seen, but once we're on it, we're totally exposed."

"Yes," Captain Mercer said. "But once we are over, they are unlikely to give chase. To do so would be to abandon their post and risk an ambush. All we must do is distract them so they are not watching the bridge when we cross."

"And how do we do that?" I asked.

He turned to me with a wolfish grin. "That, Billy, is largely up to you."

My gut tightened, as I knew what he was about to say right before he said it.

"Your orders, Lieutenant McCarty, are to draw the Jotun away from the bridge."

I swallowed hard and looked at the men in the circle. Captain Mercer's eyes were flinty hard. McNab's face filled with sympathy, and he chewed his lip, obviously holding back his words. The sergeant from First Squadron rocked on his heels, his face forcibly blank.

Jeremiah just looked resigned and saddened. He did his best to smile at me, but it was only in his lips and not in his eyes.

I let out a resigned breath. I didn't like this, but orders were orders.

"We will follow the railroad tracks," Captain Mercer said, "so you can catch up later tonight."

If I don't take too long, I thought with a grimace.

"I'd like Sergeant Freeman with me, sir," I said with a gesture toward Jeremiah.

Captain Mercer blinked in surprise, but nodded. "Very well." He turned to McNab. "Please strike camp, Sergeant-Major. We ride as soon as we are able."

McNab saluted and the circle broke up. As Jeremiah and I walked toward where Zeke had camped, he leaned over to me.

"What are you doing?" he asked.

"I have a plan," I said. "One that would've made Cassidy proud."

Mid-afternoon found Jeremiah and me slowly riding into town. He'd gone on foot the first time in an attempt to pass as a wandering farm hand, but with only two Jotun in town, there was no need.

We *wanted* these people to recognize us for what we were.

Dangerous.

We rode slowly as the light breeze picked up around us. Rain was coming, which would only help the company cross the bridge. At least I suspected that the Jotun wouldn't want to be up on the tower roof in the wet any more than we humans would. Especially if there was lightning.

But that didn't seem likely. This promised to be one of those soggy storms that started as mist and slowly grew to teardrops before finally ramping back down to nothing. It'd leave us wet and uncomfortable, but not do much more.

I'd found a way to sit that didn't hurt my ribs. They hurt less than they had a few days earlier, anyway. I'd found a way to tuck my shirt in tight, almost cinching it like a bandage. It made it a tad harder to breathe, but that was a small price to pay for not getting the occasional stab of pain from shifting around wrong.

Jeremiah had put his uniform back on. My uniform jacket was so muddied and blotched with blood that I'd left it off. Besides, riding in just my shirt was far more comfortable, even if a little bit scandalous. It wasn't my unmentionables, but I knew that the training sergeants back at Fort Chicago would not approve.

We clopped closer to the ramshackle remains of what had probably once been a cozy town. It wasn't devastated like Grand Lake back in Colorado had been, more dilapidated from neglect. The first two buildings we passed still stood, but were missing shingles and doors. The third had a collapsed wall and weeds growing three feet high right next to the opening. A few birds fluttered and twittered and flew out of a gap in the logs as we walked by.

"I still don't like the plan," Jeremiah said as he rode.

"What's wrong with it?" I asked, more curious than offended. He'd agreed to it, after all.

"I've just never seen a plan go the way it was supposed to."

I shrugged. "We'll find a way. You and Cassidy always did. You always succeeded."

"No," he said with a laugh. "I just didn't write about the failures."

"Not true. You lost that battle in *The Road to Harrisburg*. And that one outside of Saint Louis."

"True," he said with a rueful chuckle. "But I didn't write about *most* of our failures. Our losses don't make good stories."

"Yeah...," I said. I'd wanted to talk to him. Now was as good a time as any to ask. "I was talking to Maria... she said Cassidy had nightmares like me."

"He used to, back in the beginning. Especially after Saint Louis."

"But he got them to stop." It was as much a question as a

statement.

"He did."

"How?"

"He never said."

"But what do you think? I mean, you knew him as well as anyone."

We rode along a bit in silence while Jeremiah considered his answer. Finally, he pursed his lips and nodded.

"It was the Battle of Golden City," he said. "He stopped having nightmares after that."

"What happened?"

"He said he had hope once again."

I had to nod in agreement. We'd all had hope after that, the first big victory for The Army of the West. But then another memory tugged me.

"I… I remember his speech, on the courthouse steps, after the battle," I said. "He vowed to hunt down every giant and troll west of the Mississippi."

"He did," Jeremiah said.

"You never put that speech in any of your books."

"No. I never wrote about the Battle of Golden City."

"Why not?"

"Because I wasn't there."

I blinked in surprise at that. I'd just assumed that Jeremiah had gone everywhere Cassidy had.

He sensed my unasked question. "I was in Louisiana, fighting the trolls."

That raised my eyebrows. "You never wrote about that either."

"No," he said. "No, I did not." He clenched his jaw and looked away.

I decided not to ask anything else.

So we rode in quiet for a bit as the gloomy clouds continued to hang in the sky. The slow-falling mist had started, just like I'd expected. It matched my mood, but I was grateful. My head didn't hurt.

It didn't take long for us to get into the heart of the town, what there was of it. Here, more buildings were clearly kept up, with new shingles here and there and even some glass windows. Weeds didn't grown around the foundations either, and in one yard we saw a low wire fence surrounding some fat chickens.

We didn't see any people though, at least not at first. But after we'd passed two houses, a lanky boy about eight and an shaky old man stepped into the road about twenty feet ahead of us. They looked related—while the boy's yellow hair was wet and plastered down, it had the same fullness as the white mane the old man wore. The boy stood tall with his hands on his hips while the old man leaned on a cane, his pale hand gripping the knob tight.

"Who are you?" the boy demanded.

We pulled up on the reins. My horse huffed and shuffled before standing still.

"Who wants to know?" I asked.

"We're not the ones trespassin'," the boy said.

"I came through this morning," Jeremiah said. He nodded toward the old man. "I talked to your grandfather."

"You said you was lookin' for work," the grandfather said. "Looks like ya found it. You're Army."

"Army of the West," I said. I tipped my hat. "Lieutenant McCarty, at your service."

Both their eyes went wide. The boy's chin actually dropped, leaving his mouth an open oval the size of a chicken's egg.

"We need a favor," I said, "and you might be just the ones to do it for us."

The boy closed his mouth and his eyes narrowed in suspicion.

"We'll pay for it," I said. "Generously." I placed my hand on the top of my small saddlebag, drawing their eyes to its bulge.

"Your money's no good here," the grandfather stated flatly.

"You don't have to stay here," Jeremiah interjected. "We control Louisville. If you can get yourself there, they'll get you safely to the West."

The boy swiveled his head to look at his grandpa, who grimaced and shook his head.

"Too dangerous," he said.

"Not if you're clever and quick," Jeremiah said. "If you stay out of sight of the Jotun, you could be there in two days."

"No. I was born here. I'm gonna die here. I survived the war. I survived the trolls. I survived the giants. My land here is *mine*, ya hear?"

The boy pleaded silently with his eyes, but his grandpa didn't spare him a glance.

"Well, the Army will be there for a month," Jeremiah said, his voice pitched loud. "In case any of you change your mind." He slowly turned his head and scanned the town with a smile. Curtains slipped back into place as he did, but no one else came out to the street.

"We still need your help," I said. "But we were going to offer you something besides money anyway." I looked pointedly at my saddle-bag. "I'll move slow."

The boy tensed but his eyes locked onto my hand. He breathed a bit harder too.

I flipped up the top of the saddle bag and then slowly reached inside. I slowly pulled out a Colt revolver—not mine, the doctor's, since he said he didn't need it — and raised it so he could see. Then I grabbed it by the barrel and turned it to offer the stock to him.

"This," I said, "and a bagful of bullets."

The boy swallowed. "Whadda I gotta do?"

We rode through the town and then casually out the other side. We approached the tower, and when we were about four hundred yards away, I passed my reins to Jeremiah and dismounted. The rain had started, with small drops here and there, but the day was still bright enough to see that the tower's ramparts were clear.

This tower was smaller than the one at Louisville—maybe fifty feet tall, tops. The granite walls weren't as smooth, with cracks and jagged outcroppings here and there, but that was like saying the Ohio River wasn't as wide as the Mississippi. It didn't much matter as both were impassable. The door was the same design of tree trunks nailed together with a cloth-covered window.

We couldn't hear much, not that I'd expected to. I hoped Captain Mercer and the rest of the company were ready to cross. We hadn't been able to come up with a signal for them to tell us they were ready that didn't also give away their location.

Our signal was a bit easier. There's nothing quite like the crack of a Whitworth rifle, especially on a still afternoon.

I raised mine to my shoulder. Without any visible Jotun, I aimed for the window in the door. I steadied my breathing, slid my finger on the trigger, and fired.

The shot rang out. It filled the afternoon silence, and I was sure that both Captain Mercer and the Jotun had to have heard it.

"Up top," Jeremiah said.

A Jotun appeared at the roof parapet. He wore a heavy leather jerkin, but no helmet. His wavy corn-yellow hair flowed freely down to his shoulders. He scowled and his eyes quickly found us.

So I shot him.

He yowled and clapped his hands to his face.

So I fired again.

He howled as the bullet hit the back of his hand. I doubted it would do much damage, given his thick skin, but it had to sting. Then he disappeared from the roof.

"Time to go," Jeremiah said.

I slung my rifle over my shoulder and climbed back on my horse. We galloped back toward the town and intentionally veered toward the western edge, where the buildings had been all but abandoned. We slowed a bit, just as we reached the first one. Jeremiah looked back.

"He's following," he said.

"Good."

We rode around some buildings and then took a sharp right turn at an apple orchard. We paused in the trees long enough for Jeremiah to fire his Colt at a nearby trunk. The shot didn't echo as much as I'd wanted, but it was enough. We galloped hard through the orchard.

At the far side, we swerved the horses behind an old faded barn. The horses huffed as Jeremiah and I also tried to catch our breath.

The Jotun roared behind us. He'd reached the orchard fast.

And then a gunshot rang out from the woods further north, right where the kid was supposed to be hiding.

"Good timing," Jeremiah said.

The Jotun yelled again. I peeked around the side of the barn. Trees shook as he pushed through them. The rattling branches showed his path north.

"It worked," I said.

"For one of them," Jeremiah said. "Let's go." He snapped his reins and we were off.

We rode hard in a wide circle east around the tower. I kept glancing at it, but I couldn't see another Jotun. There might've been one behind the walls at the top, but it was too hard to really check while riding at top speed.

But nothing came flying at us, and nothing roared or charged out the door.

Raindrops splattered our face and more than once I had to wipe my eyes. We galloped until the horses started to flag, but urged them on. Once we were south of the tower, we turned and dashed straight for the bridge.

Still nothing.

We slowed when we reached the bridge itself. It was narrow but solid, with the tracks running down the middle. It'd been reinforced not too long ago and looked solid, but the narrowness made the horses jittery. We had to reassure them every step of the way. They were able to pick their way across the slick wood just fine, but it took forever. Jeremiah took the lead but we spent most of our time looking down at the bridge and making sure the horses were stepping only where they needed to.

When I wasn't looking down, I kept glancing over my shoulder at the tower. I couldn't believe it had been this easy. I half expected a boulder to come flying toward us at any moment. We'd only lured one Jotun out of the tower, and we knew there were at least two. Was the second looking for the gunmen too, like I hoped?

Jeremiah yanked up hard on his reins. I glanced past him.

The second Jotun stood at the end of the bridge, fifty yards in front of us, in a full iron breastplate and leather helm. It gripped a huge axe and gave us an evil grin.

TWENTY-TWO

I BECAME ACUTELY aware of the long drop off the bridge to the river bubbling far below. I didn't glance down, didn't tear my eyes away from the Jotun, actually. But I still had to suppress a shudder at the thought of falling. At least the breeze had stopped, so as to not add to my vertigo. The rain drizzled straight on down.

The Jotun remained in a battle crouch, hefting his axe easily in his hands. His fat nose looked like it'd been smashed flat in a past battle, but the glare in his eyes implied he didn't care. Instead, he grinned, and made a low, throaty chuckle.

"He's not charging," I said.

"He doesn't want to fall off this bridge any more than we do," Jeremiah replied. He tightened his grip on his reins as his horse snorted and shuffled its footing.

"We could go back," I said.

"The bridge is too narrow to turn the horses around."

My blood froze.

Turning the horses was possible but hard. I had no doubt that the moment we tried, the Jotun would attack. And we couldn't charge forward without risking the horses taking a bad step.

"We gotta dismount," I said quietly.

"I agree," Jeremiah said.

We slowly slid off our horses. Mine shuffled nervously, but kept its feet firmly planted on the planks.

Once my own feet hit the wood, I quickly reached into my saddlebag and grabbed the bottle of Maria's poppy juice. I tucked it into the ammo pouch at my waist. Then I checked that my rifle was securely strapped to my back.

Jeremiah shifted his stance and pulled his horse next to him, which partially hid me behind them.

"Can you shoot him?" Jeremiah asked quietly.

"He'll attack as soon as I raise my rifle." I kept my voice low and my body still. I didn't want to telegraph to the Jotun what I was thinking.

Not that he seemed to care. He shifted his battle axe so he held it mostly in his left hand. That's when I spotted three relatively smaller axes in his belt. They were still the length of my rifle, but with a straight handle and a wedge of a head.

"Worse," I said to Jeremiah, "look at his belt."

"Think those are throwing axes?"

"Gotta be. And we're in his range."

"No doubt."

The Jotun snarled something. It wasn't in English, so I didn't know the words, but the tone was a challenge. His right hand moved to hover over the axes at his belt.

"You fast enough?" Jeremiah quietly asked. His hand drifted toward his own rifle, still tied to his horse, alongside his saber.

"Maybe," I said, "but one bullet won't stop him."

"Then it's sabers." He unsheathed his and stepped forward, in front of his horse, holding it in front of him.

"Are you out of your mind?" I started forward to grab him and pull him back before I realized how foolish that was on a railroad bridge.

Jeremiah brought the saber up in front of him into a guard position. The Jotun snarled, but smiled. He also returned both hands to his battle axe.

Jeremiah gave me a quick look over his shoulder. "The ground slopes," he said. "It's not too far down if we get close enough to the end of the bridge. Then we can jump."

I couldn't hold back a bark of insane laughter. Of course! Why not jump off a perfectly good bridge?

But I didn't see much choice.

So I unsheathed my saber and carefully strode forward.

Once we were past the horses, Jeremiah stepped to the side so I could draw even with him. He held his sword in guard position and stared straight ahead at the Jotun.

That monster's grin was even larger than it'd been a few minutes ago. He almost danced on the balls of his feet as he waited for us to finish crossing.

We paused about twenty yards from him. I quickly glanced down—it was still a distance to the ground, but it wasn't certain death.

"Closer?" I asked.

Jeremiah shook his head. "Can't let him grab us." He shifted his stance and his right hand hovered over his Colt.

I understood in a flash. "Which eye do you want me to shoot?"

"Doesn't matter," he said. "Just as long as it slows him down."

"On three?"

He nodded. "One… two… three."

We both whipped our revolvers out and fired. I squeezed off two shots and then scrambled to the side of the bridge.

The Jotun howled with rage and pain.

I threw my saber off the bridge—no time to sheath it—and dropped to a crouch. I grabbed the rails and swung over the edge. I nearly slammed into a trestle below, but managed to get my feet up in time.

I glanced down—I was only about ten feet up and I hung over a leafy bush.

I let go.

I slammed into the bush and immediately rolled, which flipped me out of the bush and sent me tumbling down the slope a few turns. Luckily, I only rolled through grass, but my ribs still protested in pain. The dull throb in my head started anew as well.

I pulled myself up.

Jeremiah thrashed through a bush nearby. He sounded okay.

Above us, a horse screamed and then the Jotun roared. His shadow overflowed the end of the bridge but then slowly receded.

"He's coming down!" Jeremiah called. He'd gotten to his feet and looked uninjured. "Lead him toward the river." He started climbing up the slope to a shadowed spot under the bridge.

"Got it!" I half-ran, half-jogged toward the water, as fast as the uneven ground allowed.

About halfway down, a tangle of bushes hung at the top of a large sheer drop. I skidded to a stop—the cliff was too steep. I'd have to go around. I quickly turned.

The Jotun had started picking his way down the slope next to the bridge. His eyes locked on me and he snarled.

My feet froze. I was breathing hard, and my head ached.

The Jotun skidded a little on a steep part of the dirt, and then righted himself. He still took huge steps.

I wasn't going to make it to the river.

So I unslung my rifle and brought it to my shoulder. I aimed at the Jotun's face. Blood already streaked one cheek, but his eyes were fierce. He grimaced and reached for one of the throwing axes at his belt.

I shifted my aim to his right eye and fired.

He roared. One hand shot to his face, but the other still pulled out his axe.

Jeremiah leaped out of the bushes behind him and stabbed him hard in the back of the knee.

The Jotun screamed. He buckled forward.

But not before throwing the axe wildly toward me.

I threw myself down to dodge it.

And fell off the mini-cliff.

I landed on two small oak saplings surrounded by more of those leafy bushes I didn't recognize. I'd managed to roll so I smashed into them on my back, which broke my fall without breaking me. I tumbled to the ground and landed with an ooff as the air got knocked out of me.

When I'd recovered a bit, I slowly climbed out of the bushes and checked myself over. I had scratches all over my hands and one across my cheek. My elbow throbbed, but it moved easily, so I figured it was just a bruise. I'd dropped my rifle somewhere but all the rest of my gear appeared intact.

A loud, terrified scream ripped through the air. Too loud for a human.

Then it suddenly cut off.

I blinked in surprise and looked around for the best way up the mini-cliff, but my jaw dropped.

A huge hole in the side of the hill hid behind the saplings. It was almost tall enough for me to walk into standing, though only about four feet wide.

A cave. Under a bridge. I shuddered at the implications.

So I backed away from it and went sideways out of the trees. The slope to the right of the cave was more gentle, enough that I could scramble up it on my hands and knees.

I was out of breath and my hands were coated in gunky mud by the time I got high enough to see the Jotun's body. It sprawled down the slope, one arm flung to the side and the other trapped underneath. Its face was turned the other way, but a lot of blood flowed away from its head.

Jeremiah came clambering down the slope toward me. "You all right?"

I nodded. "Fine. Some scratches and bruises, but nothing bad."

"Good. We should get going before the other one comes to investigate." He reached me and I could tell he wanted to give me a relieved hug, but the slope made footing treacherous enough.

"I found a cave," I said, "under the bridge."

That wiped the relief off his face. He sucked in his breath and nodded.

"Sounds like a troll cave," he said. "Like the ones in Louisiana."

I nodded, vaguely remembering something about troll caves, but it hadn't been in any of Jeremiah's books about Cassidy, so I didn't have it clear in my mind.

"Let's take a look," he said.

He followed me back down the slope and through the saplings. We stared at the cave entrance together.

"A lot of debris," he said as he pointed to a thick layer of decaying leaves cluttered and matted around the entrance.

"Yeah," I said, "and there's no path through the bushes and trees."

He nodded. "It's abandoned. We should still go in and take a look."

I grimaced. In tight quarters, I'd need my saber if it came to a fight.

Jeremiah drew his and glanced at me. His eyes dropped to my belt.

"I dropped mine," I sheepishly admitted. "My rifle too."

"You'll need your rifle," he said. He tilted his head toward the cave. "I'll be quick. Keep an eye out for the other Jotun."

I nodded and drew my Colt. He steeled himself, and then strode into the cave.

My heart raced. I couldn't do much if Jeremiah ran into trouble, so I fervently hoped he didn't. Once again I felt the dull throb in my head growing. I closed my eyes, which helped only a little.

But I had Maria's poppy syrup!

I fumbled in my ammo bag and let out a relieved sigh when I realized the bottle had survived my fall without a crack. I unstoppered it and took a long drag. Then I remembered Maria's warning not to take too much and put it back.

I kept glancing around as I waited. I could hear the buzz of insects, and the burble of the river, and the whinny of one of our horses. I looked up and could make out the shadows of our animals, and then my gut churned.

The horse in front, Jeremiah's, had its front legs hanging through the railroad slats. No way it was still alive.

My horse still stood, but kept pacing and snorting on the bridge. It must be terrified, I realized. It couldn't turn around, but couldn't go forward either.

At least we'd killed a Jotun.

Jeremiah came out of the cave after only a few minutes. He dusted his hands off and frowned.

"Definitely a troll cave," he said, "but it's been abandoned for years. There's nothing of value inside."

"Huh," I said. "I thought all the trolls were down in Florida or Mississippi."

"Don't forget Memphis," he said, his expression grim.

I shuddered. Who could forget it? The townsfolk had surrendered, expecting to be enslaved like happened with the Jotun.

Instead the trolls had massacred them.

And then eaten them.

Except for a lucky few who'd escaped to tell the tale.

I shuddered again.

"They haven't been here in a long time," Jeremiah said. "Come on. Let's find your rifle and get back on the road."

I nodded. Even if there weren't any trolls around, there were still Jotun. Jotun with cannons. Jotun that we needed to stop, no matter what.

We had to catch up with Captain Mercer fast.

TWENTY-THREE

FOR ONCE, my luck was good. We found my rifle tangled in the limbs of a small oak tree. My saber was long gone, and we didn't see anything we wanted to take from the Jotun's corpse.

The Jotun had killed Jeremiah's horse with a throwing axe. It lay on the edge of the bridge, so we stripped Jeremiah's gear off it and he tipped the body into the ravine. I held my horse's reins so it wouldn't panic, but it strained and pulled the whole time. I had to pet its nose to keep it calm. Then we loaded Jeremiah's saddlebags on it. With all the gear, Jeremiah wasn't sure it could handle both of us, so we walked beside it as we headed down the tracks.

We walked a long time through the night. It got hard to see anything even a few feet off the road. The rain stopped, but it still felt clammy. The night birds called around us from time to time, and we heard lots of bugs, but not much else. I drank frequently from my canteen and took another small sip of poppy juice when the aches to my ribs and skull returned.

We found the company camp well after midnight. Zeke stood sentry out on the tracks and gave a huge wave when he saw us. When we got close, he trotted over.

"Bless the Lord!" he said. His earnest grin lit up the night like a beacon. "It's good to see you. We was worried!"

I couldn't help a smile at his enthusiasm. "We ran into a Jotun at the bridge."

He gave us a solemn nod. "That's what we was worried about." He explained how they'd just finished crossing the bridge when a Jotun on the top of the tower had spotted them. Captain Mercer had ordered the company to gallop as fast as they could.

"Sergeant McIlroy and the doctor didn't make it," Zeke said solemnly. "The doctor's horse stumbled, and Sergeant McIlroy tried to save him. That gave the rest of us enough time to get away."

"They're both dead?" I asked, though my gut already knew the answer.

Zeke slowly nodded. "We held their service after dinner. Captain Mercer had some nice words."

I could imagine. McIlroy had died trying to save another person? What could Captain Mercer say that wasn't nice?

"So when the Jotun couldn't catch you, he came back to the bridge and found us," Jeremiah said.

"Our bad luck," I said. "But could've been worse."

"Much," Jeremiah said. He looked at Zeke. "Is the Captain awake?"

"No," Zeke said, "but he told us to wake him when y'all arrived. *He* wasn't worried one bit."

"Of course not," I said dryly. "He probably just assumed we'd kill the Jotun."

"Did you?" Zeke asked, his eyes wide.

"Yeah," I said, "but that's not the point." I shook my head wearily. "You should probably take us to him."

The camp itself sat about five hundred yards off the tracks—far enough for the low cooking fires to not be visible through the trees and undergrowth. They'd found a small stream and a clearing that let them keep everyone's tents tight together. As soon as we got close, Zeke took the reins of my horse and said he'd get it taken care of. He pointed at a small canvas tent next to a fallen log on the far side of the camp and said it was the Captain's.

We trudged over, weaving our way through the small fire pits and low tents. Low bushes and the occasional rock kept the ground uneven, and I couldn't imagine sleeping on it, as much as my body ached for rest.

We stopped about four feet from the tent's entrance. I slumped, and then decided Captain Mercer wouldn't mind if I sat. So I lowered myself to the fallen log.

"Captain Mercer!" Jeremiah called. "Captain Mercer!"

We waited, and then heard shuffling from within. A minute or so later, Captain Mercer came out.

He stood tall, though his shirt looked rumpled and stained with sweat. As I watched, the blurriness fled from his eyes. His gaze lingered on me before turning back to Jeremiah.

Jeremiah saluted. "Reporting as ordered, sir."

"At ease," Captain Mercer said. "What happened, Sergeant?"

Jeremiah told him how we'd successfully distracted the first Jotun and made it to the bridge. Then he talked about how the second had trapped us halfway across. Captain Mercer looked at me with a raised eyebrow, but I just nodded. Then Jeremiah told him how we'd taken advantage of the slope down from the bridge.

"Billy got him in one eye," he said, "and I took out his knee. It was all over soon after that."

"Except for the troll cave," I said.

"Troll cave?" Captain Mercer asked.

"An old one, sir," Jeremiah said, "under the bridge. It'd clearly been abandoned years ago."

"Driven out by the Jotun, I am sure," Captain Mercer said. "It is of no mind." He looked at me again. "Get some sleep. We ride at dawn."

We didn't actually ride out at first light. To Captain Mercer's visible frustration, it took far too long for all the men to eat and get their gear packed.

So after the streaks of sunlight had left the clouds to slide between the trees, I was on my horse once again. I'd slept hard, without dreams, or at least ones I could recall when I'd woke. I'd nipped some poppy syrup before I'd laid down, though. I was stiff and sore in a dozen places and one of the cuts on my left hand was starting to turn an ugly inflamed red, but that was the worst of it. Despite my aches, I was eager to be on the move.

And I wasn't the only one. The whole company felt restless and annoyed. As if we'd been stung by hornets and told not to scratch, and scratching was all we could think of.

When we weren't thinking of Sergeant McIlroy and all our other dead, that is.

At least the morning was a bit cooler than the day before. Not that it would stay that way, I was sure.

We followed the railroad tracks south until almost noon. We passed a couple of small abandoned towns. At the second, we left the tracks for a small dirt road headed more southeast than southwest. The sun was high overhead when we stopped outside of a third town. We could see smoke from chimneys, so Captain Mercer had us all break for food and water while he sent two men from Company A ahead as scouts.

They reported back after an hour. The town still had a sizable human population, but also a handful of Jotun. They said there was no tower, but several large buildings that had to be Jotun homes.

"We had best not make contact," Captain Mercer told us officers, the same group he'd addressed outside of Munfordville. "We do not want word of our passing to precede us."

So we circled around the town, doing our best to stay out of sight. If anyone did see us, they raised no alarm.

We continued to avoid contact for the rest of the day. We skirted past a couple of occupied farms and two clusters of buildings that could've been towns once upon a time. Finally, about dusk, we arrived at a larger settlement that was clearly still inhabited.

We halted back in the trees and Captain Mercer gave the order to move off the road and make camp. McNab suggested sending a man in to trade for goods, especially some fresh food, but Captain Mercer refused. He did let Jeremiah take Zeke and Joe Johnson to get some apples from an orchard we could see not far off, as long as they made sure to not get caught. They didn't, and somewhere along the way Joe Johnson caught a feral chicken, so we had that as well.

That night, I had another nightmare, but it was the old one of me killing Cassidy. I awoke in a sweat, but no one else seemed to have noticed. At least I hadn't cried out.

The next day, we did much the same. We continued south, but avoided contact the entire way. More than once, a scout would ride back and talk to Captain Mercer, and then the whole company would go off into the woods for a distance before returning to the road.

The land got hillier and hillier too, which made leaving the road a bit harder. It slowed us down, and I kept worrying about running into cabins tucked away in the woods, but the scouts did a good job of spotting anything we needed to avoid.

In the afternoon, the road started to run along a stream. Our progress slowed, at least twice because our scouts spotted other humans and we had to hide. One of those times, they spotted the scouts. The other humans avoided us, so we didn't know if they were working for the Jotun or not.

"It can't be helped," Captain Mercer said, but I could tell he wasn't happy.

An hour or so before dusk, we stopped and spread out to find a suitable camping spot—relatively flat land far enough from the road or any settlements to not be seen, but with wood and water nearby. We ended up in a small abandoned sharecropper's farm, with Captain Mercer claiming the cabin for Maria. After we ate our evening meal, several men took time to visit her and get their various cuts and scrapes attended to.

I myself took a turn after I'd finished my own hardtack and apples. Joe Johnson had somehow come up with real strong coffee, which he bashfully broke out for our squadron. I was still savoring the delicious bitter aftertaste when I entered the cabin.

The dirty log cabin consisted of only a single room, with a door and an opening for a window on one side, where whatever curtains had hung there had long since disappeared. A heavy oak table sat near the window, and Maria had placed her small oil lamp on it. It gave the room a warm glow that reminded me of nights back in Golden City, reading the dime novels while Ma did her mending.

Maria sat next to the table on the lone chair, a rickety old thing of tree limbs that hadn't even been trimmed square. She smiled when she saw me.

"Hello, Billy. How are you doing?"

"Okay, I guess," I said. "My ribs are doing better. My head still hurts from time to time. Sometimes bad." I held up my left hand. "But this cut doesn't look good."

She took it in hers and held it close to the lamp. The cut itself looked purplish-black and the red flesh around it looked devilish in the low light.

"Did you wash this?" she asked. "When it happened?"

"Nah," I said. "We were in a hurry."

"You should have come earlier." She released my hand. "Get boiling water. And something for you to bite on."

My eyes went wide. "You're going to cut me?"

"To get the pus out, yes."

A little shaken, I went to get the water as I'd been told. When I returned, Maria had placed bandages and a small jar of her mold ointment on the table, next to a small scalpel I'd never seen her carry before.

"That's new," I said, pointing to it.

"An army benefit," she said with a small smile. "Hand," she demanded.

I let her take it and hold it to the table. I looked away and steeled myself. When the pain came, I winced. After the initial sharp surge, it dulled, and then flared up again as she washed the wound with a cloth she'd soaked in the water I'd brought. I looked back as she began to bandage it.

"Keep it clean," she said firmly. "You will be fine."

"Good to know," I said.

"At least for this." She tilted her head and stared intently at me. Shadows partially covered her face.

"How are your nightmares?" she asked. "Do you still despair?"

I was so taken by surprise, I jerked back. But then I remembered our last conversation, where I'd told her all my doubts about being in the army.

I took a deep breath. "I'm… I'm doing better. I *feel* better, at least. Gimme some time, though—I'll probably have another nightmare tonight." I tried to smile, but it just came off as a silly forced grin.

She nodded, but looked into my eyes as she did. *Her* smile was warm.

"Perhaps," she said, "you should ask the dreams why they come."

I snorted. That didn't make sense.

But maybe it did.

TWENTY-FOUR

I JERKED AWAKE IN A SWEAT. My heart pounded and my body shook. My mind raced with images of Cassidy and blood and darkness. They mixed and blurred together.

And I couldn't remember another thing about my dream.

I wiped my brow and slowly calmed my breathing. Then my bladder kicked in and I realized I had to get up.

The dark of night still hung on the camp as I took care of my business. I couldn't see the sentries I knew were tucked into the trees. The other tents and Maria's cabin were all quiet, with only the whir of the night insects to disturb the peace.

I wasn't going to be able to get back to sleep, I knew. I didn't want to stand around, and I didn't want to wake anyone. We'd all ridden hard the last several days, and I knew we'd be up before dawn to do it again. We weren't even in Tennessee yet, according to McNab, but he expected we'd leave Kentucky sometime during the day.

After I took care of things, I decided to walk down to the road and look around a bit. Maybe I'd get a feel for where we were going next, or I could even scout ahead. Even if I couldn't, maybe the walk would clear my head.

I took my rifle and quietly headed that way. I looked for the sentry so I could tell him I was leaving camp. I was at the edge of camp before I spotted him. He was sitting on the ground with his back against an ash tree, his rifle propped against the trunk next to him. He was doing something in his lap but turned his head as I approached.

I pulled up short. It was the Big Buffoon, Private Forrest.

After the way he'd treated Zeke, and with the problems he had with me, I didn't want him being the only one to know where I was.

He'd seen me, though, and after a minute, he tucked whatever he was doing into a pouch and scrambled to his feet.

I took a deep breath and walked forward. "You're relieved, soldier," I said. "I'll finish your watch."

He tilted his head and looked askance at me. "You sure?"

I shrugged. "Get some sleep." He looked like he was about to argue, so I quickly added, "That's an order."

He stiffened. "Yes... lieutenant." He shouldered his rifle. "The watch is yours."

With that, he marched off toward the center of camp, not looking back once.

I felt a little sheepish as I watched him leave. I'd never given an order before, and I'd done it so I could be alone? Somehow I suspected Captain Mercer wouldn't approve. Or maybe he would. I didn't know.

But since I had the watch, I decided to make the best of it. The tree the Big Buffoon had chosen was the best sentry spot around, so I took it myself.

The woods ahead were quiet. As my eyes adjusted, I could see further down toward the road than I'd expected, but nothing moved. What little noise I heard came from the camp behind me.

I sat back against the tree with my rifle across my lap. The trunk was solid and a little rough, but didn't have any knots poking into me, for which I was grateful.

My hand brushed some wood shavings on the ground. Surprised, I picked a couple up and realized they were all different sizes, and all in a small pile. The Big Buffoon must've been whittling, I realized. I wondered what he'd made.

My mind drifted to other things. How far was it to Nickajack

Cave? Another two days? Three? And then what? The answer was, nobody knew.

And then we'd have to get out of Jotun territory. That might be even harder. The Jotun we'd encountered so far didn't know where we were going. Our way back would be obvious.

I wondered if the boy and his grandpa back in Munfordville had decided to leave. I certainly hoped so—at least the boy. The way his eyes had lit up when I'd handed him the Colt made me smile, even now as I remembered it. He was a fierce little kid. He had his grandfather's stubbornness but not his devotion to lost causes.

Maybe they wouldn't leave now. But the kid would surely end up at Fort Chicago once the grandfather died, however far in the future that might be.

I liked thinking I'd see the kid again.

Except, I realized, I didn't want to go back to Fort Chicago myself. After this raid was over, I needed to do something besides march and drill and march some more.

But, I reminded myself, I didn't have to figure that out until after the raid. As Captain Mercer would say, we had a mission.

That came first.

I snorted softly. I was quoting Captain Mercer, even if only in my head.

I decided to quit woolgathering and pay attention to the woods ahead. After all, I was on watch.

We broke camp and rode out at daybreak. Like we'd done the last two days, we sent scouts out ahead and left the road whenever they reported people or settlements. I offered to take my turn at scouting, but Captain Mercer said to wait. I'd have my turn when we were closer to the cave.

By late afternoon, the creek that the road followed spread out into shallow mud flats. A brace of ducks quacked merrily and swam through the shallows. Captain Mercer called a halt while he and

McNab talked. The rest of us watered our horses and ate some food of our own.

As we rested, I sat on a small grassy patch munching apples with the rest of my squadron. Me, Jeremiah, Zeke, and Joe Johnson.

That was it.

I had a pang at the memory of the others, especially Burwell. He'd been a good man. They all had.

And they'd died.

I couldn't say they'd died for nothing, because we'd taken Louisville. Which meant we'd saved New England. That was not for nothing.

"Say Billy," Zeke said, "why're you so sad?"

I shook myself, startled. "I'm not sad."

"I don't know," Jeremiah said. "You've been moping around the last couple of days. Since Munfordville."

"I have?" I said, blinking.

"Mmm hmm," Zeke said. "You look like your dog died."

"Never had a dog," I said.

"I did," Joe Johnson said, to the surprise of us all. "Big sheepdog. He was nice."

"What made him nice?" Jeremiah asked.

"He'd bring me his bones," Joe Johnson said. "And he'd snuggle next to me at night. He kept me warm." He smiled at the memory.

"What happened to him?" Jeremiah politely asked.

"Gave him to my sister. She needed him more."

I blinked. Joe Johnson had never once mentioned a sister.

"We had a dog on the plantation when I was a kid," Zeke said. "He was kind of a mutt, but he loved to chase squirrels. Never caught any, but that didn't stop him from trying."

Jeremiah and Joe Johnson both nodded with knowing smiles. Zeke grinned back and continued his story.

"This one time," he said, "we was out in the garden, picking tomatoes. They were big and fat that year, real juicy. And if the Mistress wasn't lookin', you could quick wolf one down."

"Stealing?" Jeremiah teased. "You?"

"It wasn't stealing!" Zeke objected. "We was gonna eat them for supper. All we was doing was speeding it up."

We all laughed at that.

"Anyway…," Zeke said. "We was out there, picking tomatoes. It'd rained and mud was everywhere and we hated it. But Rusty—that's the dog, mind you—Rusty saw this big fat squirrel chitterin' on this big old tree. That squirrel was just jabberin' away like he was a traveling preacher looking for his supper. And you could tell it was messin' with Rusty's head. He was pullin' hard on the Mistress's leash and all. Finally he pulled so hard, the leash broke."

"Oh, that sounds bad," Jeremiah said.

"It was!" Zeke said. "Old Rusty took off like a shot after that squirrel. But that squirrel weren't no dummy. He zipped right up that tree faster than you could shake a leg."

I nodded. Made sense from what I'd seen of squirrels when I'd been hunting.

"Now the thing is, that didn't stop Old Rusty," Zeke continued. "He tried to run up that tree himself, except of course he couldn't. So he jumped around, all barking and yapping and howling. And the Mistress, she was yelling at him and calling him, but he was paying her no mind. He wanted that squirrel, ya see."

"Oh, we can imagine," Jeremiah said, his voice full of amusement.

"So," Zeke said, "the Mistress marched on over to Rusty, still yelling the whole time and waving her fist at Rusty, and then waving it some at the squirrel. But the squirrel musta had enough of it, 'cause he took off runnin' along a branch and then leaped to another tree right behind the Mistress."

"No!" Jeremiah said, and started to laugh.

"Yes!" Zeke said with wide eyes and a solemn nod. "Rusty ran right into her and knocked her in the mud."

Even I couldn't help laughing.

"*Then*," Zeke continued, "just as the Mistress gets up, with mud in her hair, and mud on her dress, and mud on her hands, the squirrel jumps back. And Rusty runs right into the Mistress again, pushin' her into the mud *again*. Well, that squirrel decided that if twice was good, then more was even better."

"Oh no," Jeremiah said as he fought back chuckles, "How many times did Rusty knock her down?"

"Four times," Zeke said. "Got his broken leash wrapped around her ankle the last time, just when she was trying to walk away. Pulled her down like a roped calf."

We all lost it and broke into peals of laughter. Me, I just kept picturing Zeke standing there with a tomato in his mouth, watching this dog run over the Mistress as she yelled at him. And then her getting tripped and falling splat, face first.

Maybe it wasn't funny. But maybe we just needed the laugh.

We were still sitting there, sprawled on the grass and trading funny stories, when McNab strolled up. Zeke started to scramble to his feet but McNab waved him off. He stopped and planted his feet on the ground. I think our laughter must've been contagious, because he smiled at us before turning a bit grim.

"We're almost to the Cumberland River," he said. "There's a bridge. But there's also another tower on the far side."

That sobered us all up right quick.

"Captain Mercer's decided we're going to try to sneak across at night," McNab continued. "We'll try as soon as it's dark enough."

Then he looked us all over. "He wants your squadron to cross first. Just in case there's trouble."

I swallowed. Somehow I was sure there'd be trouble.

TWENTY-FIVE

THE BRIDGE across the Cumberland River had been built for wagons instead of trains, which was a relief. Or maybe built for Jotun, given how much was granite instead of timber. It stretched gently over the water, the river itself a mere long break in the wall of oak and sycamore lining the road.

The tip of the tower loomed ahead, a dark shadow blocking out the grey clouds and scattered stars beyond. It looked narrower than the ones we'd seen so far, but I knew that distances could be deceiving.

I shivered a little as I sat on my horse. The wind had picked up enough to make it feel like a wet chill covered me. The wound on my hand itched, but I could breathe okay. My ribs felt like they were almost whole.

At the moment, my head was clear. I was getting used to the headaches that came and went. All too often, I'd ridden in pain down the trail, with my eyes shut and my hat pulled down as far over my ears as I could manage.

But now… now my heart was just beating hard. Not out of fear as much as anticipation. We couldn't see any lights in the tower, but that didn't mean the Jotun weren't there.

The road was wide enough for us to all ride side by side. Jeremiah and I were in the middle, with Zeke on my left and Joe Johnson on Jeremiah's right. At a signal from Jeremiah, we slowly rode forward.

We went as quiet as we could. We'd padded our harnesses anywhere they might've jingled. Only the clop of the horses' hooves on stone could be heard.

I kept my eyes on the tower the entire time.

We didn't see a thing.

We made it all the way across the bridge without a sound or a sight other than ourselves. Zeke and Joe Johnson moved into the woods on our right. They were thick and overgrown and promised slow going, but it kept our men out of sight. They could cover Jeremiah and me as we continued to ride forward.

We went slowly down the road. The tower sat not too far down along the left side. On the other side, the woods opened up to fields and what looked like scattered farms. Once we got past the tower, we'd have an easy ride.

But where were the Jotun?

I couldn't see any on the battlements. The handful of arrow slits were dark. There weren't any torches anywhere. It wasn't until we were almost to the tower itself that we saw something besides blank stone walls.

A rickety shack stood next to what I was starting to think of as the standard Jotun front door made of smashed-together tree trunks. The shack was human-sized, with the tower's granite wall as its back and rough hewn logs as its side and roof. It was about ten feet deep and its front stood open to the elements.

We stopped for a moment and sat quietly on our horses. We still couldn't see or hear anything other than the light wind and the occasional rustle of an animal in the trees. Slowly, we started forward once again.

We swung wide so we could look inside the shack from a distance. We could make out dark lumps, but nothing clear in the darkness. Finally we drew close, up to only a few feet away.

And heard snoring. Human snoring.

A slat wooden table blocked the main entrance, and behind it sat a simple wooden chair. The snoring came from further back in the shack, where a long lump stretched across the ground.

Jeremiah gave me a chagrined look. Without a word, we both dismounted. I drew my Colt as we approached. So did Jeremiah.

"Remember the cabin in *The Road to Harrisburg*?" Jeremiah whispered.

I nodded. I remembered the scene well. I knew what to do.

Beyond the table, a tall gaunt man sprawled between two blankets on the ground. His leathery, unshaven, and dirty face made him look like a vagrant in the moonlight. He didn't seem to notice as we quietly walked right up to the table.

Jeremiah lowered his gun to his side and I did the same. He let out a sigh of frustration and slapped his free hand down on the table.

"Hey!" he yelled. He pounded the table a second time.

The man started and jerked awake. He looked wildly around before his eyes focused on us, and then he scrambled to his feet.

"Wha—? What?" he asked as he approached the table. He wore what looked to be an old stained Confederate Army uniform, minus the hat and half the buttons. "You wanna see the Huskarl?"

"The Jotun?" I asked. "You work for him?"

He shook himself and tried to stand up straight at attention, but he just looked sloppy. Any of the soldiers in our company would look better.

"Doorman Thrall Bradford at your service," he said.

"And what exactly is a 'Doorman Thrall?'" Jeremiah asked.

"You don't have doormen?" Bradford asked. He slumped and looked confused. "I answer the door. I tell the Huskarl he has visitors."

I glanced at the door in question. Like the door at the tower in Louisville, I didn't see a way for a human to get in. But then I spotted a thin rope running up along the side to a bell.

"I see," Jeremiah continued smoothly. "Where we're from, a Jotun would be the doorman."

"Ah, well, ah." Bradford looked down at his feet for a minute before looking back at us, clearly abashed. "We only have the Huskarl. Well, and his family, but the boy's still just a babe."

I had to fight to keep my chin from dropping. His family? The boy was a baby?

My mind reeled. None of the books, none of the stories, heck, none of the news reports had mentioned anything about the Jotun having babies. They were these fierce, merciless warriors.

And they had babies?

I stared at the tower and my eyes drifted upward as I wondered where the baby might be. After a bit, I realized Jeremiah and Bradford were still talking, though I'd missed most of what they'd said.

"…but if he found out…," Bradford said. He worriedly rubbed his chin as his eyes darted to Jeremiah's rifle and saber and Colt. Particularly to the Colt, which Jeremiah hadn't quite raised to point at him.

"We'll be quiet," Jeremiah said soothingly. "In fact, if you just lay down like you were, you can truthfully claim you didn't see or hear a thing."

"Well…," Bradford turned and looked pleadingly at me.

I scowled back and tightened my grip on my revolver. His eyes widened with alarm.

"Tell you what," Jeremiah firmly went on, "Billy will stay here with you and help you watch the door while I go back and talk to our friends. Billy's got a good eye. He'll do a fine job of keeping watch while you go back to sleep."

I tried not to crack a smile at Jeremiah's acting, so instead I sneered and raised my own gun. "Yeah," I said with as much of a snarl as I could manage, "anyone gives us trouble, I'll give 'em a piece of this." I hope my implied threat was clear.

"Uh… uh…" Bradford's breathing went shallow and he seemed ready to skitter in any direction, like a cornered rabbit. "I…"

"Just go lie down," Jeremiah said. He gestured toward Bradford's bedroll. "Everything will be just fine."

"I… I, uh, don't know," Bradford said as he slowly backed up. Then he flopped down onto his blankets.

"Good choice," I said. I gave him a broad smile and then turned and leaned on the table. I could still see him out of the corner of my eye, but I hoped it looked like I wasn't paying him any attention at all. Maybe I fooled him, maybe I didn't, but after a bit, he stretched out on his back, put his hands under his head, and closed his eyes.

I couldn't help smiling to myself, though. We'd bluffed him into doing what we'd wanted just fine.

Jeremiah headed to the horses. He led mine over, and I quickly tied it to a post in front of the shack. Then he mounted his and rode off, back toward the company.

I leaned against the table. Bradford continued to lie still, his eyes scrunched up.

As I waited there in the still night, I thought about what he'd said.

The Jotun had children. Babies even. I tried to imagine what a Jotun baby looked like. Probably fat and chubby like human babies, but as big as me.

The thing was, monsters didn't have babies. Well, maybe they did. They must, if I really thought about it. But it didn't *seem* right.

The Jotun had killed a million humans, probably more. They'd certainly tried to kill more. That was the whole reason we'd attacked Louisville—to stop them from killing more of us in New England.

They were monsters. They had to be. Awful, and evil, and as deserving of death as the Devil himself.

Kill or be killed.

That was the way it was.

But did that include a baby?

My mind started doing loops.

It finally stopped when I spotted the company creeping down the road. They rode slow, in almost single file. Captain Mercer was at the head of the column and when he saw me, he peeled off and gestured for McNab to lead the rest forward. He rode close enough to be able to peer into the shack, but didn't dismount. After a cursory look, he nodded at me.

Bradford rolled on his side, facing away.

Captain Mercer didn't say a thing. The company filed by, and after the last man had passed he motioned for me to follow. I mounted and we rode away. I checked back constantly to see if Bradford would raise an alarm, but soon the tower faded in the night and the distance.

No Jotun ever gave chase.

We'd made it past a tower without a fight, and more important, without losing anyone.

We camped on an abandoned farm about an hour's ride south of the tower. The next morning, we rose before dawn and began the trek again.

Like the day before, we sent scouts ahead and avoided all contact. Twice we ducked into the trees to let human travelers pass by. We avoided the farms and towns we came across. We didn't see any Jotun at all.

The hills grew steeper and the road rougher as it wound along the slopes. More than once, we hit long muddy patches where the horses' hooves squished and sank into the muck. Still, we slogged on.

But the tediousness got to many of us by late afternoon. When we once again had to work our way through the dense underbrush to avoid a farmhouse that might or might not have people in it, I'd had enough. I wanted to *be* there.

But I held my frustration in check. We'd lost men on this trip twice. If we went slow but no one died, then slow was the way to go. The gunpowder factory wasn't going anywhere, I was sure. At least not if they didn't know we were coming.

We camped that night well off the road in a little ravine that was completely invisible from the road. My tent was on a slope and I barely slept because I kept sliding and rolling.

But barely sleeping meant I didn't dream.

The next day was just as tedious. As was the day after that. Food began to run short and we had to stop and forage more often. Just before dark, the scouts came back and reported that they'd been seen by a farmer—but he'd waved. Captain Mercer had gone with Sergeant McNab to negotiate with the farmer and returned with a freshly butchered hog.

"He's going to try for Louisville in a day or two," McNab said as we sat next to the fire and watched the pork sizzle in the skillet. "He'd been thinking about leaving since his wife died last year, but didn't know where to go. He said we gave him hope."

I snorted softly. I was beginning to lose hope. Between the sticky air and the mud and the never-ending trees and the aches in my head and my hand and the mealy food, I just felt tired.

But we'd given *him* hope. So that was something.

"He also said we're about a day from Nickajack," McNab continued. "He said we should arrive at dusk tomorrow."

And just like that, my hope returned.

TWENTY-SIX

WE SET OUT AT DAWN, like we'd done every day on this raid. The sun slowly burned off the morning chill as we ambled down the road. As always, we sent scouts ahead and avoided contact with any humans or towns we came across. We didn't run into any Jotun. Of course, by avoiding the towns, we avoided most of the places that they'd be living.

We'd been going southwest for some time, so as to avoid Chattanooga proper. There still weren't many people on the roads, which made me wonder. Was it because there weren't many people, or because no one wanted to travel?

That made me wonder more about that first traveller we'd met, way back before Louisville. The High Thrall by himself with papers but no clear business. I decided to ask Jeremiah about him.

"I don't know who he was," he said. "You need to ask the Captain." He gestured toward the front of the column where Captain Mercer rode.

I nodded and spurred my horse into a trot.

Captain Mercer gave me a warm smile as I rode up beside him, opposite McNab. He held his reins loose and looked more like a man out for a pleasant morning ride than someone off to battle. After a quick nod, he turned back to McNab, who rode with a similar casual air.

"So what happened then?" Captain Mercer asked.

"Cassidy decided we needed to find out if the Jotun were north of Harrisburg too," McNab said, continuing the story that had clearly started before I arrived. "We rode through thick woods for a day. That was tough," he said with a chuckle. "We finally found this little trail, must've been something the deer used, or maybe the Injuns back in the day. Anyway, it wasn't more than a track, almost too small for a horse."

My mind raced to Jeremiah's book *Giant Killer Cassidy and the Road to Harrisburg*. I'd read it a dozen times, huddled on the floor of Ma's laundry shop, and I remembered the scene. They'd wound their way through the woods until they'd stumbled on a ramshackle lean-to, with a nervous ten-year-old boy in front of it holding a revolver.

And a half dozen filthy children between three and six huddled inside.

"Their parents had promised to come back in two days," McNab explained. "But it'd been five, and the kids didn't know what to do."

"How did Captain Cassidy handle it?" Captain Mercer asked.

"He spent a long time thinking about it," McNab said. "Then he decided we needed to take the kids to safety before continuing on."

"Thus abandoning Harrisburg."

Captain Mercer's harsh tone got my spine up.

"It was already destroyed!" I snapped. "He couldn't have saved anyone there, and he did save the kids."

Captain Mercer turned to me with a stern raised eyebrow. "He did not know that. And he abandoned his mission."

I bit my tongue to avoid saying something that I knew I'd regret, but I still glared at him.

McNab saved me.

"Abandoned?" he drawled. "More like… postponed. We did get to Harrisburg as ordered. Eventually."

Captain Mercer's head snapped around and he rose up in his saddle, but then slowly sank back down.

"That you did," he said. "That you did."

His face was still stern and I didn't quite know what to say. Apparently the Captain had a different opinion of what mattered than I did. I decided I could ask about the High Thrall another time.

Instead, we rode without talking for some time. Maybe a half hour later, one of the scouts came riding back to us, but more at a trot than a gallop. He reported a cluster of farmhouses up ahead, so once again, the company left the road and worked our way through the trees and the dense undergrowth so as not to be seen.

It was slow going. The bushes were thick and too many of the trees clustered together, forming impassible walls to a horse. After a bit, we dismounted and led the horses at a walk, weaving them around the tight spots. McNab took the lead, his rifle out.

I kept brushing the sweat off my brow. I also kept jumping every time a squirrel shot across a branch or a bird took wing. The rattling of the branches unnerved me. My head was starting to throb and I was starting to see dark shapes behind every tree.

And then I did.

I pulled up short and stared across a small gap where a large elm had fallen and created a mini-clearing. Something big moved behind another elm. No, *someone*, I realized.

I snapped my rifle to my shoulder, but he dashed off back into the trees before I could get a clean look.

"What was it?" Captain Mercer said as he came to my side.

"Someone saw us," I said.

"Jotun?"

I shook my head. "Too small. Human, but I didn't get a good look after that. Could be a farmer out hunting."

"Or worse," he said dourly. He shook his head and frowned. "Well, if we've been seen, there's no point in skulking around. We're almost there. If it's a farmer, we've got nothing to lose. If it's something worse, we need speed now instead of stealth."

He wasn't asking my opinion, but I nodded nonetheless.

"Sergeant-Major!" Captain Mercer called. "New orders. We approach the farms!"

McNab waved in acknowledgement and began working his way toward the buildings we'd been trying to skirt not an hour before.

We left the woods and emerged into a surprisingly lush field of corn. The stalks stood shoulder-high to the horses and waved gently in the light breeze. I could see hints of golden ears peeking out wherever I looked. We rode single file through the sea of green because McNab didn't want to trample any of the farmers' crops.

The corn gave way to a garden, with tomatoes and carrots and other vegetables. They ran all the way to the edge of the farmhouse and barn.

Where three Negroes stood, armed and waiting for us.

All three wore dusty overalls over wool shirts and straw hats. The older one in the middle held an old Springfield rifle across his chest, not threateningly, but with familiarity. The burly one on the left also carried a Springfield, but held it down. He glared at us. The young skinny one on the right clutched a drawn saber at his side. He twitched as he stood there.

Captain Mercer, at the head of the line, stopped his horse a respectful distance away and gave a signal for the rest of us to wait.

"Who are you?" the older one demanded. "What do you want?"

"Just passing through," Captain Mercer said casually. He gestured at their rifles. "You get your powder for those from Nickajack?"

"And what if we did?" the Negro demanded.

Captain Mercer leaned forward on his saddle and smiled. "Then we have much to talk about." He turned his head. "Sergeant Freeman!"

The men's eyes widened as Jeremiah rode up. Their eyes darted all over, taking in his horse and his rifle and his uniform.

"Much to talk about," Captain Mercer repeated.

"Yes...," the older Negro drawled. "Perhaps we do. Inside, though." He gave Jeremiah a curious look. "Just you and the sergeant."

"Fair enough," Captain Mercer said. "Sergeant-Major," he said to McNab, "post some sentries. Then see how our men can best help these good folks with their farm." He slipped off his horse as McNab started giving orders. Then he and Jeremiah followed the men into their cabin.

Once we'd gotten the sentries posted and the horses taken care of,

McNab set us to work harvesting corn. It looked so delicious, I wasn't the only one tempted to sneak a bite, but McNab said anyone who stole from the farmers would get whipped. Not even the Big Buffoon, Private Forrest, wanted to take that chance.

We worked for a couple of hours before Captain Mercer and the others emerged. The farmers hurried toward the barn and a few minutes later, three children spilled out of the cabin and followed them. Jeremiah ambled after them. Captain Mercer looked around at the rest of us. His expression was grim, but there was a glint of satisfaction in his eyes. McNab and I were nearby, so he summoned us over.

"They had much to say about Nickajack," he said. "But at a price. We have agreed to help them get to Louisville."

"What kind of help?" McNab asked.

"We help them load their wagons," Captain Mercer said. "They'll pretend to be on their way to sell their crop until they get close. But they want guards, so Sergeant Freeman and three men will accompany them on the road."

"So we'll be down four," McNab said sourly.

"It is unfortunate," Captain Mercer said. "But necessary. They will give us a complete report on the defenses of the cave."

McNab nodded. That report could save far more than four lives.

"Tell the men to load one wagon with corn," Captain Mercer added. "They'll take that with them as part of their disguise. Our men can eat the rest."

"They'll appreciate that," McNab said. "May I...?"

"Dismissed," Captain Mercer said with a quick salute. "You too, Lieutenant," he said to me. "We have much to do."

———

We spent the rest of the afternoon helping the Negro farmer families get packed. We did take a break to enjoy some of the sweet, sweet corn, after it'd been boiled in a huge pot, along with some chickens the farmers decided not to take. I couldn't remember having such a wonderful meal, sitting in the shade of the old barn, wolfing down fresh food. It was gonna make the hardtack the next day taste horrible in comparison, but it was worth it.

Jeremiah decided to take Joe Johnson with him, along with two men from Second Squadron with dark complexions. With some dirt on their hands and faces, they could pass for Negro if no one got too close. One of the men was indignant, until Jeremiah talked quietly with him. He didn't look happy after, but he nodded and agreed. He threw his own rucksack in one of the wagons before going into the cabin to help some more.

"What'd you tell him?" I asked Jeremiah when we had a break in the wagon packing.

"That he could pretend to be a Negro and come with us," Jeremiah said, "in which case he'd almost certainly live to return to Chicago, or he could go on Captain Mercer's suicide mission."

"You really think it's a suicide mission?" I asked, though in my gut I knew the answer.

"Only if it needs to be," Jeremiah said with a dour frown. "You need to make sure it's not, you hear?"

"Well," I joked, "I have to. How are you going to get the notes for your next book if I don't take them?"

He laughed. "Who says I'm going to write a book about this?"

I was about to say, "Of course you are," but then I remembered he'd never written about New Orleans or The Battle of Golden City, so I just gave him a knowing nod.

"Just stay safe," he said. Then he turned somber. "And get rid of that gunpowder."

"We will," I said solemnly. "Count on it."

Jeremiah and the Negro farmers headed off late afternoon and the rest of us were on the road in the other direction a few minutes later. Captain Mercer ordered a canter. He kept looking to the sun and scowling. The road was wide, despite the hills, with enough room for us to ride several abreast, but the pace kept us from talking.

Instead, I scanned the trees, hoping to see something through the thick leaves. Or maybe not. One of the farmers had been hunting in the woods the way we'd come and he and Captain Mercer figured I'd spotted him. I wasn't so sure. I couldn't explain why, though.

I wanted to talk about it with McNab, but he rode up front with Captain Mercer. When we finally stopped just before dusk at a stream where we could water the horses, he and the Captain fell into deep conversation.

After they'd finished, Captain Mercer had us gather around. All eighteen of us. We were a rough crew—dirty, unshaven, and smelly. Several of us had muddy uniforms and everyone looked tired. We didn't form ranks or do much more than cluster around, but the Captain didn't seem to mind.

"Men," he said once he had all our attention. "We will arrive at Nickajack Cave at midnight."

A murmur of appreciation swept through the Company, but Captain Mercer wasn't done.

"We arrive at midnight," he said, "and we attack at dawn."

TWENTY-SEVEN

CAPTAIN MERCER and I stood in the shadowy trees a thousand yards downstream from Nickajack Cave. A shallow wide creek flowed out of the mouth of the cave and down to where it joined the Tennessee River. We'd crossed the river in the night on an unguarded narrow footbridge the farmers had told us about, and then followed a dirt road down to the cave itself.

So now we nestled in the shadows under a moonlit sky. We were well away from the creek ourselves, but the burble and tumble still soothed our ears. The night smelled of greenery and flowers I couldn't identify, which added to the false sense of tranquility.

I stifled a yawn. We'd ridden long into the night, longer than I thought Captain Mercer had expected, before we were close enough to set up a base camp in the woods. McNab had the others catching a few winks but Captain Mercer wanted a look at the cave himself and had insisted I come with him. My muscles ached with fatigue, and my head throbbed once again, but I made the best of it.

The mouth of the cave was huge. Easily fifty feet high and three times that wide, the blackness seemed to extend deep into the mountain. But the front was blocked by a large log barricade. It stood about fifteen feet high—short enough for a standing Jotun to look over the top of, but high enough to stop a human from climbing. Or at least climbing easily.

Like the towers we'd seen, this fortification had a large wooden door on iron hinges. More of a gate, really. It wasn't centered, but off to the side, away from the creek.

The cave burrowed into a small hill. The wall in front of it curved and ran up the slope around the sides of the cave and then appeared to close in the back. In that slope above the cave, the trees and bushes which overgrew the ground had been cut back for quite a ways, so the distant wall was visible. It wouldn't be hard to circle around and approach that wall from the far side if we wanted to.

The only Jotun sentry we could see sat cross-legged on the ground in the high space above the cave and before the far wall. He wore a leather jerkin and there appeared to be a large pile of something at his side, but it was hard to tell in the dark. I guessed they were boulders, ready to throw. He faced our direction but his head hung down, looking at something in his lap. I couldn't make out exactly what he was doing, as the deep shadows obscured the view, but it seemed to absorb his attention. For five or ten minutes he didn't look up once.

There wasn't much else around. The broad dirt road led to the gate, and it looked like there was a trash pile opposite the creek from it. If we hadn't been coming here specifically, we might've ridden on by without noticing a thing.

"I am surprised they only have one sentry," Captain Mercer said quietly. "The value of what they hold here is immense."

"Maybe there aren't that many of them," I said. "We've only encountered a few Jotun since that battle with Fifth Squadron."

He tensed at my words. "Perhaps."

That battle might not have been the best thing to remind him of.

"Do you think you could kill him?" Captain Mercer asked, returning our attention to the sentry.

"If I was closer," I said, "and if he looked up." A bullet or two through the eye was my only chance at this distance.

"It will be loud, though," he said, "and raise the alarm. We won't have much time to climb over the walls."

"Don't climb," I said. "Swim." I pointed to where the creek flowed out under the wall.

Captain Mercer's chuckle was most unsavory.

After the bare minimum of sleep, we gathered back in the woods just as the first hints of daylight streaked into the sky. Maria stayed in camp, along with Zeke. In the event of a disaster, his job was to save the horses and return to a designated point up the road where we could regroup. Maria's task, as always, was to help the wounded.

Of the remaining sixteen of us, Captain Mercer had sent five with McNab to circle around to the top of the cave. They were to scale that wall as soon as I took out the sentry, thereby giving us the high ground above anyone coming out of the cave. Captain Mercer would take the remaining eight to where the creek flowed out from under the wall as stealthily as possible. Once I killed the sentry, they'd attack.

It wasn't a great plan, but it was the best we could do. We didn't know how many Jotun were inside, or if there were any surprises. But the alternative was to wait around and watch for a day or two, and Captain Mercer had rejected that idea when McNab suggested it. He thought the odds of us being spotted were too great and we'd lose the major advantage we now held: surprise.

I didn't like it, but I had to agree. The sentry clearly hadn't been alerted to the fact that the Army of the West was nearby, or at least a part of it, or he'd be doing more than occasionally glancing around. The sooner we attacked, the more likely we'd succeed.

I'd found a decent shooting blind about five hundred yards from the wall. A small birch had a limb just the right height to rest my rifle barrel on as I sighted on the Jotun sentry. So while I watched the sentry, Captain Mercer and his squad crept forward quietly through the woods toward the wall.

Watching the sentry was easy. He wasn't moving. His head still hung low and I began to wonder if he was asleep, but he was too heavily shadowed to be sure. All I could tell now, that I couldn't earlier, was that he had a large sack at his side. But slowly, the light was beginning to fill the sky and ease its way down toward him. The first wisps glinted off the top of his head.

He was wearing a helmet we hadn't seen in the dark.

Before I could fully digest that, Captain Mercer and his men left the woods. They ran fast toward the wall and the creek. Captain Mercer's hair flowed behind him as he ran.

One of the men tripped and tumbled to the ground. He let out a curse.

The sentry's head snapped up.

His helmet had a visor. I couldn't see his eyes.

I fought down my panic—he had to see somehow!—and I fired where his eyes had to be. If I was lucky, the bullet might pass through an eye slit.

The bark of the rifle echoed off the hill. The giant leapt to his feet and stared my direction.

I fired again.

He flinched, but that was it. I must've hit the outside of his visor.

I could hear the men scrambling now, along with a few yells.

I fired again.

The Jotun roared. He reached into his sack and grabbed something in his meaty paws.

I fired again, but this time he didn't even flinch. He whipped his arm back and threw.

A shotgun blast of human-sized cannonballs flew toward me. I hurled myself to the ground and they smashed through the trees all around. Wood cracked and shrieked and branches exploded above me. Even after the cannonballs had passed, the trees seemed to sway and shudder.

And then a second round exploded through the trees. Four, six, eight!—I couldn't keep track of how many cannonballs came flying in. I kept my head down and tried not to tremble.

When the third round didn't follow immediately, I took five long breaths and looked up.

The Jotun had his back to me. He crouched facing the wall, his axe in his hand. He must've heard McNab and his men, I realized, but wasn't sure exactly where they were.

But that also meant he'd been distracted before seeing Captain Mercer's squad.

They were at the creek and the wall. Four or five stood in the water up to about their waists. One even leaned a hand on the wall itself. The others were nowhere to be seen.

They must be inside the wall, I realized. Which meant that they'd be sitting ducks if the sentry decided to unleash a volley of cannonballs at them.

My pulse raced. I scrambled back to my knees and lifted my rifle to my shoulder.

I looked at the sentry. His jerkin, helmet, and pants completely covered him from the back. His collar hid his neck. Even if my bullet made it through all that thick fabric, it wouldn't hurt him much. That's why we always aimed for their eyes. The only bare flesh I could see was his hands.

So I aimed for the one that held the axe.

I fired.

His hand jerked and he snarled.

I fired again.

He turned my way. His head scanned side to side and then he looked down, where Captain Mercer's men were. He stiffened and yelled something I didn't understand.

I fired again.

His hand jerked and he dropped the axe.

When he bent to pick it up, soldiers—our soldiers with McNab in the lead—appeared around his legs brandishing sabers. They stabbed at his ankles and knees. One slashed his hand before it could grab the axe.

He roared.

An answering roar came from inside the cave.

The sentry giant straightened up. He charged toward the soldiers and kicked a man, sending him flying. The others danced out of the way and kept stabbing him.

I couldn't get a clear shot of his hands. They were moving too fast as he swept around, trying to grab the soldiers. He managed to hit another one, sending him sprawling.

Another roar came from inside the cave.

I quickly reloaded my rifle while I watched the battle on the hill above the cave. Only three humans still stood and they circled the Jotun, who was down on one knee. The morning sun glinted off his helmet as he swiveled his head from one man to another.

Yells—human and Jotun—came from the cave beyond the wall.

I glanced at the creek. All the men were gone, presumably inside.

My pulse still pounded and my head started to ache, but I needed to join the fight. I scrambled to my feet and started jogging toward the wall. I watched the fight up top as I did.

I could make out McNab now—he'd lost his cap and his grey fringed bald head was unmistakable. He had his saber out, but also his Colt, which he fired from time to time at the Jotun's head. He'd feint like he was about to run in and then pull back when the giant turned to him.

The other two soldiers did the same—each darted in to attack when the Jotun had turned to face one of the others.

But despite being on his knees, the Jotun wasn't staying still. He was slowly edging sideways. It was almost a shuffle step, deliberate.

Toward the bag of cannonballs.

A blast of those would kill them all!

I ran forward. "The bag!" I shouted. "The bag!" I waved my arms toward McNab. He needed to hear me. He needed to stop him!

At first McNab didn't notice. I kept running toward the wall and shouting my fool head off. Yells and gunshots came from inside the wall, which made it hard for him to hear.

I was maybe fifty yards away when he finally spotted me.

"The bag!" I yelled and pointed. "The bag!"

He didn't understand and I started to panic. The Jotun had almost shuffled to it! He'd easily take out McNab and the others once he reached those cannon balls.

"The bag!" I yelled one last time. Then I skidded to a stop and raised my rifle.

The Jotun, still on his knees, stretched sideways toward the bag.

I fired at his hand.

He snapped it back with a roar of pain, but then he reached for it again.

One of the soldiers leapt forward and slashed at the giant's wrist. The Jotun smashed him with a fist and he crumpled to the ground.

I fired again, and missed.

But McNab had figured it out. While the Jotun was killing the first soldier, he and the other man charged.

And didn't stop.

They barreled straight into the giant's body, stabbing him and then tackling him. The Jotun was off balance reaching for the bag once again, so they knocked him backward.

Hard.

And all three went tumbling off the edge, off the top of the cave, down into the walled-off cave entrance below.

TWENTY-EIGHT

A LOUD THUMP interrupted the yells and shouts from the cave. I fervently hoped McNab had survived the fall. I threw my rifle back on my shoulder and ran toward the wall.

And pulled up short at the edge of the creek.

I couldn't swim.

I waded in, thinking maybe I could just duck under the wall, but I sank deeper and deeper, until the water was up to mid-thigh.

I couldn't swim.

I started breathing hard. I couldn't stop. Panic started to grab me. Dots floated in my vision.

I couldn't go in that way.

I waded back to shore and climbed out of the water. As I did, my head began to pound and my vision fuzzed. I started to feel sick, and then I realized it was my head and not my nerves. I fumbled in my pouch for Maria's poppy juice and gulped it down.

I needed to get back in the battle. I stumbled toward the large gate. It was the only other choice. But the headache raged through my skull. It had come on fast and hard and it was all I could do to not collapse in pain. As it was, I clutched my temples and started to stumble as I walked. I was in too much pain to run fast.

The sounds of battle dimmed. I barely noticed as I kept holding my head. I tried to count the seconds, the minutes, as I waited for the pain to fade. I couldn't, though. It was all I could do not to vomit.

The pain went on and on.

I finally made it to the gate. The thing was huge, but it didn't brush the ground. I knelt down to see how much space was underneath.

There might be enough space to crawl through on my belly, like a snake. But as I lay on the ground, I wasn't sure I could make the effort. I just lay there, taking deep breaths.

But finally, finally the pain began to fade. It eased into a floaty feeling. Like I was in a gentle hammock, rocking in the breeze.

I floated for quite some time.

Then I slowly crawled forward.

It took a long time, scraping my belly on the dirt, and my back on the wood. But I did it. At one point my shirt snagged on a splinter in the gate, but I was able to work it free.

After what seemed like forever, my head and shoulders came out from under the door.

"Lieutenant McCarty?"

I looked up but didn't see anyone right away.

"Lieutenant McCarty, are you hurt?"

I blinked and twisted around until I could see the speaker off to the side. It was a thin kid from First Squadron named Private Schneider, if I remembered correctly. He stood a few feet away, his eyes full of concern.

I groaned and extended a hand. He came over and helped pull me the rest of the way out.

"Are you injured?" he asked.

"It's my old injury," I said. I squeezed my eyes shut and rubbed my temples. "Is it over? Did we win?"

"For now, sir." He immediately turned to a set of ropes and pulleys that hung near the side of the gate. "We think these will open the door. I'm supposed to fetch Nurse Maria."

I nodded and waved him on. "Go then."

He started pulling on the ropes, and the huge gate slowly swung outward.

I didn't quite have my balance, but I was able to stand. I watched as Private Schneider tied off the ropes as soon as the gate was open wide. He gave me a questioning look, and after I gestured, took off at a run through the opening.

I turned to survey the rest of the courtyard.

What I saw was a horror. Three sprawled Jotun corpses took up most of the space between the wall and the cave entrance proper. Blood splatters covered everything, and now the rank smell of spilled guts flooded my nose.

Private Forrest, whom I still thought of as the Big Buffoon, knelt over the body of a Negro dressed in work clothes. He gave me a glance and then returned to rifling through the man's pockets.

Just inside the entrance to the cave, Captain Mercer knelt next to one of our soldiers. His head was bent and he held the man's hand. He said a few things, too quiet for me to hear.

Then he reached down and closed the man's eyes.

I quickly glanced around. Captain Mercer and Private Forrest were the only people moving. Very unsteadily, I started to walk toward Captain Mercer.

He saw me before I'd gotten halfway to him. His eyes went wide and he stood up, but faltered when he did. That's when I noticed a large bandage across his upper right arm, already soaked in blood.

"Are you hurt?" he asked me.

"No," I said. "My old injury," I tapped the side of my skull, "picked a bad time to flare up. What about you?"

He grimaced. "A Jotun nicked me. It could be worse." He gestured toward the fallen soldier he'd just left.

"I'm sorry."

He shrugged me off, but then grimaced in pain. "It was a tough fight. And it's not over, unfortunately."

"Not over?" I gasped. My head started to swim once again.

"When the outcome became clear, their survivors retreated. At least two Jotun and several Negroes fled into the cave. I have two men stationed inside as sentries."

"Two men?" I quickly did the math. "There's only eight of us left, counting Maria?"

"We also have two wounded, Private Dandridge and the Sergeant-Major."

I let out a deep breath. McNab was alive!

"How is he?" I asked.

Instead of answering, Captain Mercer just gestured for me to follow him.

We rounded one of the Jotun bodies that lay on its face. As we did, I saw more bodies of our men, sprawled like discarded dolls on some child's floor. Two other Negro men also lay among our dead, both flat on their back, completely lifeless.

The second Jotun corpse was the sentry's. Its head twisted awkwardly, and I realized it must've broken its neck in the fall, though there was plenty of blood pooling around its knees and hands.

Off to its side, McNab was stretched out on his back with his feet propped up on a folded coat. He turned his head when he heard us coming. His face was pale white and at first his eyes were vacant, but then they focused on me and he managed a pained smile.

"His arm's broken," Captain Mercer said. "He might be bleeding in his gut, too."

I sucked in my breath. That was bad, if he was. Real bad.

"Maria will know what to do," I said.

"If there's anything she *can* do," Captain Mercer murmured.

I forced my best smile on and knelt next to McNab. "How are you doing?"

"Hurts." His gritted teeth showed how much pain he was in.

"Well, next time don't fall with him," I joked, hoping to lighten the mood.

"The Jotun broke his fall," Captain Mercer said. He glanced up at the top of the cave, five times the Jotun's height. "He's lucky to be alive."

"Can't. Kill. Me," McNab spit out. "Too. Stubborn."

Captain Mercer laughed, deep and loud and full. He only winced once. "Yes," he said, as he looked from McNab to me and back, "yes, that's us. Too stubborn to die."

I snorted in soft agreement.

By the time Maria and Zeke arrived, along with Private Schneider and all our horses, my head had begun to clear. The sun had risen far enough to peek over the top of the wall. A few clouds drifted by and if you could ignore the bodies, it promised to be a nice day.

The cave itself was impressive—the roof of the front chamber stretched forever above us, into shadows where it looked like bats might be roosting. Despite being filled with mining equipment, leeching vats, and ovens, the entrance was so wide it felt like a castle courtyard. A few oil lamps flickered in stands here and there, some distant enough to be pinpricks in the back of the cave. On the way down, Captain Mercer had said the cave went for miles underground, and I could believe it.

Some of the equipment spilled out into the courtyard and surrounded a set of tents and lean-to's off to one side. It looked like there'd once been a small cabin there, but the roof and front wall were long gone. Instead, the cluster of tents and lean-to's looked like one of our camps that had been sitting for months instead of a day.

I couldn't imagine living with the Jotun the way these Negroes must've had to. At least in the cities and towns we'd passed, the humans could be on their own.

I helped Private Forrest gather our dead. We laid them out on the cave floor, about ten yards inside, next to some large wooden bins full of gunpowder bags. Each time we did, we'd check for personal items that they might want returned, and then Captain Mercer would say a few words and a prayer. Captain Mercer had Zeke get the horses settled by the gate while Maria checked on McNab. A few minutes later, she told us that he was not bleeding inside, which made us all a little relieved.

The other wounded soldier, Private Dandridge, was one of Forrest's buddies who hadn't wanted to give up his equipment after we'd crossed the Missouri, all those weeks ago. He had a crushed leg and Maria said it would have to be amputated. We made him comfortable under some blankets inside the coolness of the cave and Maria gave him some poppy juice, but he spent most of his time just staring at the wall.

After we'd finished laying out our dead, Zeke came and joined us. He looked somber and muttered a few words of prayer under his breath.

"Where we gonna bury them, sir?" he asked.

"No sir," Captain Mercer said. "We're still undercover. As for burying them, we won't." He pointed to the gunpowder. "We'll give them a Viking funeral."

"You sure about that?" Zeke asked with obvious worry in his eyes.

Captain Mercer gestured toward the equipment scattered around the cave. "We have to destroy all this—the leeching vats, the potash ovens, everything we can. We must do it before more Jotun arrive. This is the fastest way."

"Won't it collapse the cave?" I asked.

"Not likely," he said. "But if it does, what of it? It would only make their effort to start again more difficult."

"What about the others?" Zeke asked. He pointed toward the cave's depths. "Back there? Will they be trapped?"

"Perhaps," Captain Mercer said. "But they are either Jotun or traitors. Their fate concerns me not."

"But how do we know they're the only ones who know the secret?" I asked.

Captain Mercer looked at me sharply, and then let out a frustrated sigh. "Yes, of course." He stared down the cave and curled his lip into a grimace.

"What?" Zeke asked.

"The secret to making gunpowder is not in the equipment," Captain Mercer answered with a sweep of his hand to indicate the cave. "It is in the minds of men. We must ensure that those minds are not available to the Jotun."

"And we don't know if they're all down there," I added.

"We need prisoners," Captain Mercer said, "and those will not be easy to get." He turned to me. "Lieutenant McCarty, you will lead the attack into the cave."

TWENTY-NINE

I STOOD STILL for a handful of heartbeats, staring at my commander. Next to me, Zeke coughed and shuffled his feet. What Captain Mercer had just suggested was madness. His eyes seemed to know it, but they remained hard.

"That's crazy," I said. "There are at least two Jotun in there and only seven of us that can fight."

"So says the man who singlehandedly killed five Jotun." His eyes remained hard.

"I was lucky."

"Does that matter? You accomplished your mission."

"Yeah, but—"

"I cannot lead the attack." He tilted his head toward his bandaged arm. "I can barely shoot. You *must* do this. Or we risk failure of our mission."

I bit my lip as my eyes lingered on his wound. It was higher up his arm than the one Cassidy had sustained, right before our final charge. The one that would've killed Cassidy if…

…if I hadn't done it with the knife.

I couldn't stop from shuddering.

Captain Mercer misunderstood. "Yes," he said, "it will be a diffi-cult battle. They will be watching, and there will be no cover as you approach, but it must be done. If Joshua Turner is not among either the men in the cave or the dead, we must find him."

Reluctantly, I nodded. We could blow up the cave entrance, and maybe even collapse the cave, though I doubted it, and all would be for nothing if they could just start making gunpowder again.

All the deaths on the raid. All of our men, lost. For nothing, if we didn't finish this last step.

I didn't see any way out of it.

"Go talk to our sentries," Captain Mercer said. He pointed up the cave. "At least learn what's going on."

That made sense. I nodded and gestured for Zeke to come with me.

The huge maw of the tunnel went on for maybe a hundred yards before it doglegged left. The creek had broadened and filled most of the right side, and I was sure it had deep pools underneath the slow-flowing surface. Two oil lamps hung at the turn, but their flickering light barely reached the water.

Our men were a mere two hundred feet further in. One sat on an old crate and faced upstream with his rifle clutched in his hands. I searched my memory for a name: Private Williams, of First Squadron. He wore a particularly fancy black mustache and waxed the ends. It drooped pretty badly and looked frayed when he turned his head and gave us a weary glance.

The other soldier, Private... MacDonald...yeah, MacDonald, a burly dark-haired Scotsman, sat on a similar crate about twenty feet away. He faced a smaller slot in the rock wall that could've been a wide human-sized entrance, if it'd had a door.

I immediately grasped the dilemma.

Private Williams was closer, so Zeke and I headed over to him. His face brightened when he saw me.

"You're alive!" he said. "You made it!"

I blinked in surprise. "You were worried?"

"The hero of Louisville?" he said, "with you, we have a chance."

"With the Lord on our side," Zeke said, "we cannot fail."

Williams swallowed and gave Zeke a desperate look. "Pardon me, and I don't mean to blaspheme, but I'd rather have him." He jerked his thumb at me. "We don't know what the Lord's plans are."

"The Lord does move in mysterious ways," Zeke agreed, "but he is on the side of justice and righteousness."

"But are we?" Williams muttered, before looking away.

I sensed Zeke's discomfort and decided to jump in. "So," I said, "where are the Jotun?"

"Up that way," he said. He pointed across the stream, where the high cave continued. "But there might be some Negroes in there." He indicated the entry that Private MacDonald guarded.

"Did you see any go in?"

"No, sir. But we went in a little ways and it looks like it twists and forks. It'd be easy to hide in there."

That was a problem. I was sure the Negroes knew every inch of those tunnels and it'd be easy to ambush us in such tight quarters. I didn't know how we could get them out except to wait 'em out. Captain Mercer might, though.

The high cave was easier. I wasn't worried about Jotun springing out at us because there wasn't anywhere to spring out of. True, the cave might fork a ways down, but I had my doubts. Surely a cave this big couldn't stay big forever.

"So what do we do?" Zeke asked.

"We go back and get Forrest and Schneider," I replied. "Then we five," I included Williams with a look, "follow the Jotun."

I thought hard about our task as Zeke and I walked back to the cave entrance. I had no idea how we were going to sneak up on the Jotun in a cave like this. While there wasn't anywhere for them to hide, there wasn't much cover for us either.

When we arrived at the entrance, I had to blink several times as my eyes adjusted to the bright morning sunshine. The stench of the Jotun bodies still filled the air, and flies clouded thick around the corpses.

They didn't seem to bother Forrest, though. He stood at the side of the nearest one, sawing through its belt pouch straps with his saber.

My mouth was dry, so I undid my canteen and took a long drag. We couldn't wait the Jotun out, I realized. They had plenty of water and could probably go without food long enough to wait for reinforcements to arrive.

Though we had no idea when that might be.

I spotted Maria tending to McNab off near where Private Dandridge lay. Dandridge looked like he hadn't moved—still on his back, still facing the wall. McNab looked better. He sat with his back against the cave wall as she mixed something in a bowl nearby. He was still pale, but his arm was wrapped in a splint and a sling. He gave me an exhausted smile when he saw me.

"You're right. You're too stubborn to die," I teased as I walked over. Zeke trailed in my wake, but he chuckled as well.

"I just wish I was too stubborn to hurt," McNab shot back. "Thank God for Maria, though. She's a miracle worker."

"We are blessed," Zeke said, "truly."

"Amen," I added. When McNab raised his eyebrows I said, "Her poppy juice has kept me alive."

"It's all gone now." Maria said. She looked at me regretfully.

My chest tightened. How was I going to survive the headaches without it?

I forced myself to take a deep breath. They were just headaches. Yeah, I wanted to curl into a ball and sob when they hit, but it could be worse.

I looked at Dandridge. Maria had changed his bandages and the tourniquet, but it was clear. He'd lose his leg below the knee.

Yeah, it could be much worse.

I turned my attention back to McNab. "I'd like your advice on something." I filled him in on the situation with the Jotun in the cave, some of which he already knew. "You've fought more Jotun than me. What do you suggest?"

He shook his head. "Sorry, Billy. Cassidy always came up with the plans. I just made sure we had everything we needed."

I nodded. That was how the books always went. Cassidy was the hero who always came up with the plan. Too bad we didn't have a hero.

I grimaced. The words "The Hero of Louisville" immediately came to mind. I still didn't like the name, but I knew what it meant. It was my job to come up with a plan. Just like Captain Mercer had ordered.

"Well, you get better, you hear?" I told McNab.

He chuckled. "Go finish this so we can go home."

We exchanged a smile and then I turned and went looking for Captain Mercer. Zeke demurred, saying he wanted to talk to Maria.

As I walked I had to admit to myself that I wasn't sure at all how we were going to fight the Jotun back up in the cave. I doubted they'd gone back far enough for the cave to narrow in and make it hard for them to fight. They'd have picked the best place to defend.

We couldn't wait them out either. Even if they didn't like the dark, they had plenty of water. It could be days before hunger drove them to try and break out, and in days someone else could come visit.

That was the big worry, I realized. We didn't know when more Jotun would show up looking for their shipment of gunpowder and discover us. We could have weeks, but we could only have hours. There were far too few of us to put up much of a defense, especially if we had giants in the cave as well as outside the wall.

This was a raid, not an occupation. We needed to get the job done and get out quick.

I found Captain Mercer at a table under one of the lean-to's. The sun had risen further and the clouds scattered to the distance, which made it bright outside but dark where he stood. He was hunched over, looking at some papers, and seemed to be scowling.

"What are these?" I asked.

"Shipping records," he said. He riffled through the corners. "They appear complete."

"Shipping?" I said. "You mean—"

"Yes," he said. "Records of every place they have shipped gunpowder. Which will tell us everywhere they have, or at least had, cannons."

My eyes widened at the implications.

Captain Mercer saw my expression and returned a grim nod. "We need to get these to General Sanborn."

"After we destroy everything here," I said. "And deal with the remaining Jotun."

"And the traitor Negroes assisting them," he replied. "We must *not* forget them."

I swallowed hard. I hadn't forgotten them, but I didn't like the idea of killing them either. What if they weren't traitors but slaves, forced into working for the Jotun?

Slaves didn't deserve to die.

I wasn't sure human traitors did either. The blacksmith back in Louisville had been a traitor, sort of. Did he deserve to die? The farmers we'd passed certainly didn't, but they'd grown food for the Jotun. And I still had my misgivings about the merchant Captain Mercer had shot.

Captain Mercer interrupted my thoughts. "Do you have a plan yet?"

"No," I said with a shake of my head. "It's too big of a cave. There's no way to sneak up on them or surprise them. We can't wait them out either."

"No," he said, "we cannot." He grabbed a piece of paper sitting to the side of the stack he'd been flipping through. "This letter is from Baltimore and requests fifty bags of gunpowder." He almost crumpled it in his hand. "They will be here to collect the order in three days."

I actually let out a long sigh of relief. Three days was a long time.

"Presuming they are not early," Captain Mercer added.

The tension raced right back into my body.

"I..." I hesitated, not sure I wanted to say what I was thinking. But I had to. "I don't see how we can do it. The odds aren't good."

"The odds were worse when you killed the cannoneers in Louisville," he said. He tilted his head toward his wounded arm. "I can't shoot. You can."

I dismissed him with a wave as I stared into space, thinking. "I didn't shoot the cannoneers," I said. "I—"

I stared at him.

"Gunpowder bombs," I said. "We make gunpowder bombs."

Captain Mercer's eyes lit up and he nodded. "Yes… yes, we do."

THIRTY

WE SCOURED the area for things we could make bombs out of. The gunpowder was easy—we had the large bin holding bags of various weights. The casings were harder. We wanted something that would hold the powder so it exploded instead of just burned. Captain Mercer also wanted something that would give off shrapnel so as to increase the chance of penetrating the Jotuns' tough skin. I wanted something we could throw a long ways, since I didn't want to have that shrapnel flying anywhere near me or our men.

We ransacked the tents and the stoves where they made the potash. Zeke found a stack of iron pots the right size and Private Schneider found some cord we could use for fuses.

"Use some of the cord to tie two pots together," Captain Mercer instructed, once we'd pulled them all together, "with the gunpowder in between."

I nodded. It'd be harder to throw, but more likely to explode the way we wanted.

We assembled the first one and Zeke gave it a practice toss. He was only able to heave it about fifteen feet. He tried again with similar results.

"Maybe someone else?" he asked.

I shook my head. "You and Private Forrest are the biggest men here. I doubt he could do better."

"Where is Private Forrest?" Captain Mercer asked. Schneider was cutting cord to tie the pots and Maria was tending the wounded. Williams and MacDonald were still guarding the cave. So everyone was accounted for except Forrest.

Captain Mercer cocked his head and frowned. Then he looked at Zeke. "Private, please keep assembling bombs." The Captain gestured for me to follow as he marched out of the cave.

We found Private Forrest among the horses. He was furiously stuffing something into one of the saddlebags of one of the spares and looked up guiltily as we approached.

"What are you doing, Private?" Captain Mercer snapped as we strode up.

Forrest's eyes narrowed as he glanced from the Captain to me. His hands drifted down to hover over his guns.

Captain Mercer ignored him. With his good hand, the Captain flipped open the saddlebag Private Forrest had been messing with and thrust his hand in. Cold fury filled his face as he pulled a fistful of coins out.

"They don't need 'em," Forrest said. "The bastards are dead. So why shouldn't we take 'em?"

Captain Mercer let the coins trickle between his fingers back into the bag. His eyes remained fixed on the gleaming metal as they fell. "Some of this," he said coldly, "is from *our* men." He glared at Forrest. "You're stealing from our dead."

"They don't need it either," he said defiantly. He gestured at the horses around him. "We have plenty of mounts. We should take everything that we can." He shuffled nervously. "Not for me. For all of us."

He had a bit of a point, I realized. We now had three horses for every survivor.

But Captain Mercer wasn't buying it. He glared at Forrest, his eyes like fire. "We do not steal from our own." His voice was cold and precise, a knife through the air.

Forrest stepped back, his eyes wide with fear. "Wasn't stealing! Just saving it!"

"Maybe *you* should throw the bombs at the Jotun," Captain Mercer said.

The image of Forrest carrying one of our bombs into the cave quickly flitted through my mind, and I smiled at the thought before the guilt kicked in. Forrest might be a horrible person, but he didn't deserve to die for what he'd done.

No human did.

Captain Mercer continued to glare at Forrest, who was having a very hard time not reaching for his revolver. The horses around us must've sensed the tension. They shuffled in place, and a few snorted.

That's when the idea hit me.

"Captain…," I said, "I think I know how we can deliver the bombs…"

As we crept deeper into the cave, my stomach tied itself into knots. I hated the idea I'd come up with, even though Captain Mercer had loved it. I wasn't sure the other men liked it either, and Zeke kept muttering prayers requesting forgiveness under his breath.

We'd had enough kettles to build eight bombs. We'd tied them four apiece to the backs of two horses. The extra long fuses hung down their sides, and Captain Mercer had insisted we have redundant strings, in case one went out after being lit.

The plan was to get close enough to figure out where the Jotun were, light the fuses, and spur the horses forward. They'd carry the bombs close to the Jotun before they exploded. Then with the Jotun dead, we could hopefully capture some of the humans.

So much could go wrong. The horses could spook or run the wrong way. The bombs might not go off when they were supposed to. We might not see the Jotun in time. And even if we succeeded, the horses would die.

I didn't like that. Not one bit. Guilt flowed through my heart whenever I looked over at them in the flickering torchlight.

But better horses than humans.

Captain Mercer had said it was necessary for the mission. I just hadn't been able to come up with anything else.

So we all set off—me and Zeke in the lead, then the horses, then Schneider, Williams, Forrest, and Captain Mercer bringing up the rear. He said I was still in command and he was just along if there was an emergency, but I noticed that his hand never strayed far from his Colt and his eyes constantly flitted to Forrest.

Captain Mercer didn't trust him, that was clear.

We had to cross the stream in the cave as it meandered from the right side to the left. At about the middle, where it was widest and shallowest, a footbridge just wide enough for the horses still stood. It didn't have any rails and so I was a bit nervous as I walked ahead of the beasts. Fortunately, the cave ahead was straight and clear and empty as best as we could tell by the flickering light of our torches.

I worried about those torches. We needed the light to see where we were going, but it also warned whoever was ahead that we were on our way. Still, we made it to where the stream crossed back across the cave once again without hearing or seeing any giants. A few bats squeaked far above us but that was about it.

After about four hundred feet, the stream wandered back across the cave and we had to cross it again. Once again, there was a narrow bridge. This time Private Schneider and Zeke took the lead, moving slowly. The light cast by the torches of the men in back gave them long dim shadows. As they crossed, I stood to the side and waited for Captain Mercer.

I pointed at the bridge when he arrived. "They didn't destroy it."

"There must not be another exit from the cave," he said.

"Too bad we can't wait 'em out."

He nodded in agreement. But then it was our turn to cross the bridge.

Beyond the second crossing, the cave curved gently to the left with the stream on our right. Zeke crept right up along the rock wall, with the rest of us strung out behind him. As he got close to the curve, he paused. Then he looked back and motioned for me to come up.

As I did, it became clear what he'd seen.

Light.

From torches or lamps, the light flickered around the corner from ahead of us. It was dim, but unmistakeable. Apparently the Negroes or Jotun had gotten as sick of the pitch black as we had.

The problem was, I didn't see how we could sneak up on them. As soon as we rounded the bend, they'd see us. The bend was too curved to peek around without being seen, either. We didn't know how far away they were, which made it impossible to just light the fuses and send the horses ahead.

I took a deep breath. My skin felt hot and clammy, but my head didn't ache, at least.

I glanced back. Zeke was only a few feet behind me, pressed against the wall. Then about ten feet behind him, Schneider held the horses, who shuffled and swung their heads from side to side. The rest of the men were strung out behind that, all pressed to the wall, with Captain Mercer bringing up the rear. Except for the Captain, they all stood tense, their eyes on me or darting around.

I took another deep breath. It was up to me.

I unshouldered my Whitworth and handed it to Zeke. His eyes went wide.

"What're you doing?" he whispered.

"If I'm unarmed, maybe they won't shoot me." I unbuckled my gun belt and handed that to him as well.

"And if they do shoot you?"

"You shoot 'em back."

His face soured. "You know I don't shoot good."

I shrugged and gave him a looney grin. That way he couldn't see my legs shaking. Then I turned, took a deep breath, and stepped into the light.

No one shot at me.

After the gentle curve, the cave stretched ahead another four hundred feet or more before it split into smaller left and right caverns. The creek once again meandered across it, about two hundred feet in front of me. Lanterns flickered at the split in the caves—one hanging on the wall just inside each branch.

Two Jotun sat on the ground on the far side of the creek, in front of the right-hand cavern. They leaned against the right side wall and were talking with each other in low voices.

One of them was a boy!

At least I assumed he was. His body was half the size of the Jotun next to him. He had blond hair that hung to his cheeks, but not to his shoulders like most Jotun. He also lacked a beard and had a boyish face. He wore a tunic and short breeches and boots, but didn't carry a sword or axe, at least that I could see.

The adult Jotun had a full blond mane of hair and a beard, but his beard was soaked in blood. So was one shoulder and one knee. He held his right hand in his lap though an axe rested against the wall not too far away.

"Who are you?"

My attention snapped to a burly Negro in dungarees I hadn't noticed before. He stood at the entrance to the left cave branch with a rifle on his shoulder.

A rifle pointed at me.

"I said, who are you?" he loudly yelled again.

Both the Jotun had turned to look at me with wide eyes. The adult one put his arm around the boy's shoulders.

"Army of the West!" I shouted back. "I'm unarmed. May I approach?"

The Negro seemed to hesitate for a moment. Then he called out, "As far as the creek."

I slowly started walking forward. The creek was tens of feet away with about fifty feet of cave on the other side. The Negro came forward too, but he kept his rifle pointed at me.

Two more Negro men appeared out of the shadows of the left-hand cave branch. One held a pistol, the other a saber. They stood tense and watched me.

Sweat beaded on my brow as I slowly, steadily walked forward. I held my hands out to show I wasn't holding anything, but I desperately hoped Zeke or, even better, Captain Mercer, had my back.

It took an age or a week or several minutes to get to the edge of the creek. This time, there wasn't a bridge—just a rowboat pulled up on the far side. I paused a few feet back from the edge.

So did the Negro with the rifle. He was about twenty feet away now, and I could make out the bulge of his muscles and the steely glare in his eyes.

"What do you want?" he snarled.

I took a deep breath. "You could start by lowering the rifle."

He took an eon of a moment, and then did.

"Why'd you attack us?" he asked.

"We didn't attack you," I said. "We attacked them." I pointed at the Jotun, without taking my eyes from the Negro's.

He scowled.

"We're here to rescue you," I said. "To save you."

"No," he spat. "What you've done is condemn us all to death."

THIRTY-ONE

WE STOOD there and stared at each other across the creek. The light from the lanterns flickered. Despite the large size of the cave, it felt claustrophobic. Like the thick air was pressing in on me.

Worse, my head began to throb. Sweat beaded on my brow. I stared at the Negro across the creek and realized he was trembling a little too.

My throat was dry, but I forced out some words. "What do you mean?"

"The trolls," he growled. "Now we're helpless."

"What trolls?"

His eyes bulged. "What trolls?" he demanded.

"Yeah," I said. I did my best to look innocent. "I don't know what you're talking about."

He gaped at me. "You don't, do you?"

"I don't. What trolls?"

He looked disgusted as he shook his head. "This area's full of caves. Full of trolls. The only reason there ain't trolls in *this* cave is them." He jerked his head toward the Jotun.

I furrowed my brow and blinked. My head started to throb, which made it hard to concentrate. My eyes darted from the wounded Jotun and the boy to the Negroes in the back, to the one in front of me. They didn't act like slaves…

"They're protecting you," I said, "which is why you're working with them. You're thrall."

"Lord, no!" he said. "We are free men!" He glanced again toward the Jotun and lowered his voice. "We just have an arrangement."

I put my hand on my temple, as if pressing it could head off the pain that was growing. I wondered how best to talk to this man. Then I decided, why not try the truth?

"Look," I said firmly, "we know you're making gunpowder for the Jotun. We can't have that. We need you to stop."

"Or what? You'll kill us?"

I didn't say a thing. The silence stretched on, with only the beats of my heart to track the time.

The Negro twitched his arms. He started to raise his gun, but then lowered it again. Instead he settled for glaring at me. "I can't believe you'd kill other humans."

"I can't believe you're helping them kill us," I shot back.

"Perhaps we oughta talk," he said, "before the trolls kill us both."

I nodded. "Let me get my captain." I gestured back toward the cave entrance. Then I looked pointedly at the boat. "This side of the creek?"

"Sure," he said. "Just you and your captain. We'll only bring two. You can keep your guns. We'll have ours."

"Agreed," I said. I started to turn and go, but hesitated. I looked back over my shoulder and asked, "Can I tell my captain your name?"

"Joshua Turner. Chief of Nickajack Cave."

***

Captain Mercer and I met with Joshua Turner and his brother Samuel on the dusty ground on our side of the creek. Samuel was a burly man with thick muscular arms but a babyish face. He reminded me of Joe Johnson in the way he stood, but his eyes darted everywhere.

We stood in a small circle and at first each man had a hand on a gun, though I wasn't sure if Captain Mercer could even draw his. The flickering torchlight cast enough shadows to make it hard to read anyone's expressions, but everyone stood stiff, like their trousers were made of wood.

My headache continued to grow. It hadn't risen to the crippling level of earlier, yet, but I still had to concentrate to hear what was said. At first it didn't matter but after a few words of introduction and general comments, Captain Mercer was the one to get down to business.

"We're here," he said, "because your gunpowder is being used to kill our men."

"I am sorry for that," Joshua Turner said. "We did what we had to in order to survive."

"Survive the Jotun?"

"More the trolls. They're far more dangerous."

"Huh?" I said. "Jotun are bigger and better fighters."

"But the Jotun don't want to kill us every chance they can." Joshua turned back to Captain Mercer. "We started making gunpowder so we could fight off the troll packs. Those died down when the Jotun settled the area, but about a year ago the raids started again. They were worse —bigger and more determined."

"They knew you had gunpowder," Captain Mercer mused.

"Why would they want it?" I asked.

"Some trolls have figured out how to use human weapons," he explained. "Not well, thankfully. But if they knew it was here…"

"Exactly," Joshua Turner said. "They wanted it, and then the Jotun learned of it and they wanted it too."

"So you gave it to them in exchange for protection," Captain Mercer said.

"More… of a trade," Joshua Turner answered. "They stationed a small squadron here to protect us. We agreed to sell the gunpowder to them."

"Sell?" I asked.

"Yes, sell," Samuel Turner said, in a voice so deep it sounded like a cavern.

Captain Mercer dismissed the aside with a wave. "I'm more interested in the size of the squadron."

"There were eight until a week ago," Joshua Turner said. "They left four and the boy." He nodded toward the remaining Jotun.

"Any new ones expected?" Captain Mercer asked.

"No way to know," Joshua said with a shrug. Then he grew stern. "But if the trolls know what happened today, they'll be here tonight. In the hundreds."

My gut dropped. Somehow, the throb in my head jumped a notch as well.

"I... I think they do," I said. "I think I saw one in the woods the other day, following us. I'm not quite sure."

Joshua let out a long breath and shook his head in dismay.

"So perhaps we need to set aside our differences," Captain Mercer said.

"You killed a lot of us," Samuel Turner growled.

"Quiet," Joshua Turner said to his brother. "There's time for *that* later." The emphasis was slight, but I didn't miss it. A quick glance at Captain Mercer confirmed he didn't miss it either.

"Well...," Captain Mercer said. His eyes narrowed as he looked at Joshua Turner. "It appears we must combine forces if we are to survive."

"Unfortunately." Joshua Turner's eyes were hard. "The trolls will be here soon."

"How many of you remain?" Captain Mercer asked.

"Fighting men? Four, not counting the Jotun. Plus six women and children."

Oh, Lord. My gut dropped even more. Women and children? I glanced toward the Jotun once again, where the adult still held a comforting arm around the boy. Were they father and son? I had no way of knowing.

"Not enough to defend the cave." Captain Mercer waited for Joshua Turner to nod in agreement. Then he continued, "Any others? Traveling or over in Chattanooga?"

Joshua Turner shook his head. "We're all here. All that's left."

"We should have enough spare horses then," Captain Mercer said.

"We won't get far on horseback," Joshua Turner said grimly. "They'll run us down."

"Why?" I asked.

"Horses tire faster than trolls," Captain Mercer explained. "We'd have to hope they gave up first."

"We could use the boat," Joshua Turner said to his brother. "We might not all fit…"

"What boat?" Captain Mercer said quickly.

Joshua and Samuel exchanged a long look. After a bit, Joshua nodded. Samuel turned to us.

"This creek flows down to the Tennessee River," he said. "We have a boat tied up there, hidden under some trees. It's not far, but the boat's not that large."

"How many can it hold?" Captain Mercer asked.

"Ten," Samuel said. "Enough for the women and children and a couple more."

I shifted uncomfortably and looked at Captain Mercer. He frowned, and then finally nodded. "All we have to do is get far enough out into the river to be safe." When he saw the questioning look on my face, he added, "Trolls can't swim. They're too dense. They'd have to run back to the bridge."

"Don't cross the river," Joshua Turner said. "Sail down it."

That made Mercer's eyebrows rise. He pursed his lips for a moment and then nodded. "Very well. Gather your people. We'll meet you at the entrance."

We all nodded and then turned and went our separate ways.

Captain Mercer set a fast pace as we strode back toward our men. I had to almost run to keep up with his longer legs. It didn't do my head any good, but I did my best to soldier on.

Finally he slowed enough for me to catch my breath. He still looked grim.

"So how do we escape the trolls?" I asked.

"We don't." Then he paused, both in his stride and his words. "We might. But that is a worry for later. We finish our mission first."

"Destroy the equipment," I said.

"Yes." He sped up his pace once again.

We gathered our men and the horses with a few quick words. Captain Mercer sent Private Schneider ahead and told him to get on the wall and look for trolls. The rest of us kept a steadier, slightly slower pace. We didn't want to jostle the gunpowder bombs too much.

For me, I also had to walk slower because the head pain had continued to grow. My vision almost seemed blurry at times, but it could've been the low light. It fragmented my thoughts and made it hard to concentrate, which wouldn't be good. I drank some water and wished for Maria's poppy juice.

Which made me think of something I wanted, almost more than anything. After we crossed the second bridge, I pulled Zeke aside so we could talk outside of Captain Mercer's hearing.

"Listen," I said, "you gotta make sure Maria and McNab get out safe. I don't think I could live with myself if they died."

He nodded. "The Lord will watch over them."

"No, not the Lord. *You*. You're the agent of the Lord here. His hands, you hear?"

He thought for a moment, but then his lips curled up at the side. "Then what are you, Billy?"

"A lost soul, Zeke. Just another lost soul, stumbling through all this."

"Yet you're blessed." He snorted softly in amusement before looking me in the eye. "The Lord watches over you... and I will watch over Maria and the Sergeant-Major. I will be the Agent of the Lord. His hands." His face went still for a moment, as if he was lost in thought. "Yes. I will watch over them."

"Thanks." I was surprised at his serious, almost reverent demeanor, but there wasn't much more that I could say.

We walked a while longer until finally we saw the light from outside. I let out huge deep breaths of relief. My mouth was cottony and while my head still pounded, the light brought hope.

Captain Mercer began giving orders. He sent Zeke and Williams to help Maria with the wounded. McDonald and Forrest ran toward the horses to get them ready. Then he turned to me.

"Lieutenant McCarty," he said, "I am loathe to use fuses to set the gunpowder off. There is too much risk they could be cut or stamped out before they achieve their aim. We cannot have come this far to fail at the last moment."

My chest froze. Was he suggesting one of us…?

"I propose instead we use an oil lamp," he said. "If we hang it above the powder, could you shoot it from a distance and break the glass, such that the burning oil dropped into the powder?"

I let out a deep breath. For a moment, visions of Cassidy's sacrifice had filled my mind.

"I might," I said. "It depends on the range and other things."

"Of course," he said with a nod. "Please set up what you believe will work. Assume you will be firing from the gate." He gestured toward it, where I saw Schneider climbing a human-sized ladder at the gate's side that I hadn't seen before, which led to a small two-person-wide platform at the top. "Quickly, please."

"Yes, sir," I said. I turned to examine the powder bunker next to all of our dead while Captain Mercer headed toward the lean-to's and his precious stacks of papers.

I saw immediately how I could run a thin plank over the bunker and set an oil lamp on it. That way I could break the glass or just knock the lamp off and either would ignite the powder. Except I didn't see a thin plank—only a couple of wider boards. They'd work, but I'd have to set the lamps on the edges of the boards and hope for the best.

I placed two of the boards across the front corners of the bunker and checked to make sure they weren't going to wobble or fall on their own. Then I carefully added two lamps to each one. Their light danced like buzzing bees eager to be free.

Then I paused and looked at our dead. So many, laid out there next to the bunker. Zeke or Captain Mercer had tried to make them presentable, with their hands folded and their eyes closed. But there was no thinking they were merely asleep. Not with the visible wounds and the blood-caked clothes. Not with the flies and the smell.

All those moments of their lives, reduced to meat.

And soon to ash.

I could only hope their souls had gone to a better place.

I wanted to cross myself like a Catholic or bow my head and say something like Zeke would, but instead I just stood there feeling awkward.

Finally I took a deep breath and headed out of the cave.

I found the others at the horses. Somehow McNab, with his broken arm, had managed to get into the saddle. He looked pale and stiff, as if he were fighting pain with every move. They'd also managed to strap Dandridge to a horse, but he looked unconscious. He flopped forward across the saddle as MacDonald stood nearby and held the reins. Captain Mercer was speaking to Zeke, but as soon as he saw me, he broke off and strode my way. As he did, he grimaced and held his wounded arm. It'd started to bleed again through the bandage.

"Is it ready?" he demanded as soon as he was close enough for me to hear.

"Yeah," I said. "I just have to shoot the lamps."

"Can you do it from here?"

I glanced back into the cave. The bunker was in the middle, just a little ways into the cave proper. From where we were standing in the middle of the courtyard, we were only about fifty yards out—an easy shot.

"Yeah," I said, "but I'd like to be farther away."

"From the gate," he said and turned to lead the way.

We moved further out until we were right up against the horses. I saw Maria was now mounted and had taken Dandridge's reins from MacDonald. She shot me a sad smile and turned back to listen to something MacDonald said. I turned and looked back at the lamps in the cave. Bright against the dark, they were still an easy target.

"From here?" Captain Mercer asked.

"Easy."

"Then do it. Blow the cave."

I blinked in surprise. "The Negroes are still in there."

"Exactly. Blow the cave."

My heart seized with horror. I turned to face him, wide-eyed. He glared at me, his eyes cold fire.

"They're... they're still in there!" I repeated.

"Yes, Lieutenant McCarty. Every *traitor* is in there. Every *human* who betrayed us by giving the Jotun gunpowder is in there. Our mission is to stop them. Blow the cave and we finish our mission. *Do it*, Lieutenant McCarty. That's an order."

"I…," I thought of the women and children. I even thought of the boy Jotun. "I… can't. I won't."

"That's an order. This is our *mission*. Blow the cave!"

"No."

He glared at me, hard and almost with hatred. He put his hand on his Colt, though he didn't draw it.

"So help me, Lieutenant, if this mission fails because of you, I will kill you with my own hands."

THIRTY-TWO

I STARED at his hardened face. His eyes didn't blink. They didn't move. They bored into me.

He'd pulled a gun on Private Forrest back when he'd refused to give up his rifle. He'd killed that thrall merchant without a second thought. He'd kill me all right.

Without a second thought.

I couldn't look away. I couldn't speak. I could barely think. All I knew was that I would not kill those people.

Not that my death would stop Captain Mercer from killing them himself.

My world expanded beyond Mercer's eyes. Cold rage filled his face. A vein on his neck throbbed in a steady beat. His arm shook, and it looked like his wound was bleeding even more, but he didn't draw his gun. I wasn't sure he could.

But the more I saw his hidden rage, the more calm flooded through me. And then I found my voice.

"I killed Cassidy," I said with measured words, "because I had to. We don't have to kill these Negroes. So I won't."

He snarled a curse and started to draw his gun. But he didn't. He glanced at his arm, where the blood was indeed seeping out through his bandage. Then his eyes met mine again. But their icy fury just flowed through me and around me like water.

I didn't flinch.

"We can't take them with us," he said. "We can't leave them. We can't let the trolls capture them. This is a *mercy*."

"No. It's murder."

"And how many of us were murdered in Louisville because of their gunpowder? How many more will die in New England, or New Orleans? They're *traitors!*"

I stared at him. I'd never seen him lose his temper like this. I didn't know what to say. There was nothing I could say, I realized. Nothing that would change his mind. Except...

"We need them, sir."

He started in surprise, but quickly recovered. "We can find the boat without them. It won't be hard."

"No," I said firmly. "For what they know. Do you trust that those records you seized are complete? What about what things the Jotun said to them? Like where they were headed besides what was on those records?"

He glared at me and relaxed his grip on his gun.

"What would General Sanborn want?" I said. "Them dead, or them telling him everything they know?"

"Damn you to Hell," he said, but without heat. He took his hand off his Colt and glared at me. "But I'll still kill them before I let the trolls or Jotun have them."

"Fair enough, sir." I didn't like it, but it bought me time to figure something else out.

He glared at me one last time before turning and looking up toward Schneider, still on his ladder looking over the gate. "Report, Private!"

"Uh... sir," he called back down. "I can't be sure, but... I think the trolls are already here."

The courtyard between the wall and the cave fell quiet with Schneider's announcement. All of our men by the horses stared at the Captain. It was so quiet, I could hear a hawk call in the distance.

Captain Mercer himself seemed frozen, but only for a few seconds. Then he started snapping out orders. "Schneider—start a count. How many are there and where? Private Forrest, Lieutenant McCarty—to the top of the cave! We can't have them getting above us. Private Williams—to me!" He strode toward the horses and the rest without looking back.

I let out a deep breath. Somehow, I hadn't noticed my headache during the confrontation, but it was back in force. I wanted to sag to the ground but didn't dare. Instead, I looked to see if there was a way up above the cave to where the Jotun sentry had sat when we'd first attacked. The slope on the near side had giant steps carved into it. I sighed in frustration at the thought of climbing them.

Forrest was already running toward them, though. I squinted and looked closer. Human-sized ladders stretched up next to them. I took off running myself. Or running as best I could. It was more of a lope as I tried to ward off the pain.

Forrest scampered up the ladders like a squirrel. I wasn't sure he even used his feet, he moved so fast. My ascent was more labored and I panted hard by the time I was at the top. My heart seized for a second when I finally crested the top and saw him with his rifle at his shoulder, but then I realized he was still looking for enemies. I moved to his side and scanned the area above the cave as well.

The top of the cave was covered with low spiny bushes and grass. A wooden log wall rose about thirty yards from the cave lip. Like the one down below, it was fifteen feet high—good for Jotun defenses. This one spanned the entire area and then ran down the slope to complete the circle around the cave entrance with the lower wall. I didn't know if the trolls could scale it with their sharp claws, but they'd be easy pickings as soon as they stuck their heads over the top.

At least until we ran out of ammunition.

"Keep watching the wall," I said to Forrest. Then I turned to survey the area in front of the cave. I could see over the lower wall from here, much like the Jotun sentry had done.

What I saw froze my soul.

The rough dirt road we'd come down to the cave now overflowed with trolls. The horde continued to spill out of the woods where they must've been hidden before. Most wore a mishmash of human clothes but some strode naked, with their thick hides shining black or deep brown in the midday sun. All were armed with swords, axes, or spears. They milled around without any order. I tried counting and that helped me calm down. There were only perhaps twenty or thirty, which still outnumbered us badly, but wasn't horrific.

Except more and more seemed to be arriving all the time.

I looked over at Forrest. He was still watching the wall behind us, here above the cave. He had his rifle out, but everything seemed calm. If there were trolls coming that way, they hadn't arrived yet.

I glanced toward our own side. Most of the men were mounted and sat on restless horses with drawn pistols. Captain Mercer stood on the ladder overlooking the wall where Schneider had been. He seemed to be studying the trolls intently.

A huge troll, maybe seven feet tall, with two huge ugly heads strode to the front of the horde. Barrel-chested, the muscles in his arms were as big as my thigh. He raised an axe and the right head roared in challenge. The left head drooled.

My heart raced at the sight of this monster.

"Humans!" It yelled. "Humans!"

Captain Mercer cupped his hands around his mouth. "What do you want?"

"We want cave! We want powder! Give it or die!"

I blinked in surprise. Trolls really did talk the way Jeremiah had written in his books.

"If we give it to you, how do we know you won't kill us anyway?" Captain Mercer yelled back.

The troll paused and lowered its axe for a moment. Then it roared and raised it again. "Give us the powder or die!"

"So much for that," I said to no one in particular, but Forrest heard me.

"Why aren't they attacking?" he asked. His eyes kept flitting between Captain Mercer and the wall we were defending.

"Not enough of them yet." I pointed at the wall. "If they come over in ones and twos, we'll pick 'em off. They need to rush a lot at once."

"Then we gotta get out first," he said. "Now!"

"I'm sure the Captain is working on it," I pointed toward Captain Mercer who was climbing down the ladder now. "I'm sure if they ride hard enough, they can get through the trolls to the boat quickly."

"Yeah, but what about *us*? How do *we* get down to the horses? They could just leave us up here!"

My chin dropped and I looked him square in the face. "You're implying…"

He puffed out his chest and met my eyes. "I don't like you, McCarty," he said, "but Mercer don't like either of us. Not after you defied him like that. You think he put us up here just to talk?"

I swallowed hard and glanced down. Captain Mercer had mounted his own horse and was pacing it back and forth in front of the others as Zeke and Williams tried to corral the riderless mounts. Captain Mercer kept looking over at the cave.

He never once looked up where we were.

"We die up here," Forrest went on, "and Captain Mercer will say it was part of the mission. Then he'll say a few nice words at our funeral, but it won't do us no good."

My chest still remained frozen. The pounding in my head went up a notch and for a moment, I almost fell to my knees in pain. I managed to pull my canteen out and take a little water and then I closed my eyes. I couldn't help thinking, would Captain Mercer really do that? Would he really send us up here to die?

I didn't think so. But Forrest was right. If we did die, he'd say it was necessary for the mission.

I didn't want to die. Not like this.

Forrest looked pale and he gripped his rifle tight. He'd long since stopped watching the wall and had his eyes fixed on our men below. He didn't want to die, either.

And, I realized, as much as I hated him, I also didn't want him to die. He was scum, but he was human. And that's what mattered.

Voices came from the cave below. The Negroes tumbled out in a group, with packs and guns and with women in their dresses and shawls carrying a couple of kids. One woman even had a baby strapped on her back Indian style.

Then the two Jotun emerged. The wounded adult clutched his arm and walked with slow strides. The boy stuck close to the adult's side. He glanced around nervously and reached for the adult's free hand. The adult took it, and they clutched each other tight.

Beyond the wall, the troll horde grew. Growling trolls loped out of the woods onto the road. Fanged trolls with long spears marched up from behind to join their mates. There'd been maybe thirty. Now there had to be fifty. They milled around until the leader ordered the spear carriers forward. They marched to the front and planted the shafts on the ground, before tilting them forward.

A wall of sharp spikes now blocked the road. We couldn't ride horses through that!

Captain Mercer had everyone mounted except for one of the Negroes—Samuel Turner, if I wasn't mistaken. He stood next to the pulleys that opened the gate with one hand on the rope. His own horse paced the ground nearby.

Captain Mercer looked up at me and Private Forrest. He made a wide gesture with his arm. "Down here! Now!"

"You can't charge!" I yelled back. I pointed over the wall. "Spears!"

He furrowed his brow in confusion.

"Spears!" I yelled again. I pointed wildly. "Spears!"

Captain Mercer paused and said something to Samuel Turner, who quickly climbed the ladder by the gate.

The pain in my head continued. I closed my eyes and took a few deep breaths. I needed to get down.

Private Forrest was already tens of feet ahead of me, racing to get to the horses. I followed as fast as I could. It wasn't fast. I barely avoided vomiting on the ladder, but grimly pressed on.

Samuel Turner yelled something down to the Captain, who dismounted himself. All the others tried to keep their horses calm as the two Jotun tentatively approached the gate. The boy still held his dad's hand as the older giant looked over the wall.

"Humans!" came the troll leader's cry. "Time is up!"

I dropped the last few feet to the ground as a swelling roar of troll battle cries echoed off the hills. They were loudest in front, but—

—also came from behind and above us.

The trolls were scaling the wall Forrest and I'd abandoned.

THIRTY-THREE

I SHOUTED AT CAPTAIN MERCER, "The bombs! The gunpowder bombs!"

His eyes went wide and then to the sides of the gate where the bombs now rested.

"Have the Jotun throw them!"

He immediately yelled orders to Williams and Schneider. Joshua Turner dismounted too and they all ran to the bombs.

I ran as best I could over to Captain Mercer. Sweat poured from me and I had to wipe my face. My head was beginning to pound and I felt dizzy.

"Climb the wall," he said to me, pointing up. "Shoot any spearmen the bombs don't get. Take Forrest with you."

"Why Forrest?"

"He's the second-best shooter we've got." He glared at me. "You wanted to save the Negroes. Now's your chance. Then blow the cave." He turned and strode over to the Jotun.

Private Forrest appeared at my shoulder. His eyes were wide in terror. "Told you. He's sacrificing us!"

I turned to him. "I'm too stubborn to die. I won't let you die either."

"How can I believe you?"

"I swear on my soul I will not leave you."

He met my eyes. His were still filled with fear, but he slowly nodded. Then we both ran for the ladder.

He made it to the top first, as I was beginning to stumble from the pain. I had to stop at the bottom of the ladder and take a few deep breaths before I could shakily climb up. I finally made it up, dizzy and woozy the whole time. Forrest shifted sideways onto the little platform and raised his rifle to his shoulder. I steadied myself by grabbing the top of the wall as I looked out over the horde in front of us.

It'd grown! Two hundred or more trolls now spilled across the road and the woods. The wall of spears wasn't any deeper, but it now spread sideways, blocking all the land from the creek to deep in the trees.

I lifted my Whitworth to my shoulder. I scanned the area for the leader, but didn't see him.

The first gunpowder bomb flew over the wall. It arced toward the spearmen. Then it exploded above them.

Trolls screamed. Many fell to the ground. I watched a piece of shrapnel slice one's arm nearly off.

Beside me, Forrest fired.

A second gunpowder bomb exploded on the ground behind the wall of spears.

I wasn't here to watch. I picked out a spearman on the left end. Sighted down the barrel.

My arms shook.

I braced my rifle on the wall and crouched down. It was awkward, but it'd do.

A third gunpowder bomb exploded in the morass of trolls. Forrest was firing quickly. I aimed at the troll's head and pulled the trigger.

My aim was good. The troll fell to the ground.

Two more bombs flew over. Troll battle cries came from behind us. Forrest turned and started firing toward the top of the cave.

I picked out another big troll spearman, steadied my breath, and shot him.

The gates creaked open. Smoke filled the road ahead. The spear wall lay broken—a few random trolls here and there.

My vision blurred with my headache. When it cleared for a moment, I took aim at another troll. My aim was off.

Two more bombs exploded ahead of us. Then one more behind the spear wall. Forrest fired wildly.

And our men charged out of the gate.

Captain Mercer rode in front, his saber held high in his left hand. The other soldiers formed a flying wedge, their horses racing in formation. The women and wounded tucked in behind them, bent low on their mounts. They all galloped straight ahead.

"For the West!" Captain Mercer yelled. A troll tried to avoid his charge and Mercer cut him down.

I picked another spearman out and shot at him. I hit his shoulder instead of his head, but he still dropped with a cry.

Our horsemen thundered on.

But then a thrown axe caught Williams in the side and he tumbled to the ground. Two other trolls threw themselves at MacDonald's horse. He smashed into them, but it spun him out of the wedge. He was soon surrounded by a mass of stabbing trolls. Others charged through the gap he'd left, trying to reach the women and wounded.

The Jotun roared. They ran out the gate, but then turned to the side and smashed through the trees into the woods instead of following the road. The older one held back and let the young one lead. When a stray troll rushed forward with an axe, the older one kicked it and sent it flying.

But it slowed him down. Soon trolls were mobbed in front of him. Two circled behind the boy. He wasn't much bigger than they were, and he shrank back in terror as they raised their axes and strode forward.

I shot them both.

The boy's eyes went wide as the two trolls crashed to the ground. He looked up at me, his mouth open. Then the older Jotun reached over and grabbed his hand. He'd scattered the former mob and they started to run.

I lost sight of the Jotun in the trees.

"I'm out of bullets!" Forrest said. "I'm out of bullets!"

"Then go!" I said. I started to leave myself, but then saw the troll commander.

He stood on the road about fifty feet in front of our charging horsemen. He laughed, and lifted a Colt .45. He fired twice and Samuel Turner fell from his horse. Another shot, and one of the other Negroes did the same.

Then with a roar, the troll fired at Captain Mercer. The Captain flung himself forward onto his horse's neck and the bullet missed.

I couldn't take it. I sighted down the barrel at the troll commander's right head. At two hundred yards, it should've been easy, but my vision was blurred. My body ached. My gut churned and I wasn't sure I could stand.

I sighted down the barrel at the troll commander again.

Captain Mercer sat up. He raised his saber once more and directed the charging horse wedge to ride straight at the commander.

With a sneer, the troll commander raised his Colt with both hands and aimed it straight at the Captain.

I fired first.

My bullet slammed into the troll's eye and the monster crumpled to the ground. A moment later, Captain Mercer and what was left of the wedge rode right over him.

I let out a silent prayer. And then I started puking up my guts.

I wanted to keel over. Part of me wanted to die. Instead, as soon as I stopped heaving, I slowly turned around.

We hadn't blown the cave. A dozen trolls now scrambled down the ladders at the sides of the opening. Others raced in through the open gate. They'd be inside soon.

I started climbing down the ladder. My climb turned into a slide when my feet slipped, and I thumped to the ground. I turned to face the cave.

I could see the lamps.

With my back to the wall, I lifted my rifle once again. I propped my elbow on my knee and aimed as best I could. As soon as my breathing calmed, I fired.

And missed.

I closed my eyes for a moment and said a quick prayer. Then I opened them, aimed at the nearest lamp again, and fired.

And missed again.

Trolls started running into the cave. Toward the powder.

I fired a third time.

And the cave exploded.

I closed my eyes and let the rifle drop from my fingers. I sobbed in relief. It was over. I'd done it. It was over.

It was over.

Hands tugged at my shoulder, shaking me. I opened my eyes. Forrest.

"How do we get out?" he yelled. "How do we get out?"

I glanced around. The explosion had killed a lot of the trolls inside the courtyard and the others were running around not paying attention to us.

"More are coming in the gate!" Forrest yelled.

"The creek. We go out the creek. Trolls can't swim."

He grabbed my arm and pulled me to my feet. Stumbling, we ran along the wall until we reached the spot where the creek went under it. He started to pull me into the water.

I pulled back. "I can't swim either."

"Then float!" He looked around wildly and spotted a plank that the explosion had blown nearby. He ran and grabbed it and that's when I realized he'd lost both his rifle and his saber.

Holding the wood, which was about the length of my arm and the width of my thigh, I waded into the stream. The water's icy shock nearly caused me to stumble.

Forrest came after me. The current tugged and pulled at my legs. When we got to the middle where the water was up to my waist, I froze.

I couldn't do it. My head pounded. I felt sick. I wanted to run screaming, but I wasn't sure I could move.

Forrest took a deep breath, grabbed my arm, and pulled me down. I managed to take a deep breath myself before my head went under water.

I was drowning! I thrashed around. The water tugged me forward. I tried to rise up, but Forrest held me down. He was gonna kill me!

In blind panic, I started kicking. I clung tight to the wood. A moment later, my head popped out of the water, outside the wall.

I gasped for breath. We were out!

"Keep your fool head down!" Forrest hissed in my ear.

I tried to nod, but all that got me was a face full of water.

"Put your feet up! Hold onto the board across your chest!"

I did as he said, and then began to float downstream.

I was in a daze, but I forced myself to open my eyes and look on the shore. Trolls argued and yelled at each other. A few hacked at a dead horse with their axes. Several ran here and there.

None paid any attention to two bodies floating down the creek.

We bounced into a few rocks, but with our feet out in front, our legs cushioned the impact and let us push off. The chill set in quick, though. My fingers turned to ice as they clutched the board in the cold water.

We floated on. I fought to stay conscious. It was about all I could do.

I hung on until we'd floated past the trolls, past the last of the chaos. The creek meandered into some trees, and soon they were completely out of sight.

Forrest grabbed my arm again and steered us toward the shore away from the cave. Soon my feet dragged the bottom. I kicked a few rocks and a submerged log before I finally, shakily stood up.

I stumbled toward the shore. I had maybe five feet to go, but it seemed like a chasm. At last, I reached the bank and flopped forward on it. I sank my hands into the mud and pulled myself forward until all but my toes were out of the water.

My head pounded. My body was numb with cold. Glassy-eyed, I stared at Forrest as he crawled up next to me.

"We made it!" he said.

"Not yet." They could still catch us.

But my head swam before I could say anything else. And then I passed out.

THIRTY-FOUR

I AWOKE when my head whacked against something.

"Sorry," I heard Forrest mumble.

My head still throbbed, but not as much. It was more a slow pulse in my temple than the pounding everywhere I'd felt before. I was cold, though, chilled from my wet clothes. I slowly opened my eyes. The afternoon light didn't blind me, as tree limbs above diffused it. I was sitting up, with my back against something rough. An oak tree, I realized. My hands flopped in the dirt and fallen leaves by my sides. I slowly glanced around.

Forrest crouched a few feet away, looking as bedraggled as I felt. His wet hair was plastered to his forehead and he'd picked up a scratch on his cheek. Blood smeared across his face and one lip was cracked.

"You gonna live?" he asked.

I took a deep breath. A dozen aches and pains in my arms and legs made themselves known. "Yeah," I said with a nod.

"Good. We gotta find the Niggers' boat."

"On the river."

"Already looked. Can't see it."

I stretched my neck and looked around even harder. I couldn't see the river at all. Just the creek and the woods.

"You gotta save us," he said. "You know what the Captain would've done."

I raised an eyebrow. I had no idea what the Captain would've done, but Forrest's hungry desperation made me hold my tongue.

"How far to the river?" I asked instead.

"About ten minutes." He pointed downstream.

Ten minutes? That meant he'd left me to go find the boat. *Abandoned* me, in troll territory... the fury started to rise in my gut.

"You gotta save us!"

I stared at him. Wet, bloody, and shaking almost in terror. This was the man who'd bullied Zeke. Who'd refused to give up his rifle. Who'd stolen from our dead. True, he'd helped get me down the creek, but to save his neck as much as mine.

It'd serve him right if I left him behind. He was scum.

But at least he was human scum.

"Help me up," I said. I extended a hand and he took it.

I quickly checked my holster and my pouches. My Colt and saber were both gone. The pouch on my waist still had its bullets, but everything was waterlogged. I was waterlogged. Forrest wasn't much better. He had the clothes on his back and that was about it.

"Lead the way to the river," I said.

He nodded and we began winding our way through the trees.

The chills bothered me as we went. I kept trying to walk in the sun to dry off, but it wasn't happening quickly, not like it did back in Colorado. I also kept looking around for trolls. Surely they hadn't abandoned the chase.

Fortunately, we didn't run into any before we came to the river.

The Tennessee River easily stretched tens of feet wide, which made it impossible to cross. The surface was clear of boats, with nothing we could see other than water and trees in any direction.

"The boat was tied up there," Forrest said. He pointed to a shallow muddy bank with deep scrape marks leading from a nearby tree into the water.

We headed over, and confirmed that the marks had come from a wide, flat boat being pushed into the water. Dozens of footprints overlapped near the tracks.

I furrowed my brow. "Where are the horses?"

"What do you mean?" he asked.

"They rode horses here. They wouldn't've taken them on the boat."

"Maybe they set 'em loose."

"Let's look for tracks."

We slowly walked along the bank. It didn't take long to spot the horse tracks, but they were just as muddled a mess as the human footprints. Eventually we widened our sweep and it became clear that most of the horse tracks led upstream.

"They're headed toward the bridge," Forrest said.

"No," I said. "Too obvious. Captain Mercer wouldn't do that. The trolls will cut 'em off, if they're not already there."

"But where else?"

I shrugged. My headache was finally starting to fade and I could begin to think again. Except when the chills from being so wet forced me to shiver.

"Let's follow them a little ways," I said. "Maybe they don't have any riders."

"Maybe they still have their saddlebags," he said.

I nodded at that, thinking about warm clothes.

We headed upstream following the general direction of the tracks. We made it about two hundred yards before I spotted something moving in the trees. I motioned for Forrest to stand still, and he froze, one foot actually an inch above the ground.

The brown thing shuffled and moved a bit. Then I let out the breath I'd been holding. It was a horse.

We still approached cautiously. I kept scanning the area for trolls, but didn't see any. I didn't hear any either.

The horse snorted and snuffled when we approached. It still wore a saddle and saddlebags, though the bags were unbuckled and nearly flat. It shied away at first, but Forrest started speaking softly to it and was able to calm it down. As he did, I looked around through the trees.

Nothing else moved nearby. I spotted a few small broken branches, though. Went I went over to them, I found more trampled ground.

"Hey!" Forrest called a bit louder than I would've liked. "There's some clothes in here!"

I motioned for him to be quieter and walked back to the horse. He was pulling a wadded up shirt out of one of the bags. He shook it out and held it up. Then he grinned at me and starting taking off his own.

I turned and scanned the area again. Nothing else moved, other than a few branches swaying in the light breeze.

Why would only one horse be here? We were about as close to Nickajack Cave as we could get and still be along the river, I judged. If Captain Mercer was trying to make it look like the squad was riding for the bridge, he would've taken all the horses further upstream...

He did, I realized. Then he'd ridden this horse *back* here.

I turned to Forrest, who was buttoning up his new dry shirt. He looked pleased as punch and grinned at me as he did.

"I know where Captain Mercer went," I said. "He's trying to sneak back to the cave."

Forrest's eyes went wide. "Why?"

"He doesn't know that I blew up all the equipment. He's gone to finish the mission."

We slowly crept through the woods toward Nickajack Cave. We stepped lightly over the bushes and through the few fallen leaves so as not to make much noise. Sweat beaded on my brow, and I kept wanting to move faster, but caution kept tamping down the temptation. A hot-headed charge without weapons would be fatal. Our survival depended on not being noticed.

Forrest hung back about ten feet, but he stayed with me. He looked terrified every time I checked on him. It was disconcerting to see that in a seasoned soldier. Particularly one who'd been so nasty to Zeke.

So we kept going at a snail's pace. The afternoon sun had started to create large shadows through the trees, which made it harder to see ahead, but hopefully harder to see us. The whole time, I kept wondering where Captain Mercer would be.

And after a bit, I realized I knew exactly. He'd be at the lookout spot where he and I'd watched the sentry before we'd launched our raid. It gave the best view of the whole cave while being far enough back to not have a troll stumble on him.

So I started creeping that way.

Finally, after what seemed like an hour but was probably a lot less, we came within sight of it. I could hear troll shouts and yells in the distance, but still nothing nearby. I actually slowed up enough for Forrest to catch up with me. He stood at my right, trying not to breathe too hard.

Then something moved, near the lookout spot. I watched it for a little more, though I could barely make it out.

It was Captain Mercer.

"C'mon," I said to Forrest. I walked forward quickly, a little more heedless of the noise.

Captain Mercer whirled when we got close and shakily pointed a Colt revolver at us. His eyes went wide, but calmed when he recognized us. He lowered the gun as we approached close enough to whisper.

"You're alive," he said.

I nodded. "And I blew the cave."

He started. "Are you sure? I thought I heard an explosion, but… I was busy at the time."

"He did," Forrest said. "I saw it."

"Oh." Captain Mercer blinked in surprise.

"Uh…," Forrest continued, "so…where's the… uh… boat?"

"About a mile down river," Captain Mercer said. "There's a big rock outcropping there where they'll wait until dawn."

"Uh…" Forrest's eyes darted from Captain Mercer, to me, to the wall where we could hear the trolls, and back to Captain Mercer. "Shouldn't we… go then?"

Captain Mercer gave him a dirty look.

"He blew up the equipment." Forrest looked to me for help. He clearly wanted to escape as soon as possible.

"Go," Captain Mercer said with a snort of disgust. He waved Forrest away. "Just go."

Forrest blinked, took one last look at us, and then scampered off, making far too much noise for my comfort.

"The Lord has such a sense of humor," Captain Mercer said as he watched Forrest depart. "That a bully and a coward should be one of the few survivors of this raid."

My heart leaped. "Who else survived?"

"Sergeant-Major McNab, Private Zeke Washington, Nurse Maria, Joshua Turner, some of the Negro women and children. And us."

My heat pounded in shock. "That's it?"

"That's it. The trolls broke our wedge after we rounded the bend in the road. None of us would've survived if not for Private Washington."

"What'd he do?"

"He started screaming about 'The Lord's Agent' and the 'Hands of God.' He had his saber out and..." Captain Mercer actually shuddered. "The Lord was *not* merciful to those who opposed the Private."

"He got them out safe," I murmured, thinking of my last conversation with Zeke. The memory of his amazing swordsmanship before the tower in Louisville also flashed through my mind.

"He did." Captain Mercer turned back to watching the cave.

Dusk was starting to settle and the long shadows now faded into deep greys beneath the trees and across the front of the wall. The gate remained wide open and three or four trolls came out and stood in a small group in the entryway. They seemed to be talking to each other, for they barely looked around. In a similar vein, both the wall and the area above the cave were clear of sentries. The trolls didn't seem too concerned about keeping a lookout.

"Did you really blow up the equipment?" Captain Mercer asked. "All of it?"

"As best I can tell. You could sneak up and check if you want."

He nodded, as if considering it.

"But there's no point," I continued. "You have Turner. You have all his papers. Even if some of the equipment survived, the trolls won't know how to use it."

"True. All the traitors but Turner are dead, and he is safely in our charge. The trolls most certainly do *not* know how to make gunpowder. Should the Jotun know, then plenty of caves will serve for the saltpeter."

"But the Jotun *don't* know. Turner said so."

He gave me a grim smile. "Would you trust the word of a traitor? A man who sold out humanity for silver?" He shook his head. "I'm sure General Sanborn will learn the truth from Turner, even should Turner not wish to divulge much of it. Some of his men can be very… persuasive."

I willed myself to not react. In the growing gloom, I hoped Captain Mercer couldn't read the disgust on my face. Turner had done what he needed to do to survive. He didn't deserve… *persuasion.*

He turned back and studied the wall once again. In the dusk, we could begin to see the glow of fires reaching up to the sky.

"Did you see what happened to the Jotun?" he asked. "The boy and his wounded father?"

"No, sir," I lied. "I was too busy shooting trolls."

"I should have given you orders to shoot them as well, alas. But there is nothing to be done about it now."

Two trolls came out of the gate. They said something to the cluster on the road and then kept walking down the road. They headed for some of the bodies still scattered where Captain Mercer's wedge had slammed into the spearmen. They weren't close, but they were looking around quite a bit as they looted through the bodies.

Captain Mercer nodded his head. "Yes," he said. "We've done all we can do."

"We have," I said as he turned to face me once again.

"The mission is over," he said. "Let's go home."

THIRTY-FIVE

WE SLIPPED through the darkness back to the river and down the shore. Captain Mercer moved quietly, much more softly than Forrest had done, with barely a sound other than his breathing. I kept close behind. I'd gotten used to the wet and the chill, but not the way my boots still squished when I walked.

We found the rock outcropping and the boat. They'd been waiting until the Captain returned or dawn, whichever came first, and were mighty glad to see us.

It was a long, wide rowboat with slots for three oars on a side. It floated next to the rock and we carefully climbed in. Zeke and Joshua Turner manned the oars at the back, and Forrest was already seated at one in the front right. Maria huddled with the Negro women and children in the middle. I was surprised to see McNab sitting at the front left oar, but he only had his good hand on it. His grin was broad as a barn when he saw me, though.

"Too stubborn to die, right Billy?" he said.

I nodded wearily, but my heart felt lighter on seeing him.

Zeke couldn't stop grinning at me either, though he had to keep a firm grip on his oar to keep the boat from sliding too far downstream. The current wasn't fast here, but it was strong.

"Take the middle oar, Billy," Captain Mercer said. I blinked. He hadn't called me Lieutenant, but he nudged me and so I scrambled across to the oar on the far side. Captain Mercer climbed in after me and took the last one.

"Let's go," the Captain said. He pointed downstream. Then he pushed us away from the rock and we began to float.

With the strong current, we didn't have to paddle hard, which was a relief. Mostly we used the paddles to steer, at Joshua Turner's command. I didn't know what I was doing at first, but one of the Negro women with a baby moved next to me and talked me through how to use the oar. It was enough, given how weary I was, and how tired we all must've been.

Just before dawn, Joshua Turner had us steer toward shore. He picked a bank with a lot of trees that came down right to the water's edge. We tucked the boat up between them and covered it with branches that Zeke cut down with his saber. While he did, I collapsed under an oak. I could barely keep my eyes open, I was so hang-dog tired.

While I sat there, Maria approached with her medicine bag in hand.

"Are you hurt?" she asked.

"Just the usual cuts and bruises."

"Please," she said with a gesture toward an obvious scrape on my hand. "Let me see them."

I grimaced but nodded. She made me take off my shirt and smeared an ointment on every cut she found.

"How are your ribs?" she asked.

"Fine." I blinked. They hadn't hurt in days. Maybe I hadn't injured them as bad as I'd thought.

"And your head?"

I grimaced. "I nearly passed out during the battle. Since then, well, it still hurts, but it comes and goes."

"Rest then," she said. "On the boat too."

I started to object and say that I needed to row, but caught myself. We were letting the current carry us. We only really needed to row hard when it was time to come to shore.

"Rest," she repeated. "You have earned it."

"I shouldn't."

She just gave me a pointed look and continued tending to my cuts.

It turned out I didn't have anything serious wrong. I'd gotten lucky and not caught a fever, and none of my cuts had become infected. About the time Maria finished, Captain Mercer called us all together. He'd selected a watch schedule and wanted us to sleep through the day. I was more than happy to oblige, as I didn't have a watch at all, though he said I would on subsequent days. When dusk fell, we woke up, loaded back into the boat and headed downstream once again.

I managed to talk with Zeke a bit before we did. We were both worn and hungry—we hadn't loaded much food into the saddlebags and the children were fed first.

"You got 'em out," I said to him with a nod toward Maria and McNab. "Captain Mercer said you were amazing."

He shrugged and ducked his head. I thought I could see a blush spreading over his dark skin. "Wasn't me. I was just a vessel of our blessed Lord." He grew somber. "If only He coulda saved more."

I nodded in agreement. "But still... we'll get you a medal when we get back to Fort Chicago."

"That's a mighty nice idea, but they ain't gonna give a medal to a Negro like me."

"They gave Jeremiah one," I reminded him. "You never know."

Zeke shrugged, but to end the conversation as much as anything.

We continued downstream through the night, but without the urgency of before. After an hour or two, we stopped near a small farm and quietly snuck into the fields to steal some of the unharvested crops. I was the lead raider, with Forrest and Zeke with me. Captain Mercer stayed with the boat, but I thought that was mostly to keep an eye on Joshua Turner.

We found ripe corn and beans and Zeke went a little closer to the farmhouse and got some apples from a solitary tree not far from the barn. We filled the saddle bags we'd carried each time, but it still didn't feel like enough to feed us all. At the same time, I couldn't help wondering what the farmers would think when they found it gone.

When we got back to the boat, I sat with McNab for a bit while everyone ate.

"Tasty," McNab said as he bit into an ear of corn. He had a little trouble holding it with one hand, but he managed. His broken arm still hung in a sling.

"Yeah...," I said. "Um... did Cassidy ever steal food from farmers?"

"A few times we had to. But...but we learned. Cassidy'd carry some small coins and leave those behind."

I sighed in relief. Forrest's stolen coins would come in handy.

"He left coins a lot," McNab continued, "especially in the Contested Lands. He figured anyone who could survive that deserved a bit of help."

"That wasn't in the books."

"Nah. He told Jeremiah to keep it out. He felt doing good wasn't something you bragged about."

"But he didn't mind bragging about killing giants."

"Well... sort of. He figured maybe it'd give some folks hope. I mean, they called him Cassidy the Giant Killer, but it was never about the giants. It was always about the people."

I stared at him as his words sunk in. But before I could think of what to say, Captain Mercer said we should move on. I took my place at my oar and we started to row again.

I thought a lot about Cassidy for the rest of the night. When we pulled to shore at dawn to hide and sleep, I kept thinking about the man I'd known. How we'd ridden together. How he'd tried to keep me safe by sending me home. I fell asleep to the memories of us fighting side by side.

I didn't dream of him, though.

We woke at dusk and repeated the night before. We floated down the river and foraged when we saw farms close to shore. This time I made a point of leaving a few coins from Forrest's stash in a place where the farmer would find them. Forrest had glared at me when I'd taken them from the saddlebag, but Captain Mercer noticed and told me to do it. At dawn, we pulled ashore and hid.

We did float past some towns and the occasional bridge or set of docks. When we did, we kept as quiet and as still as we could.

We saw no one—human, Jotun, or troll—the entire time. I never did figure out exactly why.

Of course, my mind wasn't much on that. It kept returning to Captain Mercer. Now that we were out of danger, I couldn't stop thinking of his angry order for me to blow the cave and kill the Negroes and Jotun. He didn't seem to be holding a grudge after I'd refused, but he also kept his thoughts and emotions close to his chest.

Would he have really left me and Forrest?

I didn't think he would've, but it unsettled me that I didn't know for sure.

We'd been traveling for well over a month together and he'd never once talked about his wife and daughter. He'd never talked about his earlier life or past missions. We'd never talked about anything other than the mission.

And I didn't see a way to, either. We didn't talk in the boat unless absolutely necessary and only at a whisper. Joshua Turner said voices sometimes carried across the water. When we landed on shore, we quickly went into hiding and again there wasn't time for casual conversation. Furthermore, Captain Mercer kept to himself when he wasn't giving orders.

We floated the next day and passed by Huntsville, Alabama, just before dawn. A few fishermen saw us and waved, but that was all that happened. They didn't come close enough to make out what was left of our uniforms and they didn't turn to shore upon seeing us. Captain Mercer figured we were safe, but we went further into the day as an extra precaution before camping and hiding.

By then, our trip followed a regular pattern. We floated at night, foraged when we could, and hid during the day. The river turned north and McNab figured we'd have another week before we were out of Jotun territory. Then, he figured maybe another two weeks on foot before we could get back to Fort Chicago. Assuming no one spotted us and tried to stop us.

I got to know the Negro women a bit. The elder, Maisy, had been Samuel Turner's wife. She put on a brave face during the day, but when her little baby Rose, went to sleep, she quietly sobbed in grief. I sat with her once, as she cried for her lost husband. I think only Rose kept her going. She cradled that baby constantly on the boat, as if holding her was holding life itself.

The younger woman, Rachel, spent her time helping Maria look for herbs and other medicinal plants at each of our stops. They didn't go far, but sometimes they told Zeke what to look for. He'd smile that broad smile of his, nod his head, and do his best to find them, but he never did. Rachel seemed a mite impressed with him, but his smile was no more polite to her than it was to Maisy.

Rachel's son Jebediah was five, but I'd never met a more haunted little boy. He jumped at the slap of a paddle in water and stared into the distance for most of the day.

And that was it. The other Negro women and children hadn't survived when the trolls had torn apart the flying wedge of horsemen.

That sadness hit me harder than the loss of our own men. Had we condemned them to death? They'd been innocents—their lives destroyed and ended through no fault of their own. I could only hope their souls were at peace.

I mentioned it to McNab one dawn just before we bedded down for the day. He listened seriously, and nodded his head in sympathy when I told him of my grief for these people I'd never known.

"It's good," he said when I'd finally stopped. "It's good that their deaths bother you so. It's when the deaths *stop* bothering you that you should worry."

I snorted softly and nodded my head. I knew I never wanted to get to that place.

But as I drifted off, I couldn't help thinking. Did all the deaths bother Captain Mercer? He'd fought a lot of battles, I knew, and killed a lot of Jotun. He'd also had a lot of his men die, and surely seen a lot of innocents get killed as well.

Did it bother him?

Or was that just the cost of the mission?

THIRTY-SIX

SCOUTS from the Army of the West found us as soon as we crossed the Ohio river. They had a few horses, food, and, even better, fresh changes of clothes. It felt a little strange to put on trousers that were made for another, taller soldier, but I was so relieved to have dry ones that I didn't care. I'd had enough of boats to last me a lifetime.

The scouts were able to round up a wagon, and soon the lot of us were headed to Fort Chicago. McNab was right that it took two weeks, but it was a relieved two weeks. After being so fearful for so long, the Negro women and children were finally able to sleep. We shifted back to a regular routine, except that I wasn't assigned any night watches. I slept deep and sound each night.

Still, I grew anxious to get there. It wasn't like Fort Chicago was my home, and I certainly had no love of the barracks or the drills or the army. I just wanted this mission to be done. Complete. Finished.

I wasn't the only one. I could sense it in everyone else, even Captain Mercer. The weather had turned chilly as we entered November, and none of us cared to be outdoors. Time passed too slowly, even with the comforts of a military escort and the knowledge that we were safe from the Jotun.

We'd ridden for three days before I started to get really restless. I could sense it in Zeke too. He kept scanning the trees as if he expected trouble, but he had the hang dog look of someone who knew he'd be disappointed.

McNab noticed. He waved us over to sit next to him on the wagon.

"Y'all need to calm down," he said. "You can't go looking for danger behind every tree. It's not there."

"Yeah," I said with a grimace.

"It's hard," he said. "On the raid, you had to keep alert. But the raid's over. You gotta leave it behind now."

"We ain't in Chicago yet," Zeke pointed out.

"But we're safe," McNab said. He gestured at the army scouts riding alongside us. "Our job is done. If you never let go of the job, it'll do you something awful inside. Life's too short. Enjoy it while you can."

"Huh," I said. It made sense, but I wasn't entirely sure how to do it.

"Well, I know what I want to enjoy," Zeke said with a grin. "A nice thick steak."

McNab laughed. "I'll get you one, even if I have to bribe every cook in the Fort."

The fifth day, the sun came out bright and the wind that had bothered us off and on finally died. I'd had enough of the wagon and I mentioned it to Captain Mercer. He went and conferred with the lieutenant in charge of the scouts and a little while later, two of the scouts relaxed in the wagon while Captain Mercer and I trotted ahead on their horses.

We rode down a stretch of road that ran between old abandoned fields. The weeds and the saplings hadn't quite taken over, but it was just a matter of time. I bit back the urge to gallop, to feel the wind on my face. Instead, I basked in the pure pleasure of the ride.

Captain Mercer must've felt the same way, for he spurred his horse on, and soon we were riding fast. We'd long left the wagon behind, and soon we entered the woods, with leaves long since having started to fall. The road turned at a small creek and we slowed the horses to a walk. I looked over at Captain Mercer and saw him smiling.

"Nice to have the mission over, sir," I said.

He snorted softly and gave me a wry grin. "It is never over. This is just a pause."

"Oh? But we blew the cave, sir. They can't make gunpowder now."

"Our mission is larger than that. It will not end until the Jotun are removed from our lands."

"Uh… that'll take a while."

"Our lifetimes and maybe more." He pulled up on the reins and brought his horse to a stop. I did the same. Then he met my eyes. His were the flinty cold I'd seen before.

"My one regret at Nickajack," he said, "is that those two Jotun may have survived. I can only hope they did not."

I kept my face as blank as I could. He didn't regret the deaths of our men, or the Negro women and children, as much as the survival of an innocent boy who happened to be a Jotun?

"We should go back," I finally said. I nodded my head toward the wagon.

He nodded in agreement. "You're a fine giant killer, Billy. Cassidy would be proud."

I concentrated on the road so I wouldn't have to meet his eyes.

We arrived at Fort Chicago a few days before Sanborn returned with the army from Louisville. They put me up in one of the small shacks near Officer's Row. I wasn't sure I deserved it, but as it meant not sleeping in the barracks, I didn't turn it down. I didn't seem to have any duties, so I mostly rested or wrote some letters to Tom and my friends in Golden City. I also made notes about our raid. I knew Jeremiah'd ask for them as soon as he saw me. Captain Mercer had also warned me that we'd have to give General Sanborn a full report and the General would ask lots of questions.

I did go visit the hospital when I could. The wounded from Louisville had been sent back long before the remnants of our raiding party arrived. A lot had been discharged, and many had died, but some still hung on, neither too sick nor too well to move on. Many of them fought bad infections and fevers. I tried not to flinch when they cried out in pain.

But I did what I'd seen Captain Mercer do. I sat with each one for a few minutes and asked how they were doing. I sometimes held their hands. I always listened, and I tried not to look away when one of them recognized me and thanked me for my heroism.

That's where Jeremiah found me.

I was sitting on a small camp stool next to the bed of one of the privates with fever. He'd just fallen asleep, blessedly for him. At the sound of approaching footsteps, I looked up to see Jeremiah in his full sergeant's uniform.

"Good to see you, Billy," he said with a grin. He extended his hand.

"The heck with that!" I stood and gave him a huge bear hug. "You made it! You got out alive!"

"You too," he said with a relieved laugh. "You survived Captain Mercer!"

"It was a near thing," I said. I glanced around. No one nearby was listening, but there were still too many ears. "Let's take a walk."

He nodded and we strolled outside. As we did, he told me how Sanborn's army was almost all back from Louisville. They'd left a small guard that was to run at the first attack of the Jotun, as well as some "surprises" in the various Jotun buildings. Meanwhile, New York had received its first snows. New England was safe, at least for a while. The diversionary attack had worked, all those weeks ago.

In turn, I filled him in on the raid after he'd left. He nodded and only asked a few questions, though he promised he'd have more later.

I got to the end and my voice broke. "I… I let the Jotun live. I shot the trolls instead."

"Ah. I wouldn't tell Captain Mercer that."

"Uh, no. But what do you…?"

"Think? I wasn't there."

"But if you were?"

He shook his head. "There's no way to tell, Billy. There's no way to tell."

I pulled my coat tight around myself as I walked. The wind stung my cheeks, but I still felt warm with my friend.

Once we'd walked away from any buildings and the scurrying business of the army, Jeremiah gave me a smile.

"There's good news," he said. "Mercer's meeting with Sanborn right now. We're going to get medals again."

"As long as Zeke gets one," I said. I briefly described how he'd kept Maria and McNab safe.

Jeremiah nodded when I'd finished. "I'll tell McNab to put in a word for him."

"Good."

We walked on quietly for a few minutes.

"So," Jeremiah eventually said. "What about you? You're a hero. Again. You could be made Captain this time."

I shook my head hard. "No," I said. "No, no, no. I don't want it. I don't even want to be in the army."

"It's a little late for that."

"I could ask for a discharge."

"Is that what you really want?"

His tone made it clear it was an honest question, so I thought about it a bit. Then I thought about it hard.

"I... I don't know," I finally admitted. "I thought going into the army and killing Jotun was the right thing to do. Now I'm not so sure."

"Mmmm."

"I know it's what Cassidy wanted me to do," I continued, "or at least I thought so, but now I'm not so sure."

"He told you to be a sharpshooter because he wanted you out of the way. I'm sure he'd have invited you to join us if he'd lived."

"Yeah," I said with a nod.

We hadn't been walking anywhere in particular, but as I looked up, I realized we'd come close to the shooting range. I could hear the bark of rifles and the yell of the overseeing sergeant. A brisk breeze puffed and faded, and I idly wondered how much the recruits had to compensate for it in their aim.

"Are you still having the nightmares?" Jeremiah asked.

I blinked. "No. Not since Nickajack."

"Well there is that."

"Yeah."

We meandered closer to the shooting range. I could see the targets now—set just at 600 yards. With the wind and a Winchester, it'd be a challenge. My trigger finger itched in anticipation.

"I think I'll call my next book 'The Road to Nickajack Cave,'" Jeremiah said. "You did take notes, didn't you?"

"Of course. Since you're gonna make me out to be a hero no matter what, I figured I'd better help you get it right."

"I always get it right," he protested.

"Nah," I said. "You always make people out to be bigger heroes than they are. I wanna make sure you tell it true."

He laughed, loud and long.

"C'mon," I said with a smile at him. "Let's see if we can get some shooting in before dark."

THE END

AUTHOR'S NOTES

Sharpshooter follows Billy the Kid immediately after his adventures in *Sidekick*. I started with one basic premise and one core desire.

My basic premise was that Billy would be wrestling with post-traumatic stress disorder (PTSD) after the events in *Sidekick*. I've never been a fan of how fictional heroes so often quickly shrug off the bad things that happen in their adventures and I particularly didn't think a seventeen-year-old young man would easily get over the death of his idol. Of course, PTSD was not understood in the 1870s, so I had to ask myself how he'd deal with it and decided that he'd probably throw himself into doing what he though his idol wanted him to do.

That, of course, set up the primary conflict. Captain Mercer is exactly what Billy thinks he wants—a ruthless, nearly monomaniacal giant killer. Now Captain Mercer has his own story, that I may tell some day, but which he would never tell Billy.

It also melded nicely with another major desire. We readers didn't get to spend much time with the Jotun in *Sidekick*. I wanted to show their society and explore how they would interact with the humans they conquered. I still didn't get as deep into it as I'd wanted, but I hope it was enough to show them as more than faceless monsters.

As with *Sidekick*, my goal was to make the Universe as realistic as possible. The history up through 1865 is identical to the actual history of the United States. All the history after the rift at Andersonville was opened is my best extrapolation of what was likely to have happened. I also tried to get the economics right for a slave society where the slave holders (Jotun) need to consume a lot of calories. I'm sure there are errors, but hopefully they do not detract from the story.

Besides the Jotun, which are the size of a Tyrannosaurus Rex with the thick hide of a rhinoceros, this novel introduced the trolls. Following Norse mythology, I made the trolls human-sized with thick skins, dense muscles, and sometimes two heads. They came through the rift at Andersonville with the Jotun, but don't work with them—it's more of an uneasy co-existence. They're heavier than water so they don't swim, which has kept them living on the East side of the Mississippi, although they have tried to invade across it from time to time (Jeremiah mentions their attack around New Orleans).

I chose Nickajack Cave because it was used for the saltpeter that went into gunpowder prior to and during the Civil War. It's a huge cave, and so would have been suitable for the Jotun to reside in. It was also flooded by the Tennessee River Valley Authority in 1967 and is now home to a large colony of bats.

Finally, I wanted to capture how societies evolve. All too often, fantasy novels are stuck in the middle ages forever. In a world where gunpowder and firearms already exist, I knew the Jotun and trolls would both try to adopt them. Fortunately for the humans, they haven't quite learned the secrets yet…

ABOUT THE AUTHOR

Edward J. Knight writes fantasy and science fiction from his home in Colorado. He's put two satellites into orbit and is raising two children along with his partner, Sarah. He hates stories with idiot plots. More of his work and some occasional musings can be found at www. edwardjknight.com.

Want to keep on what Ed's writing, and when new releases will be out? Sign up for his monthly newsletter at:
www.edwardjknight.com/mailing-list/

www.edwardjknight.com

ALSO BY EDWARD J. KNIGHT

Sidekick

Gunslinger

PREVIEW OF SCOUT: THE TALE OF BILLY THE KID AND THE DEADWOOD DWARVES

The Third Novel in the Mythic West

EIGHT YEARS after the Jotunheim giants destroyed the Confederacy and most of the Union, the Army of the West stopped their last advance into what's left of the United States. Now the Army polices the borders while rebuilding its strength.

Billy McCarty hates army life. He loathes the daily regiments and rules. Strange sightings in the Black Hills offer him the chance to leave it all behind and lead his own small scout team to investigate.

But Billy's never led a team before. As they head into the wilderness where only the rules of survival matter, his every decision could mean serious injury or death.

For him or his friends.

Or both.

In the Mythic West, where gunslingers battle monsters of myth, *Scout* continues the epic adventures of the hero, Billy the Kid.

Available Summer 2021